SORRY TIME

By Anthony Maguire

A Sense of Place Publishing 2017
Copyright © Anthony Maguire
All Rights Reserved.
Published by A Sense of Place Publishing

ISBN-13: 978-0-9944791-3-6

Cover design Jessica Bell

National Library of Australia Cataloging-in-Publication entry

Creator: Maguire, Anthony, author.

Title: Sorry time / Anthony Maguire.

ISBN: eBook 978-0-9944791-4-3

Subjects: Murder-- Fiction.

Suspense fiction.

Australia, Central-- Fiction

Middle East-- Fiction.

Table of Contents

1 THE OWNER HAS LEFT THE BUILDING 1

2 DANGER: KANGAROOS CROSSING 4

3 THE PACK IS HUNGRY..............................15

4 ST CATHERINE'S 21

5 MEET ALI AND ABDUL............................27

6 HEAD OF BEHEADING 35

7 ROAST ROO 38

8 RUBY'S NIGHTMARE 45

9 SORRY TIME 48

10 DOMESTIC BLISS..................................55

11 FIREBALL..58

12 EYE OF THE STORM..............................61

13 WEEPING AND GNASHING OF TEETH 65

14 SO HELP ME GOD................................67

15 ALI'S DEMON 70

16 A SMALL PROBLEM 72

17 PAYBACK..80

18 OPAL CAPITAL....................................85

19 THE BIG BLOKE WITH A GOATEE 87

20 VENOMOUS VISITOR..............................92

21 LET'S FINISH THIS 98

22 DEATH OF A THOUSAND CUTS 104

23 GLEN OF THE OUTBACK........................107

24 MONEY TALKS 119

25 THE PIKES 124

26 THE FAMILY BUSINESS..........................132

27 ARE YOU IN THE LAND OF THE LIVING?.......135

28 RENATA, PETRA AND RUDI 138

29 AUF WIEDERSEN..................................147

30 THERE'S A MAN CALLED JIANG FENG 153

31 COLD CALLING....................................156

32 THE GODS NEED A SACRIFICE..................158

33 KISS GOODBYE....................................164

34 ROAD RAGE..170

35 DEATH COMES KNOCKING 173

36 MUM SENDS HER LOVE...179
37 THE FRIDGE...186
38 WRITING ON THE WALL 191
39 CONTROL + ALT + DEL......................................196
40 MORTAL KOMBAT 201
41 CALL TO PRAYERS 207
42 A CRUEL PLACE..213
43 INSHALLAH 220
44 EYE FOR AN EYE..223
45 DEJA VU...240

1 THE OWNER HAS LEFT THE BUILDING

DR JONATHAN CHASELING – young, bearded and hipsterish-looking – navigated his car around ruts and potholes on a relentlessly straight, orange-red dirt track stretching away to infinity. Up ahead he saw a lone tree, a ghost gum with thin, white branches reaching for the sky like skeletal hands.

A few minutes later, he parked near the tree, which was growing in a hollow beside the track. There was no mobile reception here, so he couldn't take a GPS fix or use Google Maps, but the tree was a landmark that would help him find his way back to the car, a RAV4, normally white but now coated with red dust.

A 26-year-old medical graduate on his way to Alice Springs to start a hospital job, Chaseling had detoured off the main highway to check out this place. It was renowned for marine fossils – a legacy of the time, aeons ago, when this part of Australia was covered by a vast inland sea. He got out of the car and walked into the scrub.

Taking a weaving course round scattered patches of saltbush, he kept his eyes to the ground, which was littered with small pieces of flat, rust-coloured sandstone. Every now and then he stopped to pick up a rock and look at it, turning it over in his hand, hoping to see the form of a trilobite or other long-extinct species.

He'd been walking for about 10 minutes when he saw a flat slab of stone, almost a metre long, distinctive because it was the only large rock he'd seen since leaving the track. Chaseling bent down and gripped the edge of the slab. He gave an experimental tug but it didn't budge. Then he shifted his right foot forward to give his body some leverage and put his back into the job, hauling upwards with both hands. There was a sucking noise as the slab came away from the damp earth beneath.

Holding the rock on its edge, he looked down at the patch of dirt he'd revealed – and noticed something white and rounded protruding from it. An ancient sea shell, perhaps. He set the slab down off to the side. Then he started scraping away the ochre dirt with a finger-length, sharp-edged piece of flint that had been underneath the rock. He gave a gasp. Staring up at him was the eye socket of a human skull.

His hands shaking, he uncovered the other socket, which like the first was filled with compacted dirt. Next he scratched away the earth over the mouth, revealing a perfect set of teeth. Probably an Aborigine from the times before white settlement, Chaseling thought to himself. The teeth seemed to be grinning at him. He looked down at the piece of flint in his hand. It was a dark tan colour, very different in shade and composition to the other rocks in this area. And the picture became clear. This had been the dead person's prized knife and it had gone to the grave with him. Or possibly her, although judging by the large size of the skull and teeth, it had most likely been an adult male.

Now he knew what to look for, he could see the shape of a rib cage in the dirt. And his eyes were drawn to something else. A small, disc-shaped object the size of a dried apricot, but thicker. It was caked with earth like chocolate on a Kinder Surprise egg. He picked it up – it was heavy, some kind of rock – and scratched at the dirt with the piece of flint. There was a flash of phosphorescent colour. *Opal!* His heart started thumping with excitement.

As he uncovered more of the precious stone, he saw that it had raised, spiral ridges radiating out from its centre. It glittered with a kaleidoscope of hues – now emerald green, now a brilliant magenta morphing into electric blue, each shade burning with a fire from deep within the rock. He uncapped his water bottle and rinsed the stone. He thought how 100 million years ago or even earlier, a marine snail – an ancestor of the modern-day nautilus – had lived and died in a primeval sea bed. Its shell became filled with silica-rich mud and fragments of marine life. And after the sea retreated, the contents of the shell gradually transformed into a gem which shimmered with the green of long extinct seaweeds, the blue of ancient fish scales, the iridescent purple of giant sea urchin spines and the brilliant red and orange of prehistoric jellyfish. It could well be worth of a fortune.

Chaseling put the flint back down where he'd found it. After a few moments' hesitation, he placed the opal in the pocket of his cargo shorts. *It won't be missed,* the voice of his shadowy other self whispered inside his head. *The previous owner has left the building.* He scooped up some dirt and covered first the grinning mouth, then the eyes and nose socket of the long-buried skull.

He put the slab back in place and walked towards the ghost gum, setting up a brisk pace because the sun was low on the western horizon, while in the east there was a line of ominous black clouds. He hadn't noticed them before.

2 DANGER: KANGAROOS CROSSING

THE ACCIDENT HAPPENED minutes after Chaseling steered his car off the dirt track and joined a bitumen road that would take him to the Stuart Highway.

The car was doing 100km/h and had just rounded a very gentle curve in an otherwise straight road when lit up in the headlights he saw a large, orange-brown kangaroo. It was sitting back on its haunches at the edge of the road, watching the car approach. Then it hopped onto the blacktop and into the path of the car. Chaseling stamped his foot down on the brake. But he was too late.

The tyres screeched, then *THUMP!* The nose of the RAV4 slammed into the unfortunate animal, hurling it five metres up into the air in front of the car where it did a somersault before gravity took hold and it came crashing back down. With a crack of breaking glass, it hit the windscreen – and stayed there, glued in place by wind pressure.

Pressed against the blood-smeared mosaic of shattered glass directly in front of him was the face of the kangaroo. Its teeth, stained green, were bared in a rictus of agony and one of its eyes had been crushed to red jelly. The sight was so shocking that Chaseling, for a crucial second or two, failed to take in the fact that the skidding car was veering off the bitumen towards the dirt verge. He started to correct the steering while easing his foot from the brake pedal. But once again he was too late.

The front left wheel of the car bit into the dirt and suddenly the car careered sideways onto the verge. Raising a cloud of dust, the RAV performed a 360 degree spin on the loose surface of dirt and stones. A signpost loomed. Chaseling braced for the impact. With a jolting crunch of metal against metal, the car hit the steel pole, atop which was a sign with an image of a hopping kangaroo and the words 'NEXT 20 KM.'

Chaseling's head whiplashed forward, then back again, like John F. Kennedy in the Zapruder film. Then all was still. The steel pole, bent over at a 45 degree angle, was embedded in the front of the car. Chaseling rubbed the back of his neck, which was feeling as if it had been karate chopped. With his other hand, he turned the ignition key. There was just a clicking sound. He picked up his iPhone from the floor in front of the passenger seat, where it had ended up after the accident. No bars, he was in a dead spot. He sighed and got out of the car.

There was no sign of the kangaroo which, together with the warning sign, had mangled the front end of the RAV. The hood was a concertina of tortured metal and the bumper bar and grille were bent into a V shape. Protruding from the front of the car was the steel pole. The base of the pole had gouged into the engine, smashing its way through fans, radiator and AC pipes all the way to the block. Steam was hissing from the ruptured radiator. It looked as though the car had reached the end of the road. Pity. He'd bought the second generation RAV just a month earlier in preparation for his move to central Australia from Sydney and had become attached to it.

He tore his eyes away from the devastated front end of the car and looked at the bent sign. He reflected on the irony of hitting it directly after striking the kangaroo. Perhaps it would make a good dinner table anecdote in the future. *But before I start dining out on the experience,* he thought to himself, *I've got to get the hell out of this place!*

The sun had gone down half an hour earlier and it was getting darker by the second. Chaseling's blue eyes narrowed behind heavy-framed, Clark Kent-style glasses as he scanned the landscape. No houses or other buildings. No power lines or other signs of so-called civilisation. Just large tracts of pale orange dirt, tinged a delicate shade of lavender in the afterglow of sunset. Dotted against this backdrop were the twisted, dark shapes of small mulga trees, most of them bush-sized, no taller than a person, with thin, gnarled branches and sparse, thin leaves. He walked onto the road, hoping to see the headlights of a car glimmering in the distance. But the only lights were the stars putting in an early appearance in the purple-grey sky. Soon it would be completely dark.

He heard a rustling noise coming from the scrub near the car and realised immediately what it was – the kangaroo.

Following the sounds, he walked up to a knee-high patch of saltbush just beyond the bent signpost.

The kangaroo lay on the ground weakly kicking out with its back legs, both of which were splayed out at unnatural angles. As he got closer he heard the sound of the marsupial's laboured, rasping breath. He bent down beside the stricken animal. There were pink bubbles gathered around its mouth and its undamaged eye gazed up at him with a look that seemed to say, *'Kill me! Quickly!'*

Chaseling felt a responsibility to end the animal's pain. He returned to the car and got the tyre lever.

A minute later, his grisly work done, he put the tyre iron back in the boot. His hands were shaking, and one of them was splattered with specks of blood and brain. So were his elastic-sided boots and his bare lower legs beneath a pair of navy blue cargo shorts. There were also red droplets on the lenses of his glasses. His medical training hadn't prepared him for killing animals with a tyre lever. His tall, lean body suddenly doubled up and he vomited.

He remained bent over, his stomach heaving as he supported himself with his hands against the car, for more than a minute. Slowly straightening up, he took a deep breath. He got a one litre water bottle from inside the car and rinsed out his mouth, then washed his hands and glasses. The front of his T-shirt, which had a Doctor Who-meets-Andy Warhol theme of nine identical but different-coloured Daleks, became a makeshift towel and lens cloth.

Chaseling put his spectacles back on, feeling much better now he was no longer observing the world through a filter of blood spots. There were still specks of blood and brain in his blonde hair. Other bits of kangaroo had become caught in his tawny brown beard. But it was good that he remained ignorant of the fact, because he probably would have used all or most of the water in the bottle trying to rinse himself clean. And in the Red Centre, a little water is a dangerous thing.

He got back into the car and tried the ignition again but got the same click as before, sounding very sluggish and definitely not the preliminary to the RAV's engine grumbling back to life. Stepping back out, he stood and listened for an approaching vehicle. The only sounds to be heard were the buzzing of flies zeroing in on the corpse of the kangaroo and the *clink-clink* of cooling engine parts.

But then there was a flash of light in the distance. A car. He could hear it now. Chaseling positioned himself at the edge of the road. As the lights drew closer, he saw how there was just a single main beam on the left side of the car, with a parking light shining dimly on the right. He started waving his hands.

The car was slowing down. It was an old, battered-looking Ford Falcon which sounded like it badly needed a tune-up, or possibly even a new engine. Now it was passing him, brakes squealing. He got a glimpse of dark faces looking out.

With a crunch of wheels on stones, the Falcon pulled over onto the verge twenty metres ahead of his own car. Chaseling broke into a run. As he closed the gap with the stationary vehicle, he had a fleeting but chilling thought of outback serial killers and the film *Wolf Creek*.

He slowed to a walk when he reached the car and went round to the driver's side. Looking up at him was the smiling face of an Aboriginal man, probably about the same age as Chaseling, mid to late twenties. Gazing over the driver's shoulder was a silver-bearded man aged between fifty and sixty wearing a black cowboy hat. His face also looked friendly, definitely not serial killer material. In the back seat Chaseling saw a boy of perhaps six or seven. The youngster's eyes were wide and apprehensive, regarding Chaseling as if he was some lizard-headed alien that just stepped off a spaceship.

'Need some help, *Kumina?*' asked the man behind the wheel, speaking in a husky, strangely-accented voice.

Chaseling nodded. 'I hit a kangaroo. Then I hit a kangaroo warning sign.'

The cowboy-hatted elder in the passenger seat laughed and said, 'You're a lucky fella!' His voice had the same accent, only stronger, and was also very throaty. Someone with synaesthesia might start smelling campfire smoke when they heard it.

'What happened to the kangaroo?' asked the man behind the wheel.

'Dead,' Chaseling said. 'In front of my car.'

The driver said something to the older man in Pitjantjatjara, the local language, and shifted the gear stick into reverse. As the car slowly started moving backwards, Chaseling walked along beside the open driver's window and said, 'It was critically injured, multiple broken bones, half blind. I put it out of its misery.'

The Falcon stopped in front of the RAV and the two men got out. Both were barefoot and dressed in crumpled T-shirts and jeans. Cowboy Hat ran excitedly to the dead marsupial. '*Malu!*' he said. He grabbed the kangaroo by its thick, long tail and dragged it to the Falcon, detouring around the place where Chaseling had vomited. The other man had the boot lid open. Together they hoisted the roo into the trunk and slammed the lid shut. 'Good tucker,' said Cowboy Hat, whose T-shirt bore the faded image of a loincloth-wearing Aborigine sitting cross-legged playing a didgeridoo.

The younger man turned to Chaseling and said, 'Where you going, *Kumina?*'

'Alice Springs. Starting a job there in three days.'

'Long way from here. We can take you to our community. It's not far.'

Chaseling was travelling light, with just a holdall and swag. He got these from his car. The bedroll had to share the boot with the kangaroo, but the holdall fitted on the back seat, Chaseling and the boy sitting on either side.

As they got under way an orange rim of light appeared on the horizon in front of them. A huge full moon the colour of an amber traffic light had begun to rise, lighting up the road ahead a lot more effectively than the single headlight beam. The driver maintained a moderate speed of no more than 70 km/h. Which meant he was able to take evasive action as a kangaroo, a grey one this time, leapt from the edge of the road and onto the blacktop – where it decided to stop, sitting back on its haunches, its eyes pinpoints of white light as it looked at the rapidly approaching car. The driver's bare foot massaged the brake pedal while his hands gently turned the steering wheel anti-clockwise, putting the car on a course that would take them well clear of the kangaroo. 'The trick is never drive too fast when there's roos about,' he said, then added an angry exclamation in Pitjantjatjara as the kangaroo suddenly did an about-turn and hopped in front of the car again.

'They haven't much road sense,' Chaseling remarked as the driver brought the speed down to a near-crawl and they cruised past the animal, which had paused to observe them again. To Chaseling's delight, there was the head and shoulders of a joey poking from a pouch in the middle of the kangaroo's abdomen.

The driver introduced himself as Clarrie. He had a big gap in his upper front teeth which Chaseling suspected was the result of some tribal ritual rather than bad dental hygiene. The elder was Clarrie's father and his name was Noelie. The boy was Clarrie's son, Davie.

Chaseling glanced across at the boy, who was pressed up against the side door, sitting as far away from the unwelcome passenger as possible. 'Hello Davie,' Chaseling said. The child remained silent, responding only with a quick, fearful look. Perhaps in his world, Chaseling thought, white people meant bad news. He resolved to win him over.

He said, 'Do you know how to play Yes and No?'

'No,' the boy replied in a half-whisper.

'Well, if we were playing you would have just lost that round,' Chaseling said. 'You see, how it works is that one person asks the other questions. And the one who's answering the questions isn't allowed to say "yes" or "no." Now, do you understand the rules to the game?'

'Yes,' Davie said. The two men in the front burst out laughing.

'The idea,' Chaseling said, 'is to say something like "I do" or "that's correct" instead of "yes." Same with "no." So you're totally clear about the rules?'

The boy hesitated, then said, 'I am.'

'Very good. We're playing seriously now. So what are you into Davie – do you like the footie?'

'I do. Australian Rules. Adam Goodes, he's my favourite.'

'Is he?'

'Yes.' Then Davie realised what he'd said and put his hand over his mouth, to another chorus of laughter from his father and grandfather. *These people laugh easily*, Chaseling thought to himself.

Clarrie steered them off the bitumen onto a rutted, potholed dirt track, where the wheels juddered along a series of corrugations – ribs of compacted dirt and stone. Chaseling's head almost hit the roof and he settled deeper into the lumpy seat. 'Now it's your turn to ask the questions,' he told Davie.

The boy thought for a second, then said, 'What are you into?'

'*Doctor Who* comes pretty high,' Chaseling said. 'I like watching old episodes. Do you know how many Doctors there've been over the years?'

'No,' said Davie, then put his hand over his mouth again.

'That's OK,' Chaseling said, 'it's only me who's not allowed to say the words when you're the one asking the questions.'

The boy gave a sly smile. 'What words are they?'

Chaseling decided to fall on his sword. 'Why, "yes," and "no" of course,' he said. Then he slapped himself on the forehead. '*Oh no!*'

'You said it again!' said Davie, laughing.

'Anyway,' said Chaseling, 'I know you're dying to find out how many Doctors there've been. And the answer is twelve. Unless you count the various movie spin-offs, webcasts and audio series, in which case it's around fifty. I wrote a small paper on it when I did a media course at university.'

'What's *un-iv-ers-ity?*' Davie pronounced the word slowly, blurring the last couple of consonants. His eyes were looking up at Chaseling almost hungrily, as if aware that this hitherto unheard-of place could hold the key to exciting new worlds.

'It's my turn to ask the questions,' Chaseling said, 'although when I come to think of it, the rules of Yes and No don't contain an actual ban on questionees asking the odd question. So I'll answer your question. University, also known as uni, is where you go after you finish school and study things in more detail.'

'Like *Doctor Who*?' The boy's eyes were gleaming with delight.

'If you like.'

'I wanna go to uni!' Davie said excitedly.

'Do you?' said Chaseling.

'Yeah.'

'I should have mentioned that saying 'yeah' is the same as saying 'yes,' Chaseling said.

'I'd like a turn at this,' Noelie announced from the front seat. He tilted back his hat as he looked round at Chaseling, his eyes alive with the spirit of fun. 'Ask me something, *Kumina*.'

'Well,' said Chaseling, thinking about the design on the front of Noelie's T-shirt, 'I understand you're pretty good at the didgeridoo?'

'How do you know that?' the cowboy-hatted man said with a look of astonishment, craning his head round.

'Your T-shirt,' Chaseling said, disappointed not to be unravelling, like Holmes to Watson, some more complex piece of deduction. He looked over at the driver. 'How about you, Clarrie – do you play the didge?'

'I play guitar, but I don't play the didge,' Clarrie said.

'So you play the didgeri-*don't*?' This set off a fresh gale of laughter from the two men in the front.

Chaseling gazed across at young Davie, about to get him back into the conversation, but saw the boy's eyes were half closed and his body had sunk low in the seat, his head resting against the holdall.

Clarrie said, '*Kumina*, you said you were going to Alice Springs. What were you doing out here so far from the highway?'

'I drove off the highway and went to Jarramooka. Wanted to have a look at the fossils there.'

He delved into his pocket and produced the fabulous opal he'd found. It glimmered blue and green in the moonlight. Seeing the gleaming thing in Chaseling's hand, Noelie shied away like a vampire exposed to a cross and said something in dialect to his son. Clarrie looked round and said, 'Jarramooka's a sacred place, *Kumina*, people are buried there. That's a bad luck stone. You gotta take it back where you found it.'

Chaseling slowly withdrew the hand holding the opal, regretting his mistake in showing it to the men, feeling a premonition of remorse that he may have desecrated the grave of an honoured ancient. Then he was distracted from his guilt by the Falcon's engine suddenly cutting out. It coughed, then spluttered into life again, but only for a few seconds. The engine gave a final gasp and ground to a complete halt. Clarrie turned round to give Chaseling an accusing look, as though to blame the car's malaise on the unlucky stone.

'Out of petrol?' enquired Chaseling. He gazed over Clarrie's shoulder at the fuel gauge. It was reading below empty.

Clarrie let three seconds pass before replying. 'Yeah,' he grudgingly admitted. He opened his door and got out of the car. 'We're gonna walk, it's not far.'

Chaseling got out. A warm breeze was blowing across the plain, carrying the faint sound of a dog howling somewhere out in the blackness. Clarrie had the boot lid open and was having an animated conversation in dialect with his father, who was shaking his head and apparently rebutting whatever Clarrie was suggesting. But finally the elder nodded and said: '*Uwa.*'

Clarrie turned to Chaseling and said. 'OK, you and my Dad, you're going to lift out that roo and put it on my shoulders.'

'Sure,' Chaseling replied, like someone who was called upon to hoist dead kangaroos every day. He grabbed the roo by the tail while Noelie took its shoulders and they got it out of the car boot, Clarrie standing by with his shoulders lowered ready to receive his load.

The kangaroo was a male, possessed of a large scrotal sack dangling pendulously from its loins, and was the weight of a small man, at least 65 kilos. They draped it stomach-down across Clarrie's shoulders. Clarrie's arms gripped the tail on one side and the back legs on the other. He half-straightened his body, staggering slightly under his burden. He looked like someone wearing a strange fur coat, one that still had the body attached. The mashed, bloodied head of the animal could form a nice little conversation piece as he wore his fur and accompanying corpse to a meeting of his local Greenpeace chapter, Chaseling thought, smiling at the vision and trying to suppress his amusement in case Clarrie took it the wrong way.

Hunched under the weight of the roo, Clarrie took a few experimental steps, then stopped and said something to his father before turning to Chaseling and saying, 'It's too heavy, *Kumina*. I feel like Jesus carrying his cross.'

'We could always take turns carrying it,' Chaseling suggested, without much, if any, enthusiasm.

'No, we'll leave him here and come back for him later,' Clarrie said.

They got the kangaroo back off Clarrie's shoulders and replaced it in the boot alongside Chaseling's swag, which now had a smear of blood on it. But it was nothing compared to Clarrie's T-shirt, the shoulders of which were drenched in kangaroo blood.

'How far away is the community?' Chaseling asked.

'Twenty minutes,' Clarrie said.

Davie stepped out of the car rubbing his eyes. 'We're going for a little walk,' Clarrie told him, then turned to Chaseling and said, 'If you want, you can leave your things in the car and we'll get them later.' Chaseling nodded.

The moon, round as a clock face, had risen higher, around twenty degrees above the horizon, lighting their way along the dirt road, with the vast canopy of stars providing additional illumination. 'That big fella up there,' said Noelie, pointing up at the formation that in the northern hemisphere is called the Sword of Orion and in the southern hemisphere is known as the Pot, 'he's the kangaroo man. *Malu Wati*, we call him. He go up there when he die at Kata Tjuta, after he been killed by dingoes. He live up there with *Mulumura* the lizard woman.'

'*Mulumura*,' echoed the piping voice of the boy, who was walking alongside the elder.

It turned out that the story about the clash between the roo man and the dingoes was a cautionary one. Because not far from the outskirts of the community they encountered a pack of dogs. Wild dogs.

3 THE PACK IS HUNGRY

WILD DOGS roam much of inland Australia. Hunting in packs, they prey on both native wildlife and farm animals. Every now and then, humans are on the menu.

A lot of the wild dogs are dingoes, descendants of the canines that crossed the land bridge into Gondwanaland from the Andaman Islands with their human masters 50,000 years ago or more. Others are descended from dog breeds introduced into Australia over the past two centuries. Both the native dingoes and their feral cousins are equally hated by farmers because they kill sheep and other stock, sometimes just for sport. Conservationists are more divided on the issue, giving the tick of approval to the dingo because it's 'native' while feral dogs are regarded as unholy slayers of bilbies, wallabies and other native wildlife.

To prevent wild dogs wreaking havoc in the prime sheep grazing land of Australia's southern and eastern states, the world's longest fence has been constructed. Called the Wild Dog Fence, it runs for 5600 kilometres, from the middle of the Great Australian Bight in South Australia, up through the central desert all the way to the rural hinterland of Brisbane in the north east. Most of the dog fence is 180 centimetre tall wire mesh. In South Australia, parts of it are made of multi-strand electrified wire.

The desert country where Chaseling and his companions now stood watching a dozen pairs of red eyes appear in the gloom and, as they got closer, attach themselves to shadowy, four-legged forms, was hundreds of kilometres north of the fence. This was Dog Central. Wild dogs formed part of the landscape.

The pack consisted of an assortment of skinny mongrels led by a yellow-eyed male that had the sharp, almost triangular face of a dingo combined with the long, lean body of a greyhound. His short fur was a dirty tea-brown, with darker brown stripes running down the ribcage. His tail was thin, almost rat-like.

Until now, this pack had always steered well clear of human beings. But times had been tough of late. The last decent meal – the remains of an emu – had been consumed over a week ago. And while the dogs' eyes told them that the four figures in front of them were humans, this was overridden by their olfactory senses as the irresistible aroma of freshly-killed kangaroo wafted through the air. Clarrie, his shoulders still wet with essence of roo, was *plat du jour*.

Growling from deep within his throat, Yellow Eyes slowly advanced on Clarrie, teeth bared, a tendril of drool hanging from the wolfish mouth. The dog's ears were pressed against the sides of his head. Down the centre of his back, a line of Mohawk-like hackles was rising. The rest of the pack had come to a halt, watching from the gloom as their leader moved in for the kill.

Clarrie stood solidly, his hands loosely at his sides while the animal approached. He said something in Pitjantjatjara. Noelie, who had scooped up Davie from the ground, gave a terse reply and passed the child to Chaseling. 'Gotta get a weapon.' He darted off to the edge of the road.

Holding Davie in his arms, Chaseling could feel him trembling like a leaf. He heard Noelie stepping into the scrub. And he saw how the pack leader was now just a couple of metres away from Clarrie.

With a guttural snarl, Yellow Eyes reared backwards on his haunches, then launched himself up at Clarrie, who deftly moved aside with the grace of a matador sidestepping a bull. As the animal hurtled through the air, the powerful jaws snapped shut with a percussive sound like a steel trap. The dog landed deftly on his back legs, bunched up his body for the next attack and sprang at Clarrie again. Clarrie held his ground and kicked out at Yellow Eyes, his bare foot managing to avoid the dog's slavering jaws and slam into its sternum. There was a muffled thump and high-pitched yelp. Yellow Eyes fell backwards and made an awkward landing.

The child in Chaseling's arms was rigid with fear. The other dogs were on the move, running around in an ever-tightening circle. Chaseling could smell their foetid odour, hear their excited panting. From the edge of the road, there was the sound of dry wood being broken. Out in the gloom, Chaseling saw a cowboy-hatted form snapping off the side growth of a stout, metre-long piece of mulga branch.

But now one of the dogs circling Chaseling and the child came rushing at them. A kelpie-like black dog with a white patch standing out starkly on its face, it charged towards Chaseling's legs. He lifted his foot to kick at it and the attacker lost its nerve at the last second, veering off course. Then another animal growled a challenge. It was a bull terrier cross, a barrel-chested bitch with piggy little eyes set into a big, bony head, atop which fluttered the remains of a pair of ears tattered from countless fights. From her low-slung stomach dangled half a dozen ugly nipples.

Pig Eyes had short legs, but when hunting prey, used her low centre of gravity to deadly advantage, turning herself into a canine battering ram that could knock animals off their feet.

Jaws wide open and long tongue lolling from her mouth, Pig Eyes came charging towards Chaseling's legs. Davie gave a shriek of terror and started wriggling in Chaseling's arms. As Pig Eyes attacked, Chaseling lifted his foot and kicked out, thankful that he was wearing sturdy, elastic-sided Redback work boots. The bitch's jaws clamped around the toe of his right boot with bruising force. He thought, *Maybe I should have spent a bit more and got the steel-capped Redbacks.*

Pig Eyes hauled backwards while furiously snarling and shaking her head from side to side, throwing off a spray of saliva. Chaseling pulled back his leg, frantically trying to break away as he maintained precarious balance on one foot and held on tight to little Davie, whose struggles had become so violent he was almost sending the pair of them toppling to the ground – where, Chaseling had no doubt whatsoever, they would quickly become dog food. This thought spurred him to a more spirited level of engagement in the tug of war he was having with Pig Eyes over ownership of his elastic-sided boot.

He kicked out, then pulled his foot back towards him. The vise-like grip on his foot was finally released as his boot came loose in the mouth of his attacker and Pig Eyes ran to the edge of the road, her jaws clamped around the prize.

The boot was rich with the aroma of the blood and brain matter that had splattered onto it when Chaseling put the roo out of its misery. Pig Eyes was convinced it was edible. She opened her jaws and let it drop to the ground, where she pinned it down with one of her front paws and started tearing at it with her teeth, letting loose a series of snarls that warned the other dogs to stay well away.

Meanwhile Clarrie was still under attack from the pack leader. The yellow-eyed dog had just been repelled with another kick but now the lithe body was compressed like a coiled spring, ready to relaunch itself at him.

It was then that Noelie appeared alongside brandishing the thick mulga branch. *THWACK!* The sound of the makeshift club coming down on Yellow Eyes' skull sounded like a ball being hit by a cricket bat. The dog gave a yelp, louder and shriller than before, and this time the cry had a note of fear and capitulation. Yellow Eyes slunk off, body hunched and cowed, tail tucked between his legs. At the same time, the other dogs began melting away into the scrub. All of them except Pig Eyes, who for several seconds remained just a short distance away trying to devour Chaseling's Redback. But now she released the boot from her jaws. She stepped forward, lowered her haunches and anointed the boot with a squirt of urine. Then she ran off towards the other dogs.

Seconds later there were snarls and howls so bloodcurdling you might imagine them coming from Cerberus, the multi-headed guard dog at the gates of the underworld.

Wild dog packs often turn to cannibalism to survive. Usually they go for the smallest and weakest member of the clan. But this time it was the pack leader. Having let the tribe down, he'd toppled from the top of the pecking order to the bottom. A snarling Pig Eyes rushed at him, large, bony head lowered and the little eyes glittering evilly as she used her head, and the heavy body attached to it, to knock the leader's legs out from beneath him. Yellow Eyes fell to the dirt, growling a furious challenge. But he was now at a fatal disadvantage because, after hitting the ground, he'd rolled onto his back, the pale fur on his stomach standing out in the gloom. Chaseling saw Pig Eyes lunge forward and bite into the exposed belly. Yellow Eyes gave a howl of agony as Pig Eyes jerked her head backwards, pulling out a shiny length of intestine.

Frantically windmilling his legs, Yellow Eyes tried to get back on his feet. But now the other dogs moved in, clamping their jaws around their victim's legs. Chaseling could hear the crunching of bones as they pulled in opposite directions, trying to tear the limbs off their former Top Dog.

Now Pig Eyes lunged forward again, ripping into Yellow Eyes' abdomen and hauling out something dark and glistening that Chaseling thought was a piece of liver, although it was difficult to tell for sure in the dim light.

Pig Eyes let the prize fall to the ground, placing a paw over it. Raising her bloodied snout to the sky, she let loose a loud, commanding bark that told the others, '*It's party time fellas, tuck in!*' And that's what the pack did.

Seemingly oblivious to the humans watching from less than ten metres away, the pack went into a feeding frenzy. Chaseling could hear wet snuffling noises as dogs pushed forward and ripped the rest of the yellow-eyed dog's innards out while others gnawed and pulled at legs.

Yellow Eyes gave a final, agonised cry, a dreadful ululation that seemed to go on for ever. Then, once he'd fallen silent, there was a rising chorus of growls and yelps as animals fought for prime pieces of flesh and viscera.

Chaseling and his companions had remained frozen with shock as the grisly spectacle unfolded in the moonlight. The boy in Chaseling's arms was whimpering with terror, his body shaking violently. Clarrie took his son from Chaseling's arms. The boy burst into tears.

Clarrie rocked Davie from side to side and spoke some comforting words in Pitjantjatjara. Then, looking over the child's heaving shoulders at Chaseling, his teeth flashed in the moonlight as he said, 'Welcome to central Australia, *Kumina*.'

The three men laughed. Chaseling could hear a note of near-hysteria in his own laughter. He retrieved his boot from the edge of the track, where Pig Eyes had taken it before attacking Yellow Eyes. Standing on one leg, he slipped the Redback onto his foot. There were deep teeth imprints in the toe of the boot and it was wet, slimy and rank-smelling.

They briskly walked away towards the distant lights, Clarrie carrying his son and old Noelie holding the mulga club across his chest like a soldier patrolling with his gun. Soon the sounds of the feasting dogs began to fade and Chaseling could hear the chirping of crickets and the whisper of a breeze sweeping across the plain.

4 ST CATHERINE'S

THE LIGHTS in the distance grew brighter and they soon came to some small, decrepit-looking houses beside the track. Clarrie called out to a group of people tending a fire in front of a home which had orange bin liner plastic taped across the two front windows. In the bare dirt yard, half a dozen children were playing in the shell of a derelict car. The youngsters ran out onto the track and started skipping about as though the circus had just arrived, with Chaseling playing the part of chief clown – three of the children were dancing around him in a circle. He noticed that two of them had twin rivulets of yellow mucous running from their nostrils, the result, he knew from his medical training, of a chronic respiratory infection endemic in remote indigenous Australia. A woman's strident voice sounded from the edge of the fire and the children ran back to their makeshift playhouse in the car shell.

Chaseling and his three companions continued down the track to the centre of the community. There was a general store, its cyclone-meshed window display and padlocked roller door starkly illuminated in the amber light of a sodium lamp set on a steel pole in front of the building. Dozens of large brown moths were flying around the light in frantic circles.

Next, they passed a community hall that had a huge dot painting of a multi-coloured snake along its side. 'The Rainbow Snake, *Wanampi*,' Noelie said.

'*Wanampi*,' Davie trilled.

Clarrie led them past what looked like a disused classroom. Confirming this, he said, 'Not enough kids here anymore for a school. They go to classes in another community, 40 minutes' drive away.'

They passed more houses, none of which were ever going to be featured in *Home Beautiful*. The houses stood on bases of metre-high brick, presumably to handle flooding, although Chaseling couldn't imagine this area ever being anything other than a parched desert. Above the bricks were box-like cement board structures with tin roofs.

Clarrie stopped alongside a home that was in a better state than most of the others, apart from the light green paint peeling like sunburned skin from its walls. He called something out in Pitjantjatjara. A woman appeared in an open doorway, her body silhouetted against the yellow electric light from inside. She hurried down the steps and walked across the yard towards them in bare feet, unfettered breasts swinging under a knee-length floral print dress. At the same time, young Davie ran towards her.

'His mum,' Clarrie explained to Chaseling. 'We're not together anymore.'

'The new normal,' Chaseling commented.

Clarrie introduced him to his ex. Her name was Sandy. 'What are you doing out this way?' she asked him, making shy, faltering eye contact.

'Reducing the local kangaroo population,' he said. 'My car hit a roo and Clarrie gave me a lift. And he says he's going to cook up the roo.'

'Yeah,' Clarrie said, 'but first we gotta get petrol for the car.'

They continued on through the small community till they reached a house fronted by a yard where a small group sat round a fire. A middle-aged woman stood up and approached them. She was wearing what seemed to be the obligatory floral dress. On her head was a beanie displaying the Aboriginal colours of red (for the blood that was shed), yellow (the sun) and black (the skin). After a conversation with Clarrie and Noelie, she turned to Chaseling and smiled. 'Hello, I'm Clarrie's Auntie. They call me Cookie.'

She invited Chaseling to sit by the fire. Meanwhile Clarrie and Noelie disappeared to get a jerry can of petrol and a lift back to their car. There was also mention of '*malu*,' which Chaseling, having mastered his first word of Pitjantjatjara, now knew meant 'kangaroo.'

Chaseling followed Cookie over to the fire pit, where mulga branches were crackling away, tongues of flame reaching almost a metre into the air and hundreds of orange sparks floating skywards. He sat down cross-legged alongside a young man with shoulder-length dreadlocks smoking a large, pungent-smelling joint. The man introduced himself as Lester and offered the spliff to Chaseling, who smiled and said, 'No thanks, but I'll have what he's having.' He nodded towards an old man sitting on the other side of the fire who had a long white beard and sightless eyes clouded over with a milky white film. Chaseling had just watched him put a pinch of green, leafy material into his mouth and start chewing on it. The elder spat a jet of green juice onto a burning branch, where it sizzled briefly.

'What's it called, the stuff you're chewing?' Chaseling asked from across the flames.

'*Pituri*,' the old man answered.

'What does it do to you?'

'You relax,' the man replied. 'And you can go long time with no food or no water.' He reached into the pocket of his jeans and pulled out a wad of light green leaves. He motioned for Chaseling to join him. Chaseling rose to his feet and circled round the fire pit, sitting down beside the elder.

'Get some ash from fire,' the old man told him.

Chaseling reached down and cautiously put his fingers into some powdery white ash at the edge of the pit – it was warm, but not hot. He took a pinch of it and gave it to the old man. 'Is that enough?'

'*Uwa.*'

The elder held the wad of *pituri* in the palm of his hand and kneaded the leaves into the ashes. After about a minute, he held out his hand to Chaseling, who placed the wad in his mouth. The leaves tasted hot and pungent, combined with a stringent alkaline taste from the ash.

Chaseling thanked the old man and resumed his place on the other side of the firepit. He chewed for a while, then addressed the elder. 'What's this place called?'

The old man said, 'Real name Wingalu. Then mission come. They change name to St Catherine's. Mission gone, they knock down the old buildings, but it still called St Catherine's.'

The dreadlocked man spoke up. 'This is where kids lived after being taken from their parents. Stolen generation.'

Chaseling felt a flush of shame and gazed down into the fire. It wasn't just the one generation which had been stolen, it had been several. Throughout the 1800s and three quarters of the way into the twentieth century, the authorities had taken countless thousands of Aboriginal children from their parents. Child protection officers, police and missionaries had scoured the outback, ravaging communities as they dragged screaming children away from their families. The policy was designed to protect Aborigines from themselves, to assimilate them into white society. Now it was acknowledged as a national shame, with living survivors speaking out about the tragic loss of their families and cultural identities as they were raised in white missions and foster homes.

Raising his eyes from their contemplation of the embers, Chaseling saw that Cookie had silently sat down alongside the old man. She was gazing across at him, bright points of light shining in the deep set eyes beneath the beanie. He asked her, 'Were you taken from your family?'

Cookie nodded. 'My family used to hide me from the Child Protection, but they got me when I was ten. Ended up at the mission here.'

The old man spoke up. 'I got taken,' he said. 'After Maralinga. You know 'bout Maralinga?'

'You mean the British nuclear tests?' Chaseling asked.

The old man nodded. And then he told a story.

One morning, back in September 1956, he was camped out in the desert with his parents and two older sisters. He was four at the time and already developing his hunting skills. He saw a set of tracks leading away from the hollow where they'd set up camp. They were the tracks of a perentie, the giant lizard of the desert – chevron-shaped claw marks like a sergeant's stripes, and a swirly line made by the tip of the reptile's tail.

Fascinated, he followed the narrow perentie tracks to the top of a sand dune. It was then that the sky in front of him lit up like a thousand suns. He stood at the crest of the dune rooted to the spot. All he could see was a dazzling white light, so intense that he could feel its searing heat on his face – and his eyes. He held his hands in front of his face and saw the shadowy outlines of bones. Then came the sound of the blast, a huge and extended *boom*, accompanied by a shockwave which sent him tumbling backwards from the top of the dune.

The force of the A-bomb explosion knocked him unconscious. When he came to he could hear his mother's voice. She was calling him, getting closer. But he couldn't see her. He couldn't see much of anything. A dark grey mist had descended on his world and over the following days it turned a permanent shade of black.

'My God,' Chaseling said, 'why weren't you warned?'

'They try to warn everyone and move them somewhere safe,' the old man said. 'But some people, they hide when they see the soldiers coming one week before the test. My father, he see two big green trucks maybe two mile away. He says to me, "They come to take the children." We go and find my mother and sisters – they are digging for witchetty grubs – and then we go walkabout. Army people never find us.'

'Jesus Christ!' Chaseling said. 'It sounds like you were almost at Ground Zero.'

'Two years after Maralinga,' the old man continued, 'my father get real sick. Cancer. Then he die. One year after that, my mother, same thing. Then the Child Protection people, they come and take me and sisters away. Sisters go to a different mission, I never see 'em again. But I come here to St Catherine's. The Jesuits, they bring me up. Used to flog me all the time, with a strap.'

'I'm sorry.' It was an inadequate response, but what else could Chaseling say?

The old man smiled and said, 'Don't worry, not your fault. Anyway, how you feeling now chewing that *pituri*?"

Chaseling hadn't been monitoring his state as he'd masticated his wad of *pituri*, but now he noticed that the flames and sparks from the fire seemed more vibrant. He gazed skywards and felt in awe of the stars glittering like a million jewels up in the heavens. The full moon burned almost overhead and it was now chalk white. His hearing seemed more finely tuned, picking out different sounds: the distant barking of a dog; faint music – it sounded like Bob Marley – drifting from one of the houses; the breath of the wind across the plain. He smiled. 'As James Brown once said, *I feel good!*'

There was a tap on Chaseling's arm. It was the dreadlocked man, Lester. He had a roll of canvas which he unfurled to reveal a painting, rendered in a similar style to the snake on the wall of the community hall but in a lot more detail. An impressive work, it was the vibrant image of four ants with brilliant yellow abdomens, set against a background of lines and circles painstakingly rendered with countless brown and white dots.

The largest of the circles, Chaseling noticed, was filled with a mandala pattern like that of the opal fossil in his pocket. Pointing to the mandala, he asked, 'What does that symbol mean?'

'Eternity,' Lester replied. 'The circles of life. And death.'

5 MEET ALI AND ABDUL

ABDUL AND ALI FAZIR were both part-dressed in camouflage clothing. Abdul wore a green and brown-dappled cotton vest that showed off his heavily muscled arms. A pair of faded jeans and new hiking boots completed his ensemble. Ali's large bottom and fleshy legs, meanwhile, were clad in cargo pants which were a mottled mixture of khaki and olive hues, while his stomach bulged from an over-tight black T-shirt bearing the name of his favourite death metal band, Mayhem, in spiky white letters. On his feet he wore old Converses, their once-white toe caps stained orange by desert dirt. Completing Ali's ensemble were a pair of heavy gold chains which glittered on his neck as he stood beside his brother in the moonlight contemplating a tomato red Holden utility.

The car was buried up to its axle in loose sand. Trying to control the anger he felt towards his brother for steering them into this mess, Abdul gazed towards the south, where there were the lights of several houses. He guessed they were around three kilometres away. Earlier the smell of a wood fire had wafted across the plain, but now the wind had changed direction.

Abdul pointed towards the lights. 'You're going to take a walk and find someone with a car and ropes to pull us out of this.' His Australian accent had a slightly foreign tinge.

Ali's lips formed themselves into a sulky pout. 'You want me to go there alone? We should stick together, brother!' He spoke with a full-blown Australian accent, evidence of the more tender age he'd been when their family arrived in Australia from the Middle East, but the words were delivered in rapid-fire Mediterranean bursts.

Abdul flashed him an angry look. 'My foot's too sore to walk that far and you're the dickhead who drove us into this, so you can get us out of it!'

That morning Abdul had stepped out of his tent in bare feet onto an innocuous-looking carpet of ground cover with small, waxy light green leaves. Then he took another step and let loose a yelp of pain. Hopping on one foot, he looked down and saw what he'd trodden on – a pea-sized burr with long, woody spikes radiating out of it. One of the spikes had pierced two centimetres into the ball of his foot. He'd pulled out the Devil's Thorn (so-called because some people say the spikes look like Satan's horns) and limped back into the tent to get his shoes – plus the first aid kit.

An hour later, the ute had pulled out of the clearing where they'd spent the night, leaving their campsite littered with empty plastic water bottles, beer stubbies, food cans and other rubbish. Abdul was behind the wheel. He'd been doing all the driving on their outback trip, but as now as he pressed down on the accelerator, there was a jolt of pain in the ball of his injured right foot. He braked the car and turned to Ali. 'You'll have to drive. But don't do anything stupid.'

Cautioning his brother not to do anything stupid was generally a futile exercise. Abdul was aged 35 and Ali was 29, the baby of the family, a position he'd consolidated throughout his life by acting childishly and recklessly – especially when he was at the controls of a car.

But for most of the day, everything went well. They'd crossed a vast plain, the landscape so flat that it wasn't really flat because you could see the curve of the earth. Ali had kept to a sedate speed on a 'road' which consisted of two ribbons of rust-red dirt. Then, in the late afternoon, an emu had run out in front of them. The giant, grey-feathered bird paused in the centre of the track, looking at the approaching car with bulging orange eyes. Then it hurtled into the scrub, putting on an impressive turn of speed, its long neck tilted forward like a jockey atop a horse. Ali steered the car off the track in close pursuit. The ute's engine roared as he gunned the accelerator, trying to ram the car into the giant bird. Abdul saw disaster looming. *'Slow down!'* he screamed.

Ali had eased his foot off the pedal slightly, abandoning the idea of slamming the car into the emu, but keeping up the chase. The emu suddenly changed direction, heading to the left towards a hollow of bare dirt. Ali followed – and the ute came to a halt, its wheels churning uselessly in loose sand. And then Ali made it worse by putting his foot down too hard on the accelerator and digging them ever-deeper into the morass. Meanwhile, the emu had disappeared into the scrub.

They'd tried hoisting the car with a high-lift jack but the hollow was filled with light, almost dust-like particles of red dirt. The base of the jack kept sinking deeper as they tried to raise one of the wheels high enough to place some sticks beneath it.

So now they needed to be dragged out by another vehicle. There was no mobile phone reception but the lights in the near-distance would hopefully yield a rescuer. 'A four wheel drive with good tyres should do the job,' Abdul told his brother. 'A tractor would be even better. Tell them they'll get $100 for pulling us out.'

But Ali was not relishing the prospect of a nocturnal walk through this wild country. 'I might get attacked by some animal,' he protested.

Abdul said, 'There are no man-eating animals in Australia, unless you count dingoes but they usually just go for babies.'

'I could get bitten by a snake!'

'Snakes don't come out at night,' said Abdul, who had no idea whether this was the case or not, nor whether dingoes only ate infants.

Abdul had considered the idea of camping at the spot overnight. But in the east, dark clouds loomed. Lightning flickered every now and then. They needed to get the hell out of here and make a beeline for the Stuart Highway. The whole area could be flooded by morning.

But Ali did not seem to share Abdul's sense of urgency. Abdul watched him opening the passenger door of the ute and sitting down. The interior light came on and Abdul's crow-black eyebrows creased into a frown as he saw his brother opening the glove box.

Ali got out a small zip-lock bag and delved into it with a plastic spoon fashioned from the end of a 7-Eleven Slurpee straw. Then he carefully removed a few flakes of crystal methamphetamine and placed them on the lid of a square metal tin which held the marijuana he smoked when he came down off the ice. He crushed the crystals into a white powder with the end of a plastic cigarette lighter. Then he scooped up the ice with the spoon and transferred it to a glass meth pipe, tapping the drug into a blackened round bowl. He turned off the car's interior light and sparked the lighter, the flame lighting up his face from beneath in a demonic orange glow.

Abdul limped to the back tray of the ute and got out a fold-up canvas chair. He was very different in appearance from his brother. While Ali was overweight, with long dark brown hair and an unkempt beard, Abdul was clean-shaven, bald-headed and muscular. While Ali's arms, neck, back and one leg were a writhing mass of tattoos, with a dark blue teardrop underneath his left eye, Abdul had just a single small tattoo, a Cedar of Lebanon, on his right forearm.

He unfolded the chair and set it down in a patch of bare earth a few metres away from the ute, through the open window of which he could see Ali dragging deeply at the meth pipe. Abdul didn't approve of his brother's habit, but couldn't get too self-righteous about it because the pair of them, with their older brother Mehmet, operated an enterprise which made large amounts of money from selling crystal methamphetamine, the proceeds being laundered through Mehmet's strip club in Sydney's notorious Kings Cross.

Both Abdul and Ali played pivotal roles in the family business. Abdul sourced the ice from a network of bikie gangs who manufactured the drug. He was Head of Inventory and Supply, if you like. And Ali? He had no official title either but if he had one it would be Chief Enforcer.

Although Ali was fat, he was strong. And quick with the knife. Abdul had once seen him slice open the belly of a man who'd been unable to come up with promised funds. Ali had moved so swiftly that the blade was just a silver blur. The man had looked down to see a Niagara of blood gushing onto the concrete of the McDonalds carpark where he regularly conducted business. The following week, he'd settled his debt in full. Not in person of course, because he was still in intensive care, but a relative paid the outstanding amount.

Another debtor, one who'd managed to get robbed of four ounces of ice supplied by the brothers on consignment, and who'd then insisted that the $20,000 owing should be written off, had paid with his life. On that occasion Ali's weapon had been a Glock pistol. He hid himself in a thick patch of bushes at the front of the debtor's house and lay in wait.

Through his screen of foliage Ali saw a black Maserati pulling up. The engine gave a final howl and the night fell quiet. He saw the faint shapes of a man and woman getting out and heard car doors slamming. Ali slipped on his black ski mask as he heard footsteps approaching.

When the couple were less than four metres away, Ali jumped up in the waist-high bushes like a jack-in-the-box and fired five bullets. The man collapsed to the ground and was DOA at St Vincent's Hospital. Ali had also managed to fire one bullet into the man's companion – who turned out to be the daughter of Mohammed Khaled, who'd been named in two royal commissions and countless internal NSW police reports as being the head of a crime empire which made their own family business seem like a humble cottage industry. You did *not* want to get the Khaleds offside, so it had been fortunate for Ali and his brothers that the girl's wound was superficial, a hole through her shoulder muscle. It was also fortunate that the only description of the gunman she could give police was very vague: a big man wearing a ski mask and dark clothes.

The pistol Ali had used was a cleanskin and he'd disposed of it in a canal. But recently, word had come from a source in the Middle Eastern Organised Crime Squad that he'd been pinged – DNA evidence from the paper wrapping of the felafel roll he'd wolfed down while lying in wait in the bushes, and that he hadn't been smart enough to take away with him. Their contact, a detective constable who received a monthly retainer along with free drinks and sexual services at the strip club (where some of the girls also worked as hookers), had warned that strenuous efforts were now being made to dig up further evidence implicating Ali. He'd also said it would be at least a month before detectives could put together enough material to charge him. Once that happened, he'd be a dead man walking. The Khaleds would get him long before a jury deliberated his case.

And so Ali had been ordered by his two older brothers to take a sojourn in the Middle East while the heat died down. Mehmet and Abdul had in mind the quiet village in southern Lebanon where they'd spent their very early years, and where they still had close relatives. Or Beirut, if Ali wanted some life in the fast lane. But Ali had flabbergasted his brothers when he said yes, he'd go to the Middle East – but his destination would be Syria.

Over the past year Ali had been associating with the Sydney disciples of a jihadist cleric called Sheikh Omar Halab who'd preached a few times at Lakemba Mosque before his extreme views got him banned from the lectern. A few members of the group had since joined the ranks of the 200-plus Australians who were now in the Middle East fighting for Islamic State.

Ali had been exchanging WhatsApp messages with one of his radicalised friends, Wassim Hariri, who was living in the northern Syrian rebel stronghold of Raqqa. Wassim had given Ali a contact in southern Turkey who'd help him get across the border.

But before Ali went off to fight the infidel, his older brothers were buying him a bit of life insurance. They'd organised this shooting trip so he could get some practice firing high calibre rifles at moving targets in desert terrain. Abdul, who had a clean police record and could therefore get a shooting licence, had purchased two sporting rifles. They weren't automatic assault weapons, but the Remington Model Seven Stainless rifles fired .243 bullets the size of a man's little finger with the stopping power to bring down a large animal – or a human. The family scion Mehmet had lent them his ute and they'd driven over the Blue Mountains, into the desert country beyond Broken Hill, waging war on the local wildlife along the way.

The guns clipped into a rack Abdul had built into the tray of the ute. Stepping out of the cabin after his smoke of meth, Ali went around to the back and got his rifle. It was a deadly-looking weapon with a black polymer stock, gleaming stainless steel barrel and large silver telescopic sight. He slung the gun over his shoulder by its black webbing strap.

'Leave the gun here, brother,' Abdul told him, 'It might freak people out.'

Ali cursed – it was an Arabic phrase, *bala'a il a'air*, which meant 'cocksucker' – and replaced the rifle. He took a torch and bottle of water from the cabin of the car.

'I'll flash the headlights on and off every ten minutes so you can find your way back,' Abdul called after his brother's retreating form. 'You better hurry, there's a storm on the way.'

'*Bala'a il a'air!*' Ali shouted back. He lumbered off into the gloom, the torch beam picking out a path between the sparse patches of mulga.

Ali was one of the very small number of people on earth who could get away with calling his brother a cocksucker. In fact, probably the only other person who'd be able to do that was their elder brother Mehmet.

As Ali's form disappeared into the gloom, Abdul got a bamboo mat from the back of the ute and laid it out over a patch of bare dirt, where there definitely wouldn't be any Devil's Head Thorns lurking. Then he started doing push ups. Three sets of twelve, with breaks of thirty seconds in between. This would help to ensure his pecs were in good form next time he flexed them on a Muscle Boys Afloat cruise.

Muscle Boys Afloat was a male stripper cruise that his cousin Ziad operated from a rundown old showboat on Sydney Harbour. On Saturday nights, Abdul would be a special guest. He wouldn't be an official part of the show, but between acts he liked to impress the girls who flocked on board for their hen parties by taking his shirt off out on deck and flexing his pecs. First his left pec would ripple as though a pair of electrodes had been applied to it, then the right pec would spring into action, then the left again… It wasn't exactly an act that would get him booked in Vegas, or anywhere else for that matter, but the girls liked it.

A psychiatrist might well have a field day delving into the mind of a man who liked to have women ogling his tits. And that same shrink would probably be very interested in the fact that, despite the pride Abdul took in his pecs, he suffered from a distinct degree of body dysmorphia when it came to his abs.

Abdul didn't have a six-pack. His was a four-pack. Nature had cruelly decreed that the bottom set of *glutus maximus* protrusions remained hidden. Which looked fine… to everyone else in the world except Abdul. So when he flaunted his bare torso on board the cruises or on other occasions, Abdul would hold his lower arm in such a way that it obscured his midriff, or at least enough of it for a casual observer to assume he had a full six-pack. Usually he'd accomplish this by holding a stubby of beer in front of his abs. When the time came to sip the beer, he'd casually switch the bottle to his other hand and lift it to his lips while continuing to shield the stomach which was so unjustly two short of a six-pack. Recently he'd started exploring the notion of having a two-pack surgically implanted.

6 HEAD OF BEHEADING

ALI TOOK A WEAVING PATH through the scrub, keeping to the stretches of bare earth. Every now and then he'd reach down and touch the hilt of the hunting knife at his belt. The feel of it was reassuring, calming. He was glad his brother hadn't tried to make him relinquish it along with his rifle.

He'd ordered the knife on the web and taken delivery of it a few days before they left for their shooting trip. It was called a Jungle Master and had a 10 inch blade. One side was honed to a razor-like sharpness. On the opposite edge, the blade was serrated, a vicious saw with wickedly sharp teeth. So far, four days into their trip, Ali had used his Jungle Master to decapitate three kangaroos, a dingo, a feral goat and a massive camel.

Ali's meth-tightened facial muscles creased into a smile as he recalled the death and beheading of the camel two days earlier. The beast, descended from the dromedaries driven across the outback by Afghan cameleers back in the 1800s, had represented the ultimate challenge to his surgical skills.

Abdul had managed to steer the ute close to the camel, which stood less than 30 metres away, its head down grazing on the leaves of a small bush. Before the vehicle came to a halt, an excited Ali had the door open and leapt out clutching his rifle. He put the weapon to his shoulder and pumped six bullets into the massive brown body, none of which brought it down, before a calmer Abdul stepped from the ute and aimed his rifle just behind the animal's shoulder blade. He fired a single round which penetrated the camel's heart and brought it crashing down to the desert floor like a felled tree.

Even as the camel's legs kicked in its final spasms, Ali had run to it and drawn the Jungle Master. Like a surgeon exploring the area to be operated on, he reached down and felt the camel's twitching neck around its top vertebrae. Then he lifted the watermelon-sized head by one of its ears and slashed into the throat, cutting through the windpipe and surrounding tissue. Ali then made a deep cut on either side of the neck and copious amounts of blood gushed out as the carotid arteries were severed. Next he sawed between the vertebrae at the back. Finally he put the bloody Jungle Master down and took the camel's head in both hands. With a quick jerking motion, he twisted the head anticlockwise almost 180 degrees. There was a tearing sound as the head parted from the animal's long neck and loose skin broke away. Then Ali triumphantly held his trophy aloft like a racing driver who'd just won the Grand Prix. The entire process had taken a bit over 30 seconds.

He longed for the time, not long from now, when he'd be able to practice his skills on humans. His desire to kill and maim other human beings was his real driving force in wanting to go to the front line in Syria. He wasn't in the slightest bit interested in the politics or the religion.

While some people might have an ambition to jump out of a plane wearing a parachute harness, or to climb a Himalayan peak without oxygen, Ali saw the pinnacle of his own future achievement as beheading *kufr* with his Jungle Master. Maybe he could even take over from the infamous executioner known as 'Jihadi John.'

Jihadi John was actually an ex-Londoner called Mohammad something – Ali couldn't remember the surname. Wearing a black hood, he'd wielded a knife very similar to Ali's Jungle Master in a string of Islamic State beheading videos. But lately, Jihadi John had dropped out of sight and there had been reports he'd been killed in a drone attack. Maybe there was now an opening in the Islamic State job market and Ali could become the new Head of Beheading.

As Ali made his way through the scrub, weaving between black, claw-like mulga branches, he fantasised about being the star of the latest Islamic State beheading clip. He saw himself out in the Syrian desert, framed by the camera lens, standing over the kneeling form of a blindfolded man in an orange jumpsuit. Behind them would be a line of hooded, black-uniformed warriors holding AK-47s. Ali's face would also be masked and he'd be wearing the same kind of full-length black robe favoured by Jihadi John.

The condemned man might be a Syrian soldier, an American journalist, a downed Russian pilot, maybe even an academic expert in the ancient temples, statues and other symbols of idolatry which dotted the desert. The camera would zoom in on Ali's face, just two eyes in a black hood. His eyes would burn into the lens as he said: 'We are unstoppable! Whoever stands in the ranks of *kufr* will be a target for our swords. *Allahu Akbah!*

'*Allahu Akbah!*' the faceless men behind him would echo. Then the camera would show Ali lifting his Jungle Master from its sheaf. 'Death to the infidel!' he'd shout before grabbing his victim's hair and …

Ali was suddenly jolted back to reality. *A snake!* That was what it looked like, lit up in the torch beam. Long and black, lying unmoving on its belly in the dirt, but ready to spring into attack mode and sink its fangs into his leg. Ali's heart, already pumping hard from the effects of the ice, performed a drum roll and his knees started quivering. He wasn't scared of many things, but snakes were a definite exception to that rule.

But then, as he held the beam still, he saw that the snake was really a rippling, serpentine length of fallen wood. He gave a nervous laugh and licked his lips. Despite now knowing it was inanimate and harmless, he gave the branch a wide berth as he resumed his trudge.

A small grasshopper settled on Ali's sweat-beaded face and he swatted it away. With the moon so high in the sky, there was now a lot of natural light and he would be able to pick his way through the scrub without the flashlight, and the bugs it was starting to attract. But like the Jungle Master at his hip, the torch beam was reassuring, so he kept it on. The lights of the houses were closer now, perhaps another half hour's walk. On the horizon, lightning flickered. Several seconds later, there was a faraway rumble of thunder. Ali quickened his pace.

7 ROAST ROO

CLARRIE AND NOELIE had retrieved their car, which now pulled up near the group sitting around the fire. The pair got out of the Falcon and lifted the kangaroo from the trunk, then carried it down the gloomy side passage of the house.

Chaseling was feeling very relaxed from the *pituri*, which he continued to chew like a ruminant with its cud. In his lap he was nursing a roll of canvas – the painting by the dreadlocked man, Lester. It was called *Honey Ant Dreaming* and Chaseling had purchased it for $200. Now Lester had just gone off to find another canvas, titled *Perentie Dreaming*, that he wanted to show him. Chaseling leaned back and gazed up at the night sky. It was like a divine revelation. There, laid out for him like the dots in Lester's painting, were all the wonders of the cosmos. The sky was *alive*. A shooting star made a quick, flaring journey, then disappeared. The full moon hung overhead with a yellow ring surrounding it, a giant eye gazing down.

Something flashed low on the horizon. Chaseling shifted his gaze, to the line of black clouds moving in from the east. Every second or so, there were silver flickers of lightning.

'It's gonna rain, better get this fella cooking quick.' It was Noelie, his hands gripping the tail of the road-killed roo while Clarrie clutched its forelegs. The animal had been skinned and gutted and its carcase was red, wet and glistening, as were the arms of the pair carrying it. They heaved the roo onto the fire, setting off an eruption of sparks.

With Noelie presiding, they carefully roasted the marsupial, turning it in the flames with a shovel every now and then. But they only let the kangaroo cook in the fiercely-blazing fire, the dial of the stove turned all the way up, so to speak, for a relatively brief time, no longer than ten minutes. Then they rolled it out onto an old sheet of corrugated iron. A bit later, once the flames were dying down to coals, they transferred the roo back into the pit, raking the embers so the carcase was half-buried in them.

Meanwhile, Chaseling found himself purchasing the *Perentie Dreaming* painting, so now there were two rolls of canvas in his lap. They would make excellent companion pieces on the wall of wherever he settled in Alice Springs. A stray spark settled on the edge of one of the canvas cylinders and he hurriedly brushed it away. 'I'm going to stash these in my bag so they don't get holes burned in them,' he told Lester. He got up and took the canvases to Clarrie's car.

After he returned to his spot at the fire pit, Cookie held out a battered enamel mug like a hostess offering a guest some *canapés*. 'Honey ants,' she said. 'We dug 'em up this afternoon.'

In the bottom of the cup was a squirming mass of ants with enormously-distended transparent, amber-coloured abdomens, the size of small marbles. From the tips of their dark heads to the end of the swollen abdomens, the insects were two and a half centimetres long.

Seeing Chaseling's hesitation, Cookie said, 'Here, I'll show you.' She reached into the mug and grabbed the head of an ant between forefinger and thumb, then lifted the insect bottom-upwards to her mouth before tilting her head back slightly and biting off the sac of nectar. 'Mmmm!' She ran her tongue round her lips. Flicking away the ant's head and thorax, she held the cup out to Chaseling again.

His hand slowly moved forward. 'They don't bite, do they?

She flashed a reassuring smile. 'No, *Kumina*.'

Throwing caution to the winds, he reached into the can and lifted out an ant by the head. The insect's legs moved frantically as he lifted it to his mouth. 'Bottoms up,' he said, before biting off the abdomen, which burst like a fragile grape in his mouth. But because he had his head angled downwards, and the honey was a lot thinner in consistency than the bee variety, most of the nectar ran back between his teeth, then down his fingers.

Licking his fingers, Chaseling got a tantalizing taste of sweetness offset by a smoky tang. He tried a second ant, tilting his head back this time to prevent spillage. Warm nectar flooded his tongue and he savoured it for a couple of seconds before swallowing it down. He gave the thumbs-up sign to Cookie.

After treating himself to a third ant, Chaseling urged her to share the delicacies around with the others gathered around the fire. Throwing the remains of the dismembered insect into the ashes, he said, 'I was wondering what happened to the mission. When I was over by Clarrie's car, I saw some old concrete foundations. I thought maybe that was where the mission used to be.'

'That's right,' she said.

'What happened to the mission buildings?'

'We burned 'em down.' she said. 'After the nuns and the priests cleared out. We even burned down the church.' Looking guilty, she made the sign of the cross. 'There'd been too much cruelty, the mission had to go.'

She told him about the frightful abuse of children on the mission by a priest called Father Mahoney. 'He went to jail in the end,' she said. 'I heard he died a few years back. Some of us mob celebrated. He was the Devil.'

Noelie and Clarrie rolled the kangaroo out of the fire onto a sheet of corrugated iron. Chaseling marvelled at how they were able to tread with bare feet on small embers at the edge of the fire pit without apparently feeling any discomfort. He thought how he'd like to touch the soles of their toughened, calloused feet, just to discover what they felt like. Bone? Sanded wood?

The roo was left to continue cooking in its own juices atop the iron sheet for another fifteen minutes or so. Then the ribbed sheet of metal became Clarrie's cutting board as he sliced thick juicy slabs from the haunch and shoulder with an old but evidently very sharp wooden-handled knife. He put some of these aside for himself on the edge of the corrugated sheet and placed the rest of the prime cuts on an old tin plate which he handed to his father. Next to be served were Cookie and the elderly blind man. Then a procession of people appeared fireside with an assortment of plates and bowls. One of them was a sensational looking girl in a pink mini skirt and white T-shirt which set off the dark colour of her skin. She looked shyly across the fire at Chaseling before melting back into the darkness with a segment of roo tail on a tin plate.

Finally, just when Chaseling was starting to fear that he was going to be excluded from the feast, Clarrie motioned for him to come over to the other side of the fire pit. Despite being the last to be served, the portion dished up onto a plate-sized piece of cardboard was a generous one, thick slices from the top of the roo's massive back legs. He returned to his position on the far side of the fire, where he took a piece of the dark, delicious-smelling meat and popped it into his mouth. He chewed tentatively, then greedily at the lean meat. It was tender, gamey and juicy, with a smoky aftertaste.

After dinner, Clarrie produced a battered-looking acoustic guitar. He started strumming, and even though the instrument had the top string missing, he managed to coax a good, tuneful sound from it. He played a rhythm which was part reggae, part country and part something else not so easily defined. Then he began singing in the Pitjantjatjara dialect. The old blind man hit two sticks together, producing a slow, hypnotic rhythm.

Chaseling closed his eyes as he listened, then opened them again as guitar, vocals and clap sticks were joined by a series a visceral, other-worldly sounds. Noelie had sat down alongside his son and was blowing into a two-metre long didgeridoo painted with images of animals and other tribal emblems.

Closing his eyes again, Chaseling reflected that this was the most relaxed and contented he had felt in a long time. For years, in fact. Since he'd started training to be a doctor.

Chaseling had an extremely retentive memory which had always helped him pass exams with a minimum of study. All the same, it had been a hard slog. Six years at the University of Sydney medical school, then another year as a hospital intern. He hadn't had much of a life during that time. His existence had revolved around passing the next series of exams. Then when he'd started at the hospital, the challenge had been shifts which stretched for twelve hours. It was during such a shift that Chaseling had been caught in *flagrante delicto* with a nursing assistant in a storage room. They weren't actually interrupted in the act; they'd finished their brief but intense coupling on the floor atop a makeshift bed of hospital gowns and they were getting dressed. A flushed and sweaty Chaseling was putting his foot into the leg of his trousers as the nurse, a petite blonde named Maria Vlasnik, was reaching behind her back to fasten a flesh-coloured bra.

The door suddenly opened and a male nursing assistant called Federico took a half step into the room before giving a gasp of surprise. Then his lips contorted in revulsion and he gave a little squeal of horror. 'B-but, you're married!' he said to Maria.

'Things haven't been going well at home lately,' she replied dismissively.

The male nurse's eyes lingered on Maria's cleavage as she bent down to retrieve her blue uniform shirt from the floor. Then he backed out of the room and slammed the door.

Federico hadn't reported the incident but he'd gossiped about it. Maria was transferred away from the orthopaedic ward and word of the illicit union filtered up to Chaseling's boss, the hospital's head of orthopaedics, Professor Miles McManus.

McManus was an evil-tempered tyrant who routinely shouted at doctors and nurses in the wards and operating theatre. He had a very high opinion of himself and an almost uniformly low opinion of the junior doctors and nurses in his charge. For years, he'd got away with terrible bullying and sexual harassment. He fancied himself as a ladies' man, sporting a thin, carefully trimmed moustache in the style of Hollywood heart throbs Clark Gable and Errol Flynn. Not so long ago, he'd been able to virtually take his pick of the young female doctors and nurses in his charge. But seemingly overnight, he'd grown old. And conventions had changed. These days, when he made sexual advances to the women in his workplace, they were invariably rebuffed. His last conquest, if it could be called that, had been a 61-year-old ward sister, who'd shown up for their romantic liaison with her face caked in makeup and her body squeezed into a dress two sizes and around thirty years too small. When he woke the next morning, McManus had looked across at the face of the snoring woman next to him lit up in the cold light of day – and reflected that she looked like some dreadful old whore.

And so when McManus heard how Chaseling had been caught half naked in the storeroom with the vivacious junior nurse, a woman who'd curtly rebuffed his own clumsy advances, the news made him bitter and he started singling Chaseling out for particularly vicious treatment.

In the operating theatre, McManus would snarl brusque commands to Chaseling from behind his surgical mask and find fault in everything he did. During ward rounds, he ignored him. Some of Chaseling's colleagues sycophantically followed the professor's lead and started treating Chaseling as a non-person, staring straight through him when they passed in the hospital corridor. It became a toxic workplace and he was hugely relieved when his internship came to an end.

But still McManus continued to haunt him. When Chaseling applied for jobs as an orthopaedic registrar at major hospitals in cities and provincial centres, he was continually rebuffed after the Professor was contacted and gave a damning assessment of Chaseling's abilities. The only exception was Alice Springs Hospital, which had offered Chaseling a position after interviewing him via Skype. He didn't know whether they had talked to McManus or not – probably not, although there was always the chance that the Professor had relished the idea of banishing him to the most isolated part of Australia and had thus finally given him a positive rap when contacted by the HR manager of Alice Springs Hospital.

Now, as he relaxed by the fire in the middle of the desert with his new friends, Chaseling reflected that what he'd considered to be an exile to central Australia was actually going to give him experiences that he'd never have in any city. Despite his car having been wrecked, he was relishing this adventure. He was living a life.

He stretched out sideways beside the fire, which had now all but lost its glow, just faint points of dull red light shining here and there in the otherwise dark embers. But the full moon provided a light bright enough to read by. Reclining with the edge of his head against his hand, his eyes took in a couple of empty food tins at the edge of the fire pit. They were rectangular shaped with rounded edges. Chaseling tilted his head to read the label. 'CAMP PIE,' it said.

Chaseling remembered Camp Pie from his boy scout days. Only by nomenclature was it related to the pie and its many manifestations, from Australia's humble beef and gravy offering to gastronomic delights like Beef Wellington. Camp Pie was a variety of the reconstituted meat commonly known as spam. He suspected that it figured a lot more prominently in these peoples' current diet than kangaroo or other traditional indigenous foods. At medical school he'd learned that poor diet was the prime reason for the shockingly high disease and mortality rates among Australia's indigenous communities. The life expectancy of the people he was sitting with around the fire was something like ten years less than his.

What Chaseling didn't know was that there was about to be a sudden jump in the local mortality rate here in St Catherine's.

8 RUBY'S NIGHTMARE

ALI RAPPED HIS KNUCKLES against the weather-beaten door. 'Hello?' he called. All he could hear were faint strains of music and people's voices from some other houses a few hundred metres away. But when he'd emerged from the desert into the bare dirt back yard of this house, he'd seen, lit up in an uncurtained window, a sexy-looking girl. She was standing next to the window washing dishes.

He raised his hand to the timber and knocked again. Along the first finger joints of his hand the letters 'BROS' had been inexpertly tattooed, a souvenir from Ali's incarceration in a place called Kariong Juvenile Justice Centre. The letters on the back of his fingers were rendered as part of his induction into a gang called Brothers 4 Life. The crime that had landed Ali in Kariong? Rape.

There was no response from inside the house, but he could hear the faint clatter of plates and cutlery. Ali opened the door wider and went in. He found himself in a room dimly lit by an old 1970s-style lava lamp, a glowing vermilion tube with ectoplasmic bubbles rising and falling inside. The furniture was sparse, just an old table, two wooden chairs, and a sagging couch. Ali noticed a poster of hip hop artist 50 Cent on one wall. On a shelf was a sports trophy – a dust-coated golden statuette of a man in jersey and shorts holding a rugby ball. Beside the trophy was a framed school photo of a black teenage girl, her face beaming happily into the lens. At the end of the room was an open doorway, a bright yellow rectangle of light. The washing-up sounds grew louder as Ali moved towards the doorway. 'Hello?' he said.

In the kitchen, Ruby Jakamara was washing dishes under the glare of a bare lightbulb hanging from the ceiling. She was listening to a Nicki Minaj song, *Anaconda*, through the buds of the iPhone her auntie Shirley had given her on her seventeenth birthday a month earlier. Despite her auntie's caution to keep the volume level down and thereby conserve her hearing, Ruby had it turned up high. The track was a eulogy to women with big butts, with the pneumatic-bottomed Minaj showing plenty of her own in the YouTube clip that had notched up more than half a billion hits.

Ruby's own butt was on the larger side and when she was younger she'd lamented the fact that she'd never be a super model, except possibly a plus-sized one. But Nicki Minaj was a sex goddess whose anthem delivered the message that *'anaconda don't want none unless you got buns hun.'* Which made Ruby feel good about herself. As she scrubbed and rinsed dishes and cutlery at the stainless steel sink, she wiggled her pink miniskirted bottom in time to the music and rapped along with the American artist, *'he don't like 'em boney, want something he can grab...'*

However, at this moment Ruby's thoughts were actually far from big butts, centred instead on her near future. In less than three months' time, she'd be starting a design course at Centralian College in Alice Springs, and maybe after that, once she'd got her certificate, she might start a fashion label. She could use designs from Lester and some of the other artists on this community. But by then she wouldn't be living here anymore. She'd be in Alice Springs, or maybe even Sydney, Melbourne or one of the other big cities. *I could come back here like, once a year, every Christmas*, she thought to herself.

Suddenly she noticed a large human form framed in the doorway. Her head jerked round. Standing there gazing at her was a fleshy white man with untidy dark hair and beard. His arms were a mass of tattoos. A huge knife hung from his belt. But the most frightening thing about him was his eyes – shining, unblinking pools of darkness. Underneath the left eye, the outline of a tear drop had been inked into the skin.

Tearing out her ear buds, Ruby tried to keep her voice steady as she said: 'What do you want?'

'I need help with my car,' Ali said. His eyes were fixed on Ruby's breasts under the thin cotton of a white T-shirt bearing the words LIVE LOVE DANCE. The pale tip of his tongue flicked out, then back in, like a reptile testing the air.

'You can talk to my uncle, I'll take you to him,' Ruby said.

Ali took two steps towards her.

'Or you can wait here to see my uncle, because he said he'd be here in one minute,' Ruby added, her voice shaking.

'What's your name, babe?' Ali said, taking two more steps closer.

Suddenly Ruby lashed out with her foot and tried to kick him in the balls, but Ali twisted to the side and her bare foot slammed into his hip. *'Bitch!'* he hissed, reaching down and pulling the knife from the sheaf at his belt. Then moving lightning quickly, he grabbed her arm and pulled her towards him.

'If you try screaming for help I'll cut you,' he whispered in her ear. 'I'll cut you up real bad. You understand me?' Ali's left arm encircled her neck like a tattooed python while his right hand brandished the Jungle Master. Ruby felt the needle-sharp tip of the knife on her cheek. 'I understand,' she whimpered.

Ali laughed – a high-pitched, whinnying sound. A cruel sound. And Ruby's nightmare began.

9 SORRY TIME

ABDUL WALKED over to the stranded ute, limping slightly as he favoured his injured foot, which thankfully was starting to feel a bit better. He could place more weight on it now. The Tea Tree oil he'd rubbed into the puncture had eased the swelling.

He got into the driver's seat and flicked the headlights once, twice, then a third time. After pausing for ten seconds, he repeated the exercise. He reflected, not for the first time, that his younger brother was a major worry and had been since he was a toddler, when he used to tear the wings off the flies trapped against a French door at the back of the family home. Watching them crawling around like flightless beetles on the floor, Ali would laugh with delight in the way another, normal three-year-old might chortle at the antics of The Wiggles.

Leaving the cabin of the car, Abdul helped himself to a Crown Lager from one of two drinks eskies they'd brought, along with a single cooler for food. He returned to the camping chair he'd set up in a bare patch of dirt. The storm was much closer now, a churning tsunami of dark cloud straddling the horizon. It promised untold mayhem when it arrived. In the middle there was a funnel, black as coal, reaching down to earth. Every few seconds, this eye of the storm would light up as lightning flickered inside it. The wind was picking up. Abdul was wearing open sandals and he could feel wind-borne grit on his feet and ankles. *Definitely not a night to be sleeping in a tent*, he thought to himself. Nor did he relish the thought of sheltering from the tempest alongside Ali in the cabin of the ute.

Ali gibbered and screamed in his sleep. He'd done so all his life. In their childhood Abdul had shared a bedroom with Ali. Almost every night, he had found himself being jolted from his slumbers by Ali giving vent to bloodcurdling screams and yelling out things like *'I'm gonna kill ya!'*

Their parents had tried putting Ali on various tranquillizers before he went to bed but for some reason the medication only made his nocturnal outbursts more intense. Now, of course, Ali was taking his own medication – crystal meth. And that didn't help either. During the current shooting trip, he'd heard loud shouts and groans coming from Ali's tent in the early hours. Abdul had started pitching his own tent further away, but still he'd been woken by his brother's nightmares.

Yes, Ali was a major worry.

Ali staggered out of the house. He was panting. His eyes were wild and unfocused. His T-shirt was splashed with red stains. He ran around the building and into the gloomy yard behind the house. Here he stopped for a few seconds to work out the direction back to Abdul and the car. No flashing headlights, but his brother had said he was going to flick them on every ten minutes. He glanced furtively over his shoulder. Then he set off into the scrub, moving at a half-run.

As he fled into the gloom, Ali's face wore an expression of abject self-pity, mouth turned down at the sides and eyebrows creased together. *It was her fault*, he thought. *The black bitch.* He broke through a low patch of bushes with thin, sharp-tipped leaves that stabbed through the legs of his thin camouflage pants like little needles. But Ali was oblivious to the pain as he thought, *Yes, the black bitch made me do it. Made me do it because she laughed at me.*

While methamphetamine can temporarily endow people with super strength, it can have a reverse effect on the male member, causing erectile dysfunction. After he'd toiled away, attempting to achieve penetration with his flaccid member, she'd given a snort of laughter. That's what it had sounded like, anyway, although thinking about it now it was strange how she had tears running down her face at the time. No, what she was doing was *crying with laughter*, yes that's right, crying tears of mirth, laughing at his impotence. So he'd cut her throat.

Mulga branches raked Ali's chest and arms but he barely noticed as he blundered through the scrub. He didn't know if he was going in the right direction for Abdul and the ute, all he knew was that he was heading away from the lights of the houses. His body was suddenly racked by a sob. He'd really fucked up this time. Fucked up big time. How were he and Abdul going to get out of this place? He wondered if he should turn back, try and steal a car. But at any moment someone could find the girl's body.

Abdul would know what to do. He always knew what to do. Just then Ali saw a pair of headlights flashing on and off three times. He changed direction and stepped up his pace, crashing through a patch of waist-high bushes as he tried to keep on a straight bearing.

🦘 🦘 🦘 🦘

The music recital beside the fire pit had ended. Chaseling was feeling sleepy, reclining on his side as he watched the storm getting closer. He heard a man approaching, greeting people in a booming, authoritative voice. He looked up and saw, lit up in the moonlight, a white man aged around fifty, clad in khaki shorts, work boots and a Brisbane Broncos jersey. He had a trimmed grey beard and mostly bald head. His eyes had an angry, indignant look. 'Who the hell are you?' the man demanded.

Without shifting from his semi-prone position, Chaseling angled his head upwards to look at the man. He could see that this was someone who you needed to pull rank with. 'Jonathan Chaseling,' he replied. 'Doctor Jonathan Chaseling.' He placed a slight emphasis on the 'Doctor.'

The man's expression softened slightly but his tone remained less than cordial as he said, 'Do you have a permit to visit these lands?'

Chaseling said, 'Do you mind if I ask, who the hell are *you?*'

Thunder rumbled discontentedly over the man's shoulder as he took a few steps closer and held out a large hand. 'Bruce

Fitzpatrick,' he said. 'Community general manager. Also run the shop.'

Chaseling sat up and clasped the paw-like, rough-skinned hand, which immediately clenched into a bonecrusher grip. But Chaseling was ready for it, squeezing back with all his might. While his hands were more slender than the other man's, they were strong. Fitzpatrick frowned as he realised he wasn't going to leave Chaseling with a bruised set of knuckles. He detached his hand. 'So do you have a Land Council permit?'

'I'm afraid not,' Chaseling said. 'My car hit a kangaroo and my friends here kindly gave me a lift to this place. I'm headed for Alice Springs.'

Cookie spoke up from the other side of the fire. 'How's your wife, Bruce? She better now?' She was referring to a black eye the administrator's wife Janine had suffered a week earlier, purportedly from walking into an open door in the dark. The oldest story in the wife beater's book. Everyone knew Fitzpatrick hit his wife. This was a dry community, with alcohol strictly banned. But Fitzpatrick simply travelled 30 kilometres to a roadhouse on the Stuart Highway and bought his beer there. At home he guzzled it straight out of the big 750ml bottles. And he was a violent drunk. Usually he punched his wife in the chest and upper arms so the bruises didn't show. He was also careful to dispose of the evidence of his drinking binges – the brown 'longnecks' with the green, red and white Victoria Bitter label. He could regularly be seen driving to the outskirts of the community where there were deep drill holes, made by a mining exploration crew. Perfect for disposing of his empties.

Fitzpatrick's gaze faltered under the penetrating eyes of the Aboriginal woman. He looked down into the fire. 'Janine is much better, thank you,' he mumbled.

At that point there was a bloodcurdling shriek from out in the darkness. Cookie and the other people jumped to their feet. Chaseling did the same, a tingle of danger darting up his spine.

A teenage girl with red, black and yellow-beaded dreadlocks ran into the firelight. Her face was streaked with tears. Cookie ran up to the girl and clasped her to her ample bosom.

'Ruby,' whispered the girl, 'she's dead!' Then she started wailing. Cookie took up the refrain, giving vent to an agonised cry that burst from the depths of her being. Another woman joined in, and as she wailed she picked up a stone from the ground and struck herself on the forehead. Blood started weeping from the cut she'd made. Chaseling gazed at her, open-mouthed.

Clarrie and Noelie broke into a run. 'Come with us, *Kumina!*' Clarrie shouted over his shoulder. Chaseling got up and ran after them. Fitzpatrick stood irresolute by the fire pit for a few moments before following.

The door of the house was open. Clarrie was first to run inside, closely followed by Noelie, Chaseling and Fitzpatrick.

Ruby lay on the lounge room floor. She was naked from the waist down. Her eyes were already clouding over, staring blindly at the ceiling. Blood had pooled on the floor around her head and shoulders. There was a wicked slash across her throat.

'I'll go and call the police on my landline,' said Fitzpatrick, edging out of the room. They could hear his footsteps running down the wooden steps of the house. Clarrie sank to his knees and hugged the dead girl. He wept. Ruby was his cousin.

Chaseling pulled a blanket off the couch. Clarrie moved aside to let him drape it over Ruby's body while leaving her face uncovered. The edge of the rug went up to her chin, obscuring the gaping throat wound. Chaseling said, 'I think we should close her eyes.'

Clarrie nodded. His tears were dripping onto the dead girl's face. Chaseling knelt down beside him and pulled Ruby's eyelids down, holding them in place for a few seconds. When he took his hands away, they remained shut. He pulled up the blanket so it covered her face. Then Clarrie hugged her again. '*Cuz!*' Sobs racked his body.

Noelie was also weeping, tears streaming down his cheeks into his silver whiskers. But alongside his grief, Noelie's tracking instincts leapt into action. He looked at the crimson foot prints on the scuffed lino. They led away from the body, becoming progressively fainter as they neared the front door. 'Big, heavy fella,' Noelie said. 'Wearing sneakers, Adidas maybe.' He turned to his son and said something in Pitjantjatjara. Clarrie shakily got to his feet and went into the kitchen. Chaseling heard him rummaging around.

Outside, there was a chorus of wails and shrieks. Chaseling went to the front door and looked out. There was a group of women. All of them had blood on their faces, with the exception of the dreadlocked girl who'd raised the alarm. But as Chaseling stood at the top of the steps, the girl gave a high-pitched, banshee-like screech and headbutted the front wall of the house. Blood gushed from a deep cut in her forehead.

'*Stop!*' Chaseling screamed, running up and putting his hand on the girl's shoulder. 'You need stitches on that wound!'

The girl's response was to grab the neck of her T-shirt and pull violently at it. There was a tearing sound. One of her breasts popped out. She gave another dreadful shriek.

Cookie stepped forward. Her face too was covered in blood. 'This is what we do when someone dies.'

Noelie emerged from the house carrying a battered old Maglite torch. He glanced at the bloody-faced women and took in the horrified look on Chaseling's face.

'It's Sorry Time,' Noelie told him. 'Be like this for days, till the funeral.'

Clarrie followed his father out of the house. He was carrying a slender, rusty-barrelled rifle; Chaseling thought it was probably a .22. Clarrie and his father began walking around the perimeter of the building, Noelie sweeping the torch across the ground in front of them as he looked for the same footprint he'd noticed in the kitchen. As they reached the side of the house, he gave a shout and bent down to look at tracks in the dirt. He said something to his son.

'*Kumina!*' Clarrie shouted. 'Come with us!' He and his father ran behind the house.

Chaseling stayed where he was, surrounded by the wailing, bloody-faced women. The idea of tracking a killer through the darkness did not appeal. Better to let the police deal with it. Then he noticed someone was standing beside him. It was the old blind man.

'Here's some pituri,' the old man said, pressing a twist of newspaper into his hand. 'Now go and help them.' He nodded towards the back of the house. '*Quick!*'

After a second's hesitation, Chaseling pocketed the pituri and ran to the edge of the house, where he paused and looked over his shoulder. The old man wasn't there anymore. The bloody-faced women, led by Cookie, were filing up the front steps, their wailing growing in pitch and tempo. One of them bashed her head against the door frame as she went inside. Chaseling tore his eyes away and ran around down the side of the house. He saw the flickering of a torch a short distance away out in the scrub and ran towards it.

'What kept you, *Kumina?*' Clarrie was following his father, who was walking ahead with the torch, following the killer's foot prints.

'Just a bit of good, old-fashioned cowardice,' Chaseling muttered under his breath.

'Speak up *Kumina*, I can't hear you.'

'Doesn't matter.'

Moving in single file, the three pressed deeper and deeper into the sparse scrub. Off to the east, the rumble of thunder was getting louder, the lightning flashes brighter.

10 DOMESTIC BLISS

BRUCE FITZPATRICK replaced the telephone receiver in its cradle and lifted a longneck of Victoria Bitter to his lips. He tilted his large head back as he took a massive gulp. He placed the almost empty bottle down on the scratched old table. 'They said they'll be here in about two hours, longer if that storm breaks – which it almost certainly will.'

He'd just reported Ruby's murder to the police sergeant who headed a three-officer station in the town of Nganjara, 175 kilometres away, and who had the task of trying to maintain law and order over an expanse of desert the size of Luxembourg.

Janine Fitzpatrick, sitting across the table from her husband, was 44 but looked a decade older, with the worn look of someone who has endured a hard life. The skin on her thin face was rough-textured and criss-crossed with wrinkles. Her shoulder-length dyed blonde hair was dry and dead-looking. Her tired eyes were those of someone who'd stoically suffered decades of pain. Re-enforcing this impression was the faint yellow mark of an old bruise below her left eye. 'It's not the right time to be drinking, Bruce,' she said. 'Not that there's ever a right time with you.'

The moment she said it, she knew what her husband's reaction would be, and sure enough, she saw the wet-lipped mouth twisting into a snarl, pinpoints of fury burning in the red-veined eyes. He leapt to his feet and craned his body towards her with his hand raised. But instead of cringing as she normally did, Janine held her ground, chin jutting out defiantly. This diversion from the normal pattern made Fitzpatrick pause, arm held up above his head like someone giving a Nazi salute.

'Look at you!' Janine said. 'You're not much better than the murderer!'

Fitzpatrick took a step backwards and lowered his hand. He looked down at the longneck on the table, which was just coming to a standstill after wobbling precariously as he'd lunged at his wife. He picked up the bottle and drained it, then turned and strode towards the refrigerator. 'I'll head back there and make sure things aren't getting out of hand,' he said, opening the fridge door and pulling out a fresh longneck. 'You never know what they're going to do when it's Sorry Time.'

'That's true,' Janine agreed, recalling the epidemic of self-inflicted injuries the last time the local population had gone into mourning. 'Oh, and Bruce – I'm leaving you.'

Fitzpatrick turned around and looked at her, his characteristically angry expression replaced by one of hurt, tinged with fear. 'You've said that before.'

'Yeah, just like you've said you're giving up drinking and beating me umpteen times before,' she said, her eyes cold and contemptuous. Her voice became shrill. 'Coming to this place was meant to be our new start. Remember?' She gave a bitter chuckle. 'It's over, Bruce! Don't ever touch me again!'

As Fitzpatrick let himself out the front door carrying the cold bottle of VB in a grey plastic shopping bag, his shoulders were slumped and there was a fearful look in his eyes as he stared into a lonely future.

🦘 🦘 🦘 🦘

Abdul saw Ali's bulky form approaching in the moonlight. His brother was panting loudly. As Ali got closer, Abdul took in the blood that soaked the front of his shirt. 'What have you *done*, brother?' he shouted, leaping out of the canvas chair.

Ali burst into tears. Between sobs, he told Abdul what had happened. Or at least, his twisted spin on what had happened. How he'd just been trying to be friendly. How the girl had kicked him, made him lose control …

Abdul slapped his brother's face. 'You fucking psycho! Instead of coming back with a car, you murder someone!' He glanced over at the marooned ute, then switched his gaze to the approaching storm. 'We're fucked!'

'I'm sorry!' Ali blubbered. He covered his stinging face with his hands and broke into a fresh bout of weeping.

'Too late to be sorry,' Abdul said. 'We'll have to ditch the car and hike out of here, then hijack a car.' He went to the back of the ute and delved into a toolbox, pulling out a hammer and chisel. 'Get the bonnet up,' he told his brother.

Seconds later they were shining the torch under the raised hood of the stranded car and locating the identification code stamped into the side of the engine block. As Ali shone the torch, Abdul hacked into the nine character combination of numerals and letters with the chisel, and the code was soon unreadable. Next he chipped away the VIN number on the inside panelling of the driver's door, then obliterated the chassis number stamped into the dashboard.

'OK,' Abdul said, 'you unscrew the numberplates and I'll pack up the gear we'll be taking.'

Ali's face had retained the same confused, fearful look it had displayed when he'd made his appearance. His eyes slowly focussed on his brother. He got a screwdriver from the toolbox and started removing the rear licence plate.

11 FIREBALL

THE WIND had suddenly picked up. A knee-high carpet of sand particles was being blown along the desert floor, prickling Chaseling's bare legs below his shorts. Noelie was finding it increasingly difficult to follow the killer's footprints, which were fading under the onslaught of the wind. But there were other signs – trampled clumps of salt bush, broken mulga branches – that enabled him to keep tracking the monster who'd killed his niece Ruby. He kept up a brisk pace as he led Clarrie and Chaseling deeper into the stretch of desert between St Catherine's and a line of weathered hills four or five kilometres away. Off to their right, a boiling mass of black clouds loomed on the horizon. A lightning bolt seared down to earth, lighting up the sky. Chaseling counted to seven before thunder rumbled. He'd heard somewhere that you could calculate the distance between yourself and an approaching thunderstorm through a simple formula: three seconds between lightning and thunder equals one kilometre; so the storm was just over two kilometres away. And approaching fast. He heard a bird's wings going *wup-wup-wup* as it fled before the storm.

Noelie had taken off his hat and was carrying it, otherwise it would have been snatched off by the wind. He broke into a half-run, his son and Chaseling hot on his heels. Within a couple of minutes, Chaseling was panting with exertion and starting to fall behind. There was now an almost continuous rumble of thunder as the storm moved in.

Then they came to a startled halt as, less than a kilometre away, a column of flame whooshed out of the earth like a fiery geyser. It was followed a few seconds later by the deep rumble of a powerful explosion.

The brothers had unloaded some food and water from the car and placed it in their day packs. Now they got their rifles and a box of bullets. They put these behind a termite mound thirty paces from the car. The termite hill was a four metre high, stalactite-like cone of compacted red earth hardened to an almost cement-like consistency by the saliva of the tiny insects that had been building it over the course of decades.

Abdul and Ali returned to the ute and got two twenty litre drums of petrol. They poured the contents of one drum into the cabin of the car, the tray in the back and under the bonnet. Abdul unscrewed the cap of the ute's petrol tank. Then he picked up the second fuel drum and walked backwards away from the car, pouring petrol onto the ground. He stopped just in front on the termite mound and recapped the lid of the petrol tin. He turned to Ali. 'Do it brother.'

Ali reached into his jeans pocket and got his cigarette lighter. He lowered it to the ground. Because of the wind, he had to strike it several times before the petrol ignited. With a *'whoosh,'* flames leapt up, singeing Ali's beard. A line of fire streamed towards the car. The brothers ran behind the termite mound, Ali giving a strange little giggle. He'd always enjoyed setting fire to things.

As they sheltered behind the thick base of the termite hill, a roaring column of red flame leapt from the car, extending fifty metres into the sky. Then an explosion rocked the earth as the petrol tank ignited. Abdul peered cautiously around the edge of the termite hill. The car was a fireball and a thick plume of dark smoke was spewing from it, being blown sideways by the wind.

Abdul nodded in satisfaction. Burning the car would destroy any evidence linking them to the murder his brother had committed. Unfortunately the fire would also act as a beacon to anyone searching for Ali. So now they had to get the hell out of there, to the road that ran along the base of the hills. And hijack a car. Which might be a challenge since this was such an isolated place. However, he'd seen the headlights of at least half a dozen vehicles travelling along the road earlier while he'd been waiting for Ali.

Picking up the empty petrol tin, Abdul approached the blazing car. He hurled the fuel drum into the flames. While he didn't have a police record, he'd been fingerprinted by New South Wales police. Returning to the termite mound, he wondered if Ali had left any fingerprint and DNA evidence at the scene of the murder. He probably had. But no time to worry about that now. 'Let's go,' he told his brother. They put on their packs and picked up the rifles. Then they headed quickly into the gloom, Abdul still walking with a slight limp.

Maybe, Abdul thought to himself, if they managed to get out of this mess and Ali made it to Syria, it might be a good thing if he didn't come back.

12 EYE OF THE STORM

THE WIND was starting to howl as the three men reached the burnt-out car, its cabin still well ablaze. Noelie followed the smouldering trail of scorched ground to the termite hill. He circled round to the other side of the mound and saw two sets of footprints, protected from the wind by the raised mass of earth.

'There are two bad fellas,' he said, leading them into the scrub. The wind had all but destroyed the footprints. But Noelie could make out enough to know that the second man had an injury on the upper sole of his upper right foot because the imprint of his heel was deeper. And he could also see that this was slowing the man down, forcing him to take shorter steps.

In the sky above them, the clouds seethed like boiling ink. The eye of the storm was almost upon them, an ominous tower of blackness with electricity pulsing like strobe lights inside. Every few seconds, a blue bolt would sear down to earth. And now there was just a one second gap before thunder, painfully loud like blasts from a cannon, shook the ground.

The ute, if it hadn't got stuck in the sand, would have been insulated from the lightning by its tyres. But now the car's metal body became an irresistible target. Night became day as a gigantic finger of electricity shot down to the burning car and one hundred million volts found its way to earth. The three men were a hundred metres away and Chaseling just had time to put his hands over his ears as thunder exploded. His nostrils flared as he inhaled the acrid scent of ozone, mixed with burning steel, rubber and petrol. Now the wind suddenly whipped up, and with it came a wall of sand. Chaseling felt as though a porcupine was rolling across his face and arms, while his lower legs, closer to the heavier wind-borne particles, were getting a taste of what a sandblaster feels like. He wished he was wearing jeans instead of cargo shorts. A big fat raindrop splattered on his head.

Ahead of him, Noelie and Clarrie were shadowy figures in a red haze, the torch beam flickering from side to side as they took a meandering path through the mulga. Then a lightning bolt blasted the earth so close to them that the hair on Chaseling's head stood on end and the heat almost burned his skin. The thunder, exploding almost immediately, created such a powerful shockwave it made him stagger backwards. Plus there'd been the sound of a different percussion, a crack like a rifle shot, a split second before the thunder. He couldn't see the torch beam any more, but maybe his eyes were just dazzled by the lightning flash. Flames danced in a patch of scorched scrub.

Abdul looked over his shoulder and saw the light of a torch. 'Shit!' he said. Then suddenly the landscape was lit up by a blast of lightning. He saw the figures of three people, too close for his liking.

He got Ali to stand stock still and then rested the barrel of the rifle on his right shoulder. He slammed a bullet into the breach. 'Cover your ear, brother,' he said. Ali raised the index finger of his left hand to his right ear.

Through his telescopic sight Abdul could see the beam of the torch, but he couldn't see the men. Then the landscape lit up as another bolt of lightning blasted into the ground a few hundred metres beyond the trio, thrusting them into silhouette just long enough for Abdul to get the crosshairs on the man holding the torch, aim slightly to the left to compensate for the wind, and press the trigger. A microsecond later he saw the man drop, then the lightning flash died and again all he could see was the torch beam, which had fallen still. Then heavy rain started to pelt down and a grey curtain of water obscured his view. The brothers turned tail and ran towards the line of trees that grew along the edge of the muddy road.

Noelie lay dying. There was a finger-sized hole in the front of his chest. But the exit wound in his upper back was the width of a hen's egg. It was bleeding copiously and a cluster of pink bubbles formed around the wound, before being washed away by the cascading rain. Chaseling turned to Clarrie, who was kneeling in the dirt on the other side of his prone father. 'Help me get my shirt off!'

He stood up and held his arms in the air while Clarrie peeled the rain-sodden T-shirt from his chest. Then he balled it up to plug the hole in Noelie's back. Lying on his stomach in the muddy dirt, the old man groaned as pressure was applied to the wound. Clarrie was crying, his tears mingling with the rain that was getting heavier by the second. He gripped his father's hand. There was a rattle of breath in Noelie's throat, followed by a long sigh.

Chaseling felt Noelie's neck for a pulse. 'He's gone. I'm sorry,' he told Clarrie.

Clarrie raised his face to the sky and the rain. His face was contorted and the tendons in his neck bulged like ropes. He gave a tortured howl. His shoulders heaving, he bowed his head for a few seconds. He gently rolled his father onto his back. Next he took the old Akubra hat that was clenched in his father's hand and placed it over Noelie's face, then looped the chin strap round the back of his head, tightening the toggle so the hat didn't blow off. He said some words in Pitjantjatjara. Then he picked up the Maglite and rifle. 'Let's go,' he said.

Bruce Fitzpatrick steered his Nissan Patrol past the blackened, smoking wreck of the burnt-out ute, wondering whether it had been the target of the lightning strike he'd seen a few minutes earlier. Massive raindrops were starting to splatter on the Patrol's windscreen. Lit up in his headlights was a trail of scorched dirt. He stopped alongside a termite mound. There was another lightning flash, and the crash of thunder. Fitzpatrick thought he might have also heard a rifle shot.

Fitzpatrick reached down to the gap between his seat and car door and pulled out a longneck of VB. He twisted the top off, lifted it to his lips and guzzled away like a baby drinking milk. The big brown bottle was soon empty. He put the transmission back into drive and released the brake. Then he steered the Toyota in the direction of the gunshot, flicking the windscreen wipers to maximum speed as sheets of rain fell from the sky.

13 WEEPING AND GNASHING OF TEETH

PASTOR HANS VAN OOSTREM drove along the dirt track that linked a string of Aboriginal communities along this line of hills. Today he'd distributed almost fifty Bibles and a large amount of other religious literature. Perhaps he'd saved a few souls. But perhaps not. Religion, like so many other things, was a numbers game, he thought as he tugged at his silver goatee beard. Complementing the goatee was a carefully-trimmed moustache and a full head of white hair. He wore black, heavy-framed, old fashioned glasses. People had observed, more than once, that he looked like the late Colonel Harland Sanders. If ever KFC wanted a lookalike for an ad campaign, Pastor Van Oostrem would be a strong contender.

He fiddled with the dial of his radio but all he could get was country music. Van Oostrem had never been partial to country. Now *folk* music, that was another thing. The folk music that he'd grown up with in his childhood: The Seekers; Peter, Paul and Mary. Now that was good music. Wholesome and simple. No profanities or metaphors for sex and drugs. Except possibly in Peter, Paul and Mary's *Puff the Magic Dragon*, which he had it on good authority was about marijuana smoking.

Van Oostrem was keeping his Mitsubishi Pajero to about 60 kilometres an hour along the dirt road. The rain was easing but the road surface was dangerously wet and muddy. He had another 50 kilometres to drive before he reached the community of Tjamu, where he was going to stay the night with the principal of the local school.

Suddenly two men were lit up in the headlights of his car. Both were pointing rifles at him. Their faces had looks of murderous intent, particularly the bearded one. The bald one had his arm raised palm outwards like a traffic policeman. The Pastor put his foot down on the brake pedal and the car skidded to a halt. Then the driver's door was being wrenched open and the shaven-headed man was dragging him out of the car.

Abdul jabbed the barrel of his rifle into the pastor's stomach. Van Oostrem let loose a hiss of air and fell to the muddy road. Abdul got into the driver's seat while Ali opened the front passenger door and grabbed an open holdall of clothes and other personal effects. He threw the bag out onto the road and got in the car. Abdul slammed the transmission into drive and the tyres spun in the wet dirt for a few seconds before they gained traction and the Pajero shot forward.

Still winded from the blow to his stomach, Van Oostrem stood up shakily in the middle of the road and watched the tail lights of his car disappearing down the track. Instead of Christian thoughts, but found himself wishing the men a swift and painful demise. Plus an agonising afterlife. *'They will be cast into the fiery lake of sulphur!'* he shouted at the already-distant car. *'And there will be weeping and gnashing of teeth!'*

14 SO HELP ME GOD

THE RAIN AND WIND were dying down as the storm rumbled off to wreak havoc elsewhere and the sky was clearing, the moon peering out through ragged clouds, stars re-establishing their places in the firmament. Chaseling was shivering. He was bare-chested now after using his shirt to plug Noelie's bullet wound and the rain was proving surprisingly cold. He saw headlights behind the line of mulga at the edge of the road. An engine roared and the lights began moving off quickly to the left. He looked over at Clarrie, who broke into a run. Chaseling sprinted after him.

A few minutes later they broke through the mulga onto a dirt road. About 50 metres away they saw a man. They ran towards him. As they approached, the man, who looked like Colonel Sanders, glanced apprehensively at the gun in Clarrie's hands.

'Have you seen two fellas?' Clarrie asked.

'Yes, I have. They took my car.'

At that point they noticed headlights slowly approaching from out of the scrub. Clarrie flashed the Maglite. A couple of minutes later, Fitzpatrick's Nissan Patrol was driving onto the road and pulling up beside them.

Clarrie went up to the driver's window, which slid open. A waft of alcohol fumes drifted out.

'My dad's been killed,' he told Fitzpatrick.

'Jesus Christ,' Fitzpatrick said dully. 'What happened?'

'No time to tell you now,' Clarrie said. 'We need your car.'

'What for?'

'To chase the fellas who killed my dad and Ruby.' He nodded his head towards Pastor Van Oostrem. 'They took his car.'

Fitzpatrick frowned. 'I called the police on the landline and they're on their way. Best if they deal with it.'

'We need the Patrol,' Clarrie repeated.

Fitzpatrick shook his head. 'Out of the question,'

Clarrie slowly lifted the .22 rifle so it was pointed into the cabin of the car at Fitzpatrick's face. 'Very good of you to lend us the car,' he said. He turned to Chaseling. 'Don't you think so *Kumina*?'

Chaseling paused for a moment as he considered the ramifications of taking part in a carjacking. But normal codes of behaviour no longer applied. 'Yes, a very generous gesture,' he said.

Clarrie pulled open the driver's door and the empty beer bottle fell out onto the dirt. A furious-looking Fitzpatrick slowly stepped out of the car. 'The police are going to throw the book at you blokes,' he said.

'I don't think so,' said Chaseling. He turned to Van Oostrem. 'Colonel, you want to get your own car back in one piece, don't you?'

'I do indeed,' Van Oostrem said.

'And so before we set off in pursuit of those men – and your car – you agree that you've witnessed this gentleman offering to lend us his vehicle?'

Van Oostrem looked down at the beer bottle on the road, then at Fitzpatrick, who he had met a number of times on visits to St Catherine's. He hadn't warmed to him on those occasions. And now, as he looked at the angry-faced man standing with a hand resting possessively on the door of his car, he decided to show him no mercy. 'Yes, that's exactly what I've witnessed,' the Pastor said. 'He lent you his car, totally voluntarily – so help me God.'

Clarrie shouldered Fitzpatrick aside and got into the driver's seat of the Patrol. The shirtless, shivering Chaseling glanced down at the holdall of clothes that had been thrown out of Van Oostrem's vehicle. 'You wouldn't happen to have a spare shirt, would you Colonel?'

Thirty seconds later, Clarrie was gunning the Patrol down the uneven dirt track. Beside him sat Chaseling wearing a too-large white T-shirt. Across the front, the word 'JESUS' was spelled out in big red letters. The 'S' in the centre was the Superman emblem. Pastor Van Oostrem had bought a thousand of the T-shirts from China for just $500 and hadn't been concerned about any copyright infringement issues. The saving of souls took precedence over man-made laws.

Fitzpatrick watched the tail lights of his car disappear into the distance. He turned to Van Ooostrem and shouted, 'You're a man of God, and you lie! Doesn't it say something in the Bible about "bearing false witness?"'

'God will forgive me!' Van Oostrem yelled back in a voice filled with the thunder of the pulpit. He pointed an accusing finger down at the empty bottle of VB at their feet, then levelled the finger at Fitzpatrick. 'He might even forgive you, too, if you open your heart to Him.'

Fitzpatrick's angry expression morphed into a look of guilt. 'The rain's almost stopped,' he observed unnecessarily. He bent down and picked up the bottle. 'I'll give this a Christian burial.'

'Good, I'll be happy to officiate at the funeral,' Van Oostrem said.

They walked into the scrub and headed for the lights of St Catherine's. Pastor Van Oostrem thought to himself that he might yet save a soul this day. And hopefully his car would be saved too.

15 ALI'S DEMON

CLARRIE DROVE the Patrol without lights. And at breakneck speed. The road was straight, and lit by the full moon. The storm had passed as quickly as it arrived; the sky above them was now clear of all but some thin tendrils of cloud. The dirt road had sucked up the rain like blotting paper and looked dry in most places, with just the occasional shallow pool of water.

'Don't you get animals on the road at this time of night?' asked Chaseling, all too clearly remembering the kangaroo's sudden and catastrophic appearance in front of his car.

'Not many,' Clarrie replied, none too reassuringly. 'Usually get them around sundown.'

They fell into silence, each man preoccupied by his own thoughts. After driving for three quarters of an hour, Clarrie exclaimed, 'There they are, the mongrel bastards!'

Like two red eyes, a pair of tail lights shone faintly in the distance. Chaseling got out his phone and saw that it had reception again. 'We should call the police now.'

'No police!' Clarrie said. 'This is personal.'

Chaseling thought to himself, *What the hell am I doing chasing down a double murderer? Or perhaps it's two murderers, maybe one murdered Ruby and the other shot Noelie.*

His thoughts were interrupted as Clarrie said, 'They've turned onto the highway.' He pressed down harder on the gas pedal. 'Don't wanna lose 'em.'

Chaseling reached into the pocket of his cargo shorts and pulled out the twist of newspaper the old man had given him. 'I'm going to have some pituri,' he said. 'Care to join me?'

'Not while I'm driving,' Clarrie said.

As he chewed the wad of pituri, Chaseling wondered how this night would end. Not well, he feared. He had a premonition: there would be more blood, more death.

Abdul steered the Patrol off the dirt road onto the Stuart Highway, two lanes of bitumen cutting through central Australia from north to south. Before being tarred the highway was simply known as 'The Track.' On the eastern horizon to their right, the sky was the gunmetal grey of pre-dawn.

Ali finished tapping out a message on his mobile phone and pressed the send button. There was just one bar of signal showing on the screen, but the text seemed to go through OK. He opened his day pack and got out his ice pipe and the stash of the drug in its zip-locked plastic bag. He reached into the bag and got out a shard of meth, which he crushed between his fingers above the bowl of the pipe. Flakes of the drug spilled onto his lap and he swore. Then he put the lighter to the bowl of the pipe and sparked it up. His eyes rolled back in his head as he dragged the smoke into his lungs.

Watching his brother from the corner of his eye, Abdul thought about the demon inside Ali, the demon that had always been there, the demon that screamed and snarled during the night as it manifested in Ali's nightmares. The demon that had despatched Ali to the boys' home and overseen his decline ever since.

Ali exhaled and then took a deep breath of fresh air. His eyes opened and focused on the GPS stuck to the windscreen. It was showing the way to a place called Coober Pedy.

16 A SMALL PROBLEM

VASKO NITARSKI stood in a windowless, cave-like room with rough-hewn sandstone walls. The dome-shaped ceiling was also bare rock and, as with the walls, it was etched with striations like the claw marks of some giant, burrowing animal. These had been made by the teeth of the tunnelling machine that bored into the desert bedrock in search of precious opal.

In front of Nitarski was a long wooden work table covered with grungy-looking laboratory equipment and containers of chemicals. Lengths of rubber tubing had lost their original coral colour and turned a mottled grey. Glass beakers had thick brown crusts of crystalized residue around the lips. The labels on some plastic drums had become so badly stained the wording was barely legible.

Nitarski wore elbow-length safety gauntlets. On his broad face, black eyes glinted behind safety goggles. The lower part of his face was covered by a chemical cartridge respirator, the twin straps of which snaked round his creased, bull-like neck. An exhaust fan hummed away in the ceiling, feeding foul air up a round ventilation shaft to the rocky hilltop ten metres above. But the fan could only do so much; without the goggles and gas mask, the fumes from the chemical cocktail he was mixing would sear his eyes and mucous membranes like mustard gas.

Very slowly, Nitarski poured hydrochloric acid from a cylindrical glass container into a 1000 millilitre beaker containing the meth base he'd prepared the previous day. It had to be poured slowly otherwise the mixture could overheat, with disastrous consequences. The beaker stood on top of a unit called a stirring hotplate containing a rotor with magnetic arms. Inside the beaker was a plastic pellet containing another magnet. As the rotor in the hotplate revolved, the pellet whirled around like a dervish inside the mixture. And now, as Nitarski let the acid trickle down into the witches' brew, he nodded with satisfaction. While the inside of the beaker was stained a coffee-like colour, the discolouration was patchy, the glass relatively clear in places, so that Nitarski was able to see what looked like a white tornado coming to life and growing ever-larger.

Steam was starting to rise from the mixture as it approached boiling point. Nitarski turned down the temperature dial on the stirring hotplate. The trick was to keep it just below boiling while the water in the solution evaporated away. Once all the water was gone, he would pour the contents into a bucket containing 4.5 litres of frozen acetone and put the mix in the freezer for a week to crystallize into the precious substance commonly known as ice.

Then he'd make a delivery run down to Adelaide, where he would stock up on raw materials. Plus he'd relieve the sexual tensions built up while living alone for long stretches in his dugout. He was a regular at a brothel in Kent Town and on his last visit the Madame had told him there were some new girls arriving that she thought he might enjoy.

He stepped away from the lab bench and pulled off one of his gauntlets to look at his watch. It was just after six-thirty AM. In ten minutes, he'd check on the brew. Now for a cigarette. He left the room through a pair of heavy transparent plastic curtains that hung from ceiling to floor.

Nitarski emerged into an open-plan living area. As with the lab, the walls and ceilings were brown sandstone. Running through the rock were white flecks and veins of fossilised marine material. One wall had a deep rectangular recess carved into the rock and it had been just the right size for Nitarski's 60 inch TV. Opposite the screen was a black leather recliner. Except for an office chair behind a small desk, the recliner was the only seat in the room. Nitarski hadn't set this place up for entertaining. A small kitchen nook completed the living area. A passageway at one end of the room led to two bedrooms and a bathroom. Opposite was another wider, much longer passageway leading to the entrance of his dugout.

Nitarski took off his eyeglasses and respirator, revealing a flat face, hook nose and acne-scarred cheeks, and stripped the gloves from his massive hands. The rest of him was also big – he was just a few centimetres short of two metres tall, with broad shoulders and a barrel chest. His hair was shaved at the sides and back, with an inch long crew-cut on top. Add a pair of obsidian black eyes and a cruel-looking mouth, and he definitely didn't look like the kind of person you'd want to get into an altercation with.

He put the protective gear down on his desk, then picked up his cigarettes and lighter and walked out of the room and down the front hallway of the dugout. With its concave walls and curved ceiling, it was more of a tunnel than a hallway, testament to the dugout's genesis as an opal mine, and it was long, running for 15 metres.

Stepping through the front doorway, he gazed out onto a strange landscape. Lit up in the grey dawn light was a panorama of low, rocky brown hills, completely devoid of vegetation. But on the tops of these bluffs 'grew' TV antennae, satellite dishes and cylindrical metal chimneys. Below, at ground level, were the front facades of dugouts. All that you could see of these were front doors, windows and garages, beyond which were cavernous dwellings like the one he inhabited.

Nitarski's nearest neighbour was 100 metres away, at the foot of a hillock set lower than his own, so the noxious fumes from his meth manufacturing operation drifted up into the atmosphere undetected. That was what got most meth manufacturers unstuck. The smell. Plus there were the fires which frequently broke out, a stray spark of static electricity or excessive temperatures transforming your lab into an inferno.

Nitarski lit a cigarette, his pitted cheeks sinking into his face as he took a deep, extended drag. He thought back to the time he saw a bikie called Chook stagger from the charred, smoking ruins of his backyard shed with the skin on his face and arms melted away like plastic. Chook's lips had been fused together on one side, making it look as though he was sneering as he whispered '*Water,*' in a dreadful, sub-human voice. Then he collapsed to the ground. His voice, much weaker now, repeated, '*Water.*'

As it happened, Nitarski had been holding an almost full 600 ml bottle of Mount Franklin mineral water in his hand at the time. But instead of going to Chook's assistance he'd shoved the bottle into the side pocket of his leather jacket and ran round to the front of the house. He thought he could hear a siren in the distance as he kick-started his Harley. Then he roared away. He'd heard later that Chook had died on his way to hospital. A shame. Good bloke.

Nitarski was drawn back to the present as he watched an old four-wheel drive covered with red dust snaking down a dirt track. It was an opal miner named Pino who left at this time every morning for his diggings five kilometres north of town. Pino and Nitarski had once exchanged a few friendly words, but that was the extent of their acquaintance. And that was the way Nitarski liked it. This wasn't the kind of place where your neighbour arrives with a plate of lamingtons the day you moved in.

Weighing against all the advantages of producing ice out in the desert was a single, but substantial, negative factor – the tyranny of distance. The nearest capital city, Adelaide, was 845 kilometres away. But the good thing was that Sydney was much more distant, 2090 kilometres to be precise. And in Sydney there were people who wanted to kill him. His move to central Australia had been a matter of necessity.

It had started out as a simple turf war between two outlaw bikie gangs over drug distribution in western Sydney. Nitarski had been sergeant-at-arms with the Bandidos, who had a well-established distribution chain through two tattoo parlours. Then a rival gang called the Finks decided to end this arrangement and firebombed both tattoo shops in a single night. Nitarski's response was to march into a pub where the leaders of the Finks were drinking and blast them with a sawn-off shotgun.

One of the Finks died on the spot, most of his head blown away. Another expired in the ambulance on the way to Westmead Hospital. The third survived, but before beginning an extensive series of plastic surgery operations, he'd looked like Two Face from the *Batman* movies and comics, his left cheek reduced to tattered ribbons of flesh, the lidless eye bloodshot and weeping.

The police hadn't been able to find any witnesses who'd give a description of the gunman, despite a dozen drinkers and two staff being in the bar at the time. Meanwhile, the Finks had sought retribution.

Three days after the pub attack, he started to head out the front door of his home one evening, carrying a gym bag, looking forward to a workout at his local fitness centre. It had just got dark. As he stepped out of the doorway, there was a flash of light from across the road and a loud bang. A bullet zapped past so close to his head that he could feel its heat on his ear.

He dived to the ground. There was the roar of a car engine and the shriek of tyre rubber. A black four-wheel drive zoomed off down the street. Lying on the concrete path in front of the doorway, Nitarski heard a man's voice yell, *'Next time!'*

A week later, a huge man with a tattooed face followed him into the lift at Bankstown Central Shopping Centre. There was a violent struggle which swung the elevator car from side to side as it descended from the rooftop carpark. When the doors opened one floor below, Nitarski stepped out over the man lying senseless on the floor and shouldered past shoppers waiting for the lift. 'He had some kind of seizure,' he said, pulling his phone out of his pocket. 'I'm going to call an ambulance and get centre management.' He did neither. Instead he found his way back up to the carpark via a set of stairs and got the hell out of there.

The third and final attempt had been a car bomb planted in his black Jaguar XJS. The device's trigger was a motion sensor made from a modified car alarm. Trouble was, it was a bit too sensitive.

Nitarski rode a Harley which he'd customised with a pair of ceramic-coated 'shotgun' exhausts. The result was a throbbing roar, so loud that pedestrians often covered their ears when he rode past.

And so when Nitarski rode his matt black 'Fat Bob' Harley down his street, a woman who lived across the road frowned as the visceral growl of the bike drowned out a piece of dialogue in her favourite TV soap, *Home and Away*. Still, she thought, at least it wasn't the sound of gunshots, like the other night.

The Harley had just got its front wheel onto Nitarski's driveway when the thumping vibrations from its exhaust set a pea-sized steel ball into motion inside the cylindrical housing of a shock sensor planted underneath his car. As the ball moved it broke the connection between two contact points and triggered a detonator set to go off after one millisecond. And three sticks of powergel, an explosive commonly used in mining, blew up with an earth-shaking boom that shattered windows up and down the street and sent bits of flaming Jaguar flying through the air.

Nitarski was thrown from his bike, which was fortunate because two seconds after the massive blast, the petrol tank of the Jag ignited and a fireball seared everything within a ten metre radius. Lying winded face down on the road, his body protected by helmet, leather jacket, gauntlets, heavy jeans and boots, the inferno passed over rather than engulfed him.

As he shakily picked himself up from the road, there was a ringing in his ears. Apart from that, he was physically unscathed. But he knew that his luck was not going to last. He decided it was time for a change of scenery. He liked the idea of living a lone wolf existence somewhere far from his enemies. And he knew just the place, having once stayed in an underground backpackers hostel there when he rode his hog from Adelaide to Darwin. He hired a truck, filled it with his Harley, meth-making equipment and other essential possessions and drove to central Australia. He did it quietly, and even his fellow-Bandidos were taken by surprise. Since then he'd been in touch with only a very small number of trusted friends and associates.

But he remained ever-alert to the dangers of his past catching up with him. Now, as he stood watching the rocky bluffs of Coober Pedy getting lighter as dawn approached, his ears were tuned in for a particular sound – the growl of motorcycle engines as the Finks arrived to wreak bloody vengeance. There was also a chance the bikes could be ridden by his former compatriots, the Bandidos.

Bikie gangs don't like it when members leave the clan. It's called 'patching out' and there are hefty 'exit fees.' The standard amount is $10,000. Some gangs, like the Bandidos, demand that you surrender your beloved hog. With a top-of-the-line Harley costing $20,000 or more, and the price tag of some other suitable steeds soaring much higher (an Indian Roadmaster is worth more than $40,000) this was a very painful sacrifice to make.

As insurance against Finks, Bandidos, or for that matter the long arm of the law reaching out to grab him, Nitarski had prepared for a swift getaway, keeping his Toyota LandCruiser packed with water, food and other supplies including a pair of 20 litre drums of fuel. The LandCruiser would be able to travel a long way before it needed a refill because it had a 145 litre fuel tank with a range of 800 kilometres.

Nitarski took a final suck at his cigarette before grinding it into the dirt with an old work boot coated with a patina of chemical stains. The phone in his jeans pocket vibrated against his thigh as it signalled an incoming message. He pulled out the device. The message was from Ali. '*Morning bro, will be calling in to C U again around 6am, maybe earlier,*' the screen said.

Sausage-sized fingers began tapping out a reply to Ali's message. High up on the back of the fingers of Nitarski's right hand, the letters 'BROS' had been crudely tattooed in blue ink.

He'd met Ali 13 years earlier at Kariong Juvenile Justice Centre, where they'd both become members of Brothers 4 Life, a group of hardcore inmates, all of them serving time for crimes of violence. Both Ali and Nitarski had cut their ties with the gang after leaving the institution, which was fortunate for them because most of its members were now in Goulburn's Supermax jail serving long sentences for drive-by shootings, kidnappings, firearms possession and rape. But Ali and Nitarski's friendship, borne out of necessity in the jungle-like environment of the boys' home, had endured and they'd kept in touch after getting out of the correctional facility. When Nitarski started manufacturing ice from a warehouse on the outskirts of Sydney, Ali introduced him to his brother Abdul and they entered into a supply agreement that had been lucrative for both sides.

Ali and Abdul were two of the handful of people who knew about Nitarski's relocation to central Australia. Three weeks earlier, Ali had sent him a Facebook message saying that he and Abdul would soon be setting off on a hunting trip to the Centre. *'Luv 2 see ya bro,'* his former boys' home buddy had written.

Two days ago, the brothers had become the first guests to cross the threshold of Nitarski's new pad, spending a night there. He'd enjoyed their company and, supplementing their host's meagre furnishings with their fold-out picnic chairs, the brothers had revelled in some home comforts after the deprivations of camping in the outback.

Nitarski finished keying his reply to Ali's latest message. *'OK, see you soon. BTW, how was the hunting?'* He pressed the send button. Replacing the phone in his pocket, he went back into the dugout, his feet crunching as he walked down the hallway, which, unlike the rest of the dugout, had no floor covering, just bare dirt and small stones.

Just over a minute later, Nitarski was halfway through putting his protective gear back on when the reply came back: *'Hunting was good. Just had a small problem, hope you can help, bro.'*

The eyes behind Nitarski's safety goggles looked troubled as he read the text. With guys like Ali, 'a small problem' usually meant nothing of the kind.

17 PAYBACK

ALI AND ABDUL KNELT barefoot at the roadside on prayer mats. Facing northwest, the sides of their faces lit up by the sun rising on the eastern horizon, they chanted their *Fajr*, or dawn prayer. *'Master of the Day of Judgement, You alone we worship, You Alone we ask for help …'*

As they chanted, a crow perched in a mulga tree joined in with its own dawn recital: *'Aaah! Aaah!'* Other desert creatures also stirred. A fly with an iridescent green abdomen circled Ali's head before settling at the edge of his mouth, where it managed to suck up a droplet of moisture before he swatted it away. A huge, chocolate-coloured ant crawled onto the fringed edge of Abdul's prayer mat and paused there for a couple of seconds. Detecting the vibrations from the voice of the man on the mat, it decided to detour around him.

The brothers prayed for five minutes, alternating between standing, kneeling and prostrating themselves. Normally they recited the words parrot-fashion, without thinking about them. But today they put more fervour into it. *'Oh Allah I take refuge in you from the punishment of the grave, from the torment of the fire, from the trials and tribulations of life and death ….'*

A kilometre away, Clarrie and Chaseling sat in the Patrol. Clarrie had driven behind a patch of mulga. Through a screen of twisted, dark branches he watched the two men at prayer. Chaseling, meanwhile, squinting from behind his glasses, could barely see the tiny white dot of the Pajero, let alone the figures of the men beside the car. But Clarrie's forbears had been scanning horizons for hundreds of generations. His eyes were able to see the enemy. While his mind focused on payback.

Payback forms the backbone of the tribal justice system in many Aboriginal communities. It is the law of the spear. If you hurt a member of the tribe, and the elders declare you guilty, you'll be taken out to a sacred area of the desert and speared. If your infraction was a minor one, you'll be speared in the leg and hopefully the sharpened, fire-hardened point will miss your femoral artery and you'll survive the punishment. But if you've taken a life, the spear will be aimed at your heart. If perchance the aim of the elder hurling the weapon isn't up to scratch and the point hits rib or sternum, you'll be put through the ordeal a second time, a third time … until justice is done and you fall to the earth with your life blood pumping away into the ochre sand. These days, payback has largely been displaced by the white justice system. But it still goes on in more remote communities, and is deeply entrenched in the Aboriginal psyche.

Clarrie could see the men getting back into the Pajero. He re-started the engine of the Patrol and watched as the other car pulled out onto the highway. He waited for a minute or more before putting the Patrol in drive and steering it out of the scrub. As the tyres crunched onto the verge he suddenly braked. Chaseling looked across at him, wondering why they'd come to a stop. Clarrie was looking straight ahead, towards the road. Following the line of his sight, Chaseling gazed out the windscreen. Basking on the warming bitumen of the highway was a large snake.

The serpent had its body extended to maximise the radiant exposure. It was at least two metres long and its scales were a shiny dark brown. The eyes had bright orange irises and big black pupils, set in sockets that were cast downwards, giving the reptile a mean, don't-mess-with-me look. The snake was an Inland Taipan.

Also known as the Fierce Snake, the Inland Taipan is the world's deadliest snake. One bite contains enough venom to despatch up to 100 humans. As for the marsupial rats that form its staple diet, they expire in under a minute after the taipan's two centimetre long fangs inject their poison, a classic case of overkill because the taipan dispenses 40,000 times the amount needed to snuff the life out of these half kilo animals.

Clarrie quietly opened the car door and got out. Then he ran towards the snake screaming at the top of his lungs. This was the technique Clarrie's people used to surprise and catch the taipan's reptile cousin, the perentie. The idea was to create a kind of wall of sound that threw the animal's senses into temporary overload and it remained frozen to the spot for a few seconds, giving you sufficient time to bash it over the head with a *nulla nulla* stick.

Unlike the perentie, the taipan did not form part of the traditional indigenous diet. Clarrie had never tried the wall of sound technique on a snake before, so he was taking a dangerous gamble as he charged towards the taipan shouting at a volume that carried far across the desert plain.

The aural assault was successful and the taipan lay still, except to flick out a forked, jet-black tongue. And then Clarrie's bare foot was pressing down behind its blunt head and the powerful body started wildly thrashing, the tail whipping against Clarrie's legs. Watching horrified from the cabin of the idling car, Chaseling saw Clarrie reach down and grab the snake just behind its head. He released his foot and the fingers of his spare hand tried to close around the tail, which was a frantic blur of movement. And before Clarrie could grab it the tail encircled Clarrie's upper arm like a mega-sized tourniquet.

While taipans are not constrictors that squeeze their prey to death (who needs to do that when you've got one of the most lethal venoms in the animal kingdom?), they often coil their bodies around their victims to keep them immobilised as they chomp into them with their fangs. Paralysis and unconsciousness set in, and then it's dinnertime as the snake swallows its prey whole. The taipan's jaws were working away furiously, opening almost 180 degrees then snapping shut, the movements of its head throwing off little droplets of venom as it tried to twist round and sink its fangs into Clarrie's hand. Clarrie turned away so the poison didn't get in his eyes. He called out to Chaseling, 'Come and help me *Kumina*, we need to get this thing off my arm.'

Chaseling got out of the car and slowly approached Clarrie and the snake, stopping on the edge of the verge around three metres away from them. 'If you don't mind me asking,' he said, 'out of idle curiosity, what are you going to do with the snake?'

'Taipan can be a good weapon,' Clarrie answered. 'Now *Kumina*, can you please come here and unwind him from my arm?' Seeing the shocked expression that engulfed Chaseling's features, he added, 'You'll be safe – I got him. It'll just be better if he's off my arm.'

As if in reply, the taipan opened its jaws and let loose a hiss like a steam train, its tongue flicking in and out. At the same time, it began to shake its head violently from side to side and as Chaseling stood there trying to pluck up the courage to do what Clarrie had asked, he saw how the snake was starting to wrestle out of Clarrie's grip, its powerful neck muscles expanding and contracting so that the head was able to reach round, snapping its jaws shut just a centimetre or two from the back of Clarrie's hand. 'Quick, *Kumina!*' he shouted.

Overcoming his dread, he ran to Clarrie's side. He grabbed the end of the tail and pulled it away from Clarrie's arm, twisting it anticlockwise. Coil by coil, he unwound the tense, muscular body of the reptile from the other man's bicep, trying to ignore the hissing, biting head in Clarrie's grip. He blinked rapidly as a droplet of venom landed on the left lens of his glasses. *First time in my life I've been grateful for the fact that I wear glasses,* he thought.

Once he'd uncoiled the snake, it went into a fresh bout of manic struggles, its body whipping from side to side as Chaseling gripped it two-handed by the tail. Meanwhile more of its neck had squeezed from between Clarrie's fingers and its fangs were almost brushing his skin as it furiously struck out at his knuckles and wrist. 'OK, you get your hand behind mine and pull him by the neck, and I'll get a better grip. *Quick now!*'

Chaseling altered his grip so he now had one hand gripping the upper part of the snake, just behind Clarrie's hand. He gave the body a sharp tug and saw Clarrie's hand momentarily loosen its hold on the snake's neck before his fingers closed securely behind its head.

'Thanks *Kumina*, all under control,' Clarrie said. 'He's tired now, he won't get away. OK, you'll be driving, so just give me that loop of tail you've got there… Yeah, that's right, very good, *Kumima*. OK, now you can let go your other hand.'

Having gratefully released his grip on the snake, Chaseling took a couple of backwards steps. He took off his glasses and reached in the pocket of his cargo shorts for his handkerchief to wipe the venom off the lenses.

'Let's get outta here now *Kumina*,' said Clarrie, walking to the car and sliding in the passenger side with his new pet. Chaseling closed the door behind them and went round to the driver's side. Seconds later he was steering the Patrol out of the scrub and across the dirt verge. 'Now drive like the Devil's on your tail,' Clarrie said.

Chaseling plunged his foot down on the accelerator and with a squeal of rubber, the Patrol took off down the highway.

18 OPAL CAPITAL

AFTER ABOUT HALF AN HOUR of fast driving, their speed averaging 140-150 km/h, the Pajero came back in sight, although at first it was only Clarrie who could see it. 'OK, slow down now *Kumina*,' he said.

Another few kilometres later, a sign saying 'WELCOME TO COOBER PEDY' appeared on their right. Below was more text which Chaseling couldn't read at first because a graffiti artist had tagged over it in bold black sweeps of a black spray can. But just before they passed, Chaseling figured out that it said 'Opal mining capital of the world.'

'Turn off here, *Kumina*,' Clarrie said. Chaseling performed a right turn and they drove through the modest-sized heart of Cooper Pedy, a low-slung strip dominated by opal dealers, restaurants and underground hotels. A dusty four wheel drive with swags, eskies and multiple water drums strapped to its roof drove past and a red Greyhound bus with a destination sign saying ALICE SPRINGS was pulling out of its bay. It was good, thought Chaseling, that there were other vehicles on the move, so hopefully the occupants of the Pajero wouldn't notice them following. Not that he'd personally spotted the Pajero for a while; he was relying on Clarrie's eagle eyes.

At the end of the main street, Clarrie instructed him to turn right. They passed a drive-in theatre, then a series of above-ground houses built of board and brick. In the near distance were rounded, rocky outcrops with doors and windows set into their bases and cars parked out front. Now Chaseling could see the Pajero, raising a cloud of dust as it took a dirt track off towards one of the hillocks.

'Stop here and see what they do,' Clarrie said, indicating a driveway to a weatherboard building with a cyclone-fenced yard full of heavy mining machinery.

Abdul switched off the ignition of the Patrol and turned to his brother. 'We're the same blood, but I've got to think of my own neck. I killed a man last night because of you. Now we'll both be headed for Supermax unless Vasko gives us replacement wheels and we get the fuck out of central Australia. It might already be too late – the cops might be putting roadblocks up on the highway. So I'm warning you, if you drag me down you won't be my brother anymore.'

Ali sat, eyes cast downwards and lips pursed in what he hoped was a penitent look. Abdul got out of the car and Ali followed. They were at the bottom of a bare hillock of red-brown rock. Set into the rock face was Nitarski's front door, made of stained timber with an ornate brass handle and knocker that looked out of place in this rugged setting. Alongside was a brown-painted garage door.

The front door opened and Nitarski appeared, his face lit up in a welcoming smile which faded as he saw the grim expressions on his guests' faces – and the dried blood on the front of Ali's T-shirt. His deep set eyes gave Ali a look that would make a flower wither.

Abdul was first to speak. 'Hi.'

'What's happened?'

'Tell you about it inside.'

The brothers got their day packs from the back of the Pajero and Ali also grabbed his rifle. Abdul turned around and looked to see if there were any cars approaching. It all looked quiet. He and Ali followed Nitarski into the dugout.

19 THE BIG BLOKE WITH A GOATEE

ABDUL AND ALI stood behind the kitchen bench. On the other side, Nitarski was dispensing coffee into cups from a machine. 'So what was that little problem that you ran into?' Nitarski said, looking at Ali, taking in the fact that not only was there blood on his shirt front, but on the fingers that were tapping nervously on the laminex of the kitchen counter.

The brothers had rehearsed their story on the drive to Coober Pedy. 'We ran into these three guys,' Ali began. 'Aussie rednecks, they were in a Patrol. They said we looked like terrorists.'

'There was this big bloke with a goatee,' Abdul broke in. 'Mean motherfucker. He saw our rifles in the back of the ute. He had a rifle of his own. He pointed it at us and one of his mates took our guns. Then he shot out all the tyres on the ute.'

Now Ali picked up the story again. 'And then the big bloke pointed to my gold neck chain and said he wanted that too. So I took it off and went to give it to him – and grabbed his rifle.'

Abdul now took over as narrator again. 'The fucking gun went off – almost hit me. But you know how quickly Ali can move in a fight. He pulled the rifle away from the bloke and next thing he was hitting him over the head with it.'

'But the big bloke had a thick skull,' Ali said. 'He stayed standing. So I hit him again and put him down.' He paused to take a sip of Nitarski's reasonably palatable coffee and looked across at Abdul, who took up the thread again.

'The other two guys just stood there scared shitless,' Abdul said. 'We took the gun and we also took their car – after we'd got the plates off the ute, destroyed the ID numbers and set it on fire.'

Nitarski's face was inscrutable. 'Why did you have to cover your tracks like that? You were just defending yourselves and self-defence is legal.'

There was a couple of seconds' silence. Ali appeared to be studying a line of ancient sea shells embedded in the opposite wall. Abdul's eyes were half closed as he savoured a mouthful of coffee. Then his eyes opened fully.

'The problem is,' Abdul said slowly, 'that Ali kept laying into the bloke with the rifle butt after he went down. Caved in his skull, the brains were coming out. He died. We need to ditch their car, get some replacement wheels and disappear from this part of the world. Fast.'

Nitarski didn't believe a word of it. But he saw an opportunity for financial gain. Sure, he and Ali were old friends, with matching symbols of brotherhood that had been painfully rendered by a blunt sewing needle and blue biro ink all those years ago. But now Ali and his real brother were asking him to risk his skin helping them escape a murder rap. 'You can have my LandCruiser and all the supplies that come with it,' he said. 'But it'll cost you a hundred grand.'

Abdul had a DNA-ingrained urge to haggle going back to when his forbears bartered in the casbahs of ancient Arabia. 'That's a very expensive LandCruiser, brother.'

Nitarski locked eyes with Abdul, who threw in the towel after a few seconds and looked down at his bulging day pack. His voice sounding pained, like someone about to donate a kidney less than willingly, he said, 'OK, you're in luck because I always carry a hundred grand worth of mad money. A hundred and twenty grand, in fact, but Ali and me will hang on to the twenty.' He unzipped the day pack and got out five fat wads of $100 notes.

🦘 🦘 🦘 🦘

'What we're gonna do, *Kumina*, is go round to the back of that hill.'

Chaseling nodded and released the Patrol's handbrake, steering it down the dirt track that skirted around the outcrop. His heart was beating rapidly, adrenalin surging through his veins. He was afraid, but excited.

As they reached the back of the outcrop, Clarrie said, 'OK, let's get out here.' Chaseling got out of the car, went round and opened the front passenger door. He had a feeling Clarrie was going to do something with the snake – which began a fresh bout of violent struggles as Clarrie stepped out of the Patrol. 'Grab the rifle, *Kumina*,' he said. Chaseling got the .22 from the back seat and slung it over his shoulder by its ancient leather strap.

With one hand clamped behind the taipan's head and another clasping its tail, Clarrie started walking up the side of the rocky little hillock, his toes splaying out to give his bare feet a good purchase on the loose, gravel-like stones that littered the surface. Even when the snake broke into another round of frenzied struggling, he managed to keep his footing as he ascended the hill.

Chaseling didn't have the same kind of mountain goat abilities, and he'd got less than halfway up the side of the bluff when his boots slipped on a mass of little stones that acted like ball bearings. He landed awkwardly on his knee, giving a grunt of pain as his kneecap crushed into a pebble. Then when he got up and put his foot forward to continue the ascent, both feet lost their grip and suddenly he was sliding backwards down the hill. Scrabbling at the surface with his hands, he managed to halt his descent after a couple of metres. He got to his feet again and resumed his ascent, treading more carefully this time and, on the final, steepest stretch, crawling on all fours as he used his hands to maintain his tenuous traction.

Reaching the flat summit of the outcrop, his eyes took in a TV mast and half a dozen knee-high aluminium chimneys, with overhanging conical tops to prevent rain and dust getting in. Clarrie was standing beside one of these chimneys holding the snake, which had now fallen still again, except for the forked tongue, which kept flicking out as Chaseling approached. Clarrie bent down and put his ear to the top of the chimney, which was exuding an unpleasant chemical odour. He shook his head and walked to another chimney and listened. Then he stepped away from the silver-grey pipe and speaking very quietly, said, 'Come over here, *Kumina*.'

Chaseling crunched across the stony surface till he was standing alongside Clarrie, who pointed to his ear, while nodding his head down at the chimney, which was actually not a conventional chimney but the protected mouth of a ventilation shaft down to the dugout below. Chaseling put his head down and listened. He heard the faint, echoey sound of voices.

'*Kumina*, can you pull this thing out?' Clarrie said, pointing a foot at the base of the chimney.

Chaseling put his hands around the grey-silver length of piping, which was about the diameter of an old 45 rpm record, its base sunk into the galvanised iron sleeve of a flange. He gave an experimental tug. It didn't give. He took a tighter grip and pulled harder. It shifted slightly, perhaps an inch, then refused to move any further.

Looking exasperated, Clarrie took a step back and kicked at the top of the chimney with the horn-hard heel of his bare foot. His kick knocked the piping sideways, giving it a list like the Leaning Tower of Pisa. He walked round the other side, where he gave the chimney another kick. 'Now try,' he said.

🦘 🦘 🦘 🦘

The sound of Clarrie's foot crashing into the chimney was amplified as it travelled ten metres down the sandstone shaft. It reverberated across the room below like a snare drum. 'What the fuck was that?' Ali's voice was nervous as his eyes fixed on the source of the noise, the dark round mouth of a ventilation shaft set into the uneven ceiling at the end of the room, near the tombstone-shaped entranceway to the front hall.

After a couple of seconds' silence, there was a new sound – the scrape of metal against metal.

Nitarski strode around the other side of the serving counter and wrenched open a kitchen drawer. His hand came out holding a Colt .45 revolver with a long silver barrel. He broke it open and reached into the drawer again to get a handful of three centimetre long, blunt-nosed bullets. He quickly loaded the chamber of the Colt with six of them. Then he started walking purposefully towards the other side of the room, ready to blast some welcoming cheer up the shaft at the intruder on the roof. *Maybe this is it*, he thought. *The Finks have tracked me down. Or possibly the Bandidos …* But his gut told him there was a far greater likelihood, indeed a near-certainty, that Ali and Abdul had been tailed here. *Thanks brothers*, he thought. *Thanks heaps!* He pulled back the hammer of the revolver with his thumb.

20 VENOMOUS VISITOR

LIKE A DENTIST extracting a tooth, Chaseling pulled at the chimney, wincing as the metal shrieked against the flange. Then the chimney came loose and he staggered backwards, almost falling. As he laid the aluminium pipe on the ground, he watched Clarrie feed the taipan's head down the shaft. 'OK,' Clarrie whispered, not that there was likely to be much need for stealth after making so much noise kicking in the sides of the chimney, 'help me get the rest of the snake down this hole.'

Chaseling gingerly took a coil of the snake in his hands. The muscles beneath the rough scales tightened and the taipan tried to wind its body round his arm. But acting decisively, he pushed the coil of writhing reptile down the shaft, followed by another coil. Meanwhile Clarrie had the snake's tail, which he now plunged into the hole.

The entire body of the snake was now in the shaft. But it had bunched itself up and didn't look like it was going to obligingly drop down into the dugout below. 'Get the rifle and use it to push him down,' Clarrie instructed. '*Quickly!*'

Chaseling picked up the rifle, which he'd placed on the ground when he started grappling with loops of snake. Holding it by the rusty barrel, he placed it butt-end into the hole and pushed downwards. He'd got the rifle stock an elbow's length down the shaft when it met resistance and the snake signalled its unhappiness about the situation with a hiss. Chaseling pushed down harder, putting his body weight into it. The snake lost its hold and tumbled downwards.

🦘 🦘 🦘 🦘

Ali stood holding his rifle. Abdul, alongside him, was regretting leaving his own weapon in the ute. He stood with his hands clenched into fists. Nitarski, carrying the Colt .45, was cautiously approaching the far end of the room. He thought he could hear voices coming down the shaft. Something told him not to stand directly underneath it. A second later, it turned out that his intuition was spot-on as a large, dark-coloured snake suddenly came tumbling out of the round opening in the ceiling and landed on the chequerboard-patterned lino floor in a writhing, hissing, scaly tangle. For two or three heartbeats, it lay there stock still, before suddenly rearing up in striking position like a cobra, the upper body swaying from side to side and head extended right back.

Nitarski, who was just two metres away from the snake, slowly started walking backwards. From behind him, he heard the metallic snap of a rifle bolt slamming home. Too late, he shouted a warning over his shoulder. *'No, don't!'*

The sight of the snake rearing up had been all too much for Ali. After pumping a bullet into the breech of his rifle, he darted to the side so Nitarski wasn't in the line of fire, raised the stock of the gun to his shoulder, took rough aim at the snake's swaying head and pulled the trigger.

The percussion of the rifle discharge, massively loud inside the stone chamber, was accompanied by the howl of a ricochet as the shot missed the snake by several centimetres and rebounded off the wall behind. And now, travelling low, the bullet tore through the plastic drapes and into the meth lab – where it hit a 20-litre plastic drum of acetone stacked against the opposite wall. The bullet punched a hole in the front of the drum, then the other side of it before hitting the sandstone rock face behind. As the metal slug slammed into the rock, it set off a spark of static electricity.

With a mighty *whoosh*, a column of angry red flame shot up to the ceiling of the lab room. Liquid fire erupted from the ruptured drum and a rivulet of flames started making its way across the lab floor towards the transparent door flaps.

Nitarski released the hammer of the Colt .45 and let the weapon fall to the floor as he dashed towards the lab. He burst through the two plastic curtains and, coughing as he inhaled the black smoke billowing from the blazing acetone, tore a fire extinguisher from the left hand wall. Stepping nearer to the core of the flames, he pressed down the handle on the extinguisher and white fire retardant blasted from the nozzle onto the core of the fire. Meanwhile the rivulet of flame moving across the floor became a torrent as the sides of the acetone drum completely melted away. Nitarski danced aside and pointed the extinguisher at the liquid fire, but it had already surged across the floor of the lab and one of the door flaps was alight, the flames working their way hungrily upwards. Then the other flap caught fire. Another moment later, the whole doorway was engulfed in flames and black smoke.

Nitarski frantically directed the extinguisher at the burning plastic curtains, forgetting momentarily about the second 20-litre drum of acetone he'd been trying to protect from the flames. Now the contents of this drum reached flashpoint and ignited.

There was a mighty roar and the entire lab was engulfed in fire. Nitarski was thrown out through the flaming, molten remains of the plastic curtains and into the adjoining living area, his clothes ablaze. He landed face down on the lino, where, giving a dreadful, prolonged scream, he began frantically rolling back and forth, trying to extinguish the flames that danced on his shirt and jeans and seared into his skin.

Abdul was hurled to the floor by the force of the blast but Ali remained standing, pressed against the wall that he'd backed into to maximise the distance between himself and the snake – which continued to command his attention because it was on the move, wriggling across the floor. And it was making a beeline for Ali.

He lifted his rifle to his hip and fired a second shot at the taipan. Like the first one, it missed. But the bullet did halt the snake's advance. With an enraged hiss, it reared up into striking position again. Ali turned tail and fled the room, heading down the passageway leading to the bathroom and two bedrooms.

Meanwhile Abdul had escaped the explosion unscathed. As he picked himself up from the floor, he gazed across at Nitarski, who had fallen still, lying on his side. His body was no longer on fire but it was smoking, his clothes reduced to tattered black rags. The skin on his face and arms was also black, except where the blisters had burst to reveal patches of dark pink skin like rare steak. Abdul ran to the kitchen counter, where he scooped up the wads of $100 bills and thrust them back into his day pack.

Starting to gasp from the chemical smoke spewing from the lab, Abdul went and joined Ali, who he found sitting on the edge on Niitarski's king-sized bed sparking up his meth pipe. The air in here was much cleaner, except for the fumes of burning meth. 'No time for that, bro, we gotta get out of here!' Abdul screamed.

Ali took his lips away from the glass stem of the pipe and exhaled some smoke. His eyes, bulging with fear, looked up at his brother and he said, 'The snake?' The words were uttered in the trembling, high-pitched tones of a frightened child.

Abdul could see that his brother was near-hysterical and that the snake would have to be dealt with before anything else. Ali's rifle was propped up against the bed. Abdul grabbed it and pulled out the magazine to check it had bullets in it. Seeing the gleam of brass cartridges, he slammed the magazine back in. 'Wait there,' he told Ali, who had sparked up the lighter again and gave a slight nod of acknowledgement as he sucked smoke into his lungs. Abdul ran out of the room holding the rifle.

The living area was thick with toxic black smoke. The river of burning chemicals had flowed out of the lab area and was now starting to move like molten lava across the floor towards the prone form of Nitarski. The taipan was on the move again, wriggling towards Abdul, whose eyes were streaming from the smoke. He blinked rapidly a few times as he put the rifle scope to his eye. He squeezed the trigger and a bullet howled from the gun. It hit the taipan in the middle of its body and almost blew it in two. There were the whines of several ricochets as the high velocity bullet tore down the main hallway of the dugout and exited through the solid front door. The snake thrashed around in a pool of blood on the floor, its struggles so violent that the halves of its body, held together just by flaps of skin, broke apart, but continued to show plenty of life as, like an earthworm cut in two, they whipped back and forth. The lethal jaws opened and closed convulsively. Which was inconvenient because this part of the snake was blocking the passage out of this place.

The fumes were burning his eyes and lungs. Pulling up the bottom of his T-shirt to cover his mouth, Abdul stepped closer to the snake and aimed the rifle one-handed. The shot blew off the snake's frantically snapping head and the bullet screamed on down the tunnel-like hallway. Then Abdul's body gave a jolt as a bloodcurdling screech reverberated off the stone walls and ceiling. He turned around.

Abdul had thought that Nitarski was dead. But now the river of fire from the blazing lab had engulfed his head and shoulders and he began a series of violent movements, writhing on the floor and screaming as orange-red flames spread down his body. Then he gave a final howl of agony and fell still, his whole body ablaze.

The stench of burning chemicals combined with the smell of barbecuing meat as Abdul detoured around the burning man, scooping up the Colt .45 that was about to be engulfed by the flames spreading across the floor. Coughing violently, he made his way to the desk in the corner where he grabbed Nitarski's respirator and goggles. Then he rejoined Ali.

The air was still relatively clean in the bedroom where Ali had taken refuge. He was sitting bolt upright on the bed. His eyes were wide, their pupils hugely dilated. Speaking in a hoarse voice, Abdul told him, 'The snake's dead. So is Vasko. Go into the garage and see if he's left the keys in the LandCruiser. If they're in there, give one honk on the horn, and I'll come down and join you and we'll get the fuck out of here.' He handed his brother the Colt pistol. 'Take this with you.'

Abdul placed the respirator in front of his face and snapped one strap around the back of his head, followed by the second strap higher up. 'Maybe hold your breath as you're going through the main room – and watch out for the flames on the floor.' His voice sounded muffled and inhuman through the gas mask.

Ali got to his feet and started to leave the room, pausing just before he reached the door. 'What will you be doing?'

'Finding Vasko's stash – and cash,' said Abdul, ever the opportunistic criminal. Tendrils of black smoke were floating into the room. 'Hurry, brother – whoever put that snake down the hole will probably have some other tricks up their sleeves!' He snapped on the safety goggles, then pulled out the top drawer of a dressing table and tipped its contents onto the bed. No cash or drug stash, just socks and underwear. He wrenched out a second drawer. More clothes, neatly folded. Very quickly, he searched the rest of the room. Nothing. He should have known that Nitarski would be too street-smart to conceal his valuables anywhere obvious. He heard the sound of a car horn. Time to go.

He was halfway out of the room when all the lights went out, plunging the dugout into stygian darkness.

21 LET'S FINISH THIS

CLARRIE AND CHASELING slid down the side of the hill. It was faster that way, besides which Chaseling, who started descending first, and doing so carefully, was forced into it as Clarrie, sliding on the soles of his Teflon feet like a skier or snowboarder, rammed into him and set him skidding down the side on his hands and knees. At the base of the hill he stood up and looked at the fingertips of his right hand – he had lost the top half of a nail as he clawed at the rocky slope. His right knee, which had blood seeping from a nasty graze, wasn't feeling too good either. During the descent he'd heard the faint crack of a gunshot from inside the hill. 'Sounds like the snake worked a treat,' Clarrie said as they ran to the car

They'd left the doors of the Patrol open. Clarrie jumped into the driver's seat and had the car crunching across the rocky surface before Chaseling threw himself in beside him. The car's wheels spat gravel and raised a plume of dust as they took off down the track that skirted the side of the hill.

A rumble shook the car. And as the car crunched down a dirt driveway leading up to Nitarski's dugout, there were two loud bangs, spaced a few seconds apart, which sounded very much like gunfire. Clarrie pulled up behind the Pajero they'd tailed, boxing it in, and turned off the ignition.

'Do you know,' Chaseling said, 'that *"pajero"* means "wanker" in Spanish?'

'No,' replied Clarrie, reaching round to the back seat and getting the rifle. He opened the driver's door. Then he turned to Chaseling, his brow creased with concern. 'You better stay here in the car, *Kumina*.'

Although it was a cool morning, a slight sweat had beaded on Chaseling's brow. He forced the tight muscles around his mouth into a smile. 'I don't want to miss the end of the movie.'

Clarrie's face was creased with worry. 'Seriously *Kumina*, this isn't your fight.'

Chaseling pushed down on the door release. 'You can do the fighting, I'll just cower behind you,' he said as he pushed the door open and slid out of the car.

Seconds later they were fanning out sideways as they approached the dugout entrance. The hill which the dugout had been built into was steep, almost sheer, on this side. It was as though the entrance was built into the base of a little cliff. Chaseling's white-knuckled hand clutched the rubber-sleeved Maglite torch. Clarrie carried the .22. They paused on either side of the front door. Near the top of the door was a round, finger-width hole with sharp white splinters radiating out from it.

'A car horn, startlingly loud, sounded from behind the garage door to their right. Chaseling's knees were shaking slightly. He hoped Clarrie didn't notice. But Clarrie was looking at a metal electricity box bolted onto the bare rock between the front door and the garage. He wrenched open a little galvanised iron door and reached inside. Chaseling heard the click of a switch. 'Lights out, boys,' Clarrie said.

Keeping his body glued to the outside wall of the dugout, Clarrie pulled down on the door handle. There was a creak as he opened the door far enough for a person to slip inside. Then he gave Chaseling a quick nod before disappearing into the dugout. Chaseling followed, closing the door behind him. They found themselves in a dark tunnel of bare rock. It was perhaps three metres wide. Chaseling could hear Clarrie making his way along the right hand wall. So Chaseling started to move cautiously along the opposite rock face, his hand touching the scoured surface for guidance. The only light was coming from the end of the tunnel, where there was a dull, flickering orange glow. Chaseling wrinkled his nose as he inhaled noxious fumes. 'Don't turn on that torch just yet,' he heard Clarrie whisper. They edged their way down the dark, rocky passageway.

The shadow of an open doorway loomed halfway down, on the right. Clarrie's nostrils suddenly flared and he came to an abrupt halt. He was getting a waft of a familiar body odour.

The foul scent he'd smelled at the scene of Ruby's murder. Stale sweat and spicy foods. He crouched down on the ground on all fours like a cat. Then he edged towards the dark recess in the wall. The smell was overwhelming now, and he could hear the man's uneven breathing …

Ali stood in deep shadow just inside the doorway to the garage with his Jungle Master held above his head. While snakes made him quake in his boots, people were a different matter. He felt a hot flush on his throat as the berserker devil inside him clamoured to be unleashed. The heat started engulfing his face. He was going to turn himself into a human threshing machine and cut the enemy to pieces. From the sound of the voices he'd heard filtering up the rock corridor, there were two of them.

Out in the passage, Ali saw a figure slowly come into view, a person with very light hair which stood out in the near-darkness. Ali could also just make out that the person wore a pair of dark-framed glasses and had a beard which was a darker shade than the scalp hair.

Like a striking trapdoor spider, Ali launched himself through the doorway. But his lower legs came into contact with something solid – the crouching Clarrie – and Ali ended up making an inelegant entrance into the tunnel on his stomach, belly flopping onto the dirt floor. He broke the fall with his hands and dropped the knife in the process. He came to rest with one of his hands resting against Chaseling's ankle. Ali grabbed hold of the ankle. Chaseling gave a frightened shout. Ali's other hand searched for the knife. And he found it. His fingers closed around the hilt of the Jungle Master, then he pulled at the man's leg to bring him closer for the kill. Chaseling frantically kicked out with his foot, but Ali's grip was like an iron shackle, encircling his ankle just above the top of his boot, the fingers clamping down with bruising force on his Achilles tendon. He found himself being pulled closer to the near-invisible attacker. Then he saw a silvery flash of reflected light – a knife!

Ali had reared up into a sitting position and was drawing his arm back to stab his victim in the groin. But suddenly the bone-hard sole of Clarrie's foot slammed into his chest. Ali gasped as he was thrown against the rough cut wall of the passage – and he released his grip on Chaseling's ankle.

Chaseling's fight or flight response kicked in, releasing a cocktail of adrenalin, cortisol and testosterone into his bloodstream. Fight won out over flight. He lunged forward with the Maglite raised above his head. A shadowy form loomed in front of him. 'Fuck *off*, you bastard!' he screamed as he brought the torch down on the top of the figure's skull.

Unfortunately the figure happened to be that of Clarrie, who was in the process of lunging at the knifeman. On the positive side, the Maglite's rubber sheathing was quite thick and cushioned the blow. But the concussion was substantial, not unlike a sock filled with sand, and Clarrie fell to the ground.

Meanwhile the attacker darted away. Chaseling saw the silhouette of his large figure disappearing into the smoky, flame-lit portal at the end of the tunnel. He heard Clarrie groan.

'Sorry Clarrie!' he hissed, helping him get back on his feet. Clarrie winced as he touched his hand to the top of his head but he said, 'I'm OK, *Kumina*. Let's finish this.'

From the end of the tunnel, there was the sound of violent coughing, followed by a pair of male voices speaking in Arabic.

At that moment a frightening-looking figure appeared in the glowing end of the tunnel, the silhouette of a man wearing a gas mask and goggles. And pointing a rifle at them. There was a red flash and an ear-jarring percussion.

The bullet would have torn right through Chaseling's head if Clarrie hadn't dragged him down to the ground a split second before it tore down the tunnel. And now, from a squatting position, Clarrie took careful aim with his own rifle and fired a single shot. The .22 sounded puny, like a small firecracker, compared to Abdul's high velocity .243. But the pea-sized bullet tore between the third and fourth ribs on the left side of Abdul's chest, and ploughed into his heart. He fell backwards.

There was silence. Ten, twenty, thirty seconds. Then a dreadful, guttural scream rang out and echoed off the walls of the tunnel. The final reverberations were still subsiding when Ali made his reappearance.

Shrieking like someone possessed, Ali came charging down the corridor, his left hand spitting fire as he fired the Colt .45, his right hand slashing the Jungle Master through the air.

Clarrie was catapulted backwards as a bullet slammed into his face. Then Ali loomed in front of Chaseling and slashed at his neck. Chaseling dodged aside and the serrated edge of the Jungle Master sliced into his upper arm, just below the shoulder. The steel felt cold as it cut deeply into the muscle. Then Ali was disappearing through the doorway from which he'd earlier made his knife-wielding entrance.

'Clarrie?' Chaseling said in a trembling voice. He flicked on the Maglite.

The bullet had hit Clarrie in his forehead. He was very dead, lifeless eyes staring vacantly and blood pooling around his head. Chaseling heard the roar of a car engine, followed by a mighty crash. It came from the room the man had disappeared into. It was no longer in darkness. Chaseling walked unsteadily through the doorway, blood flowing down his arm and dripping onto the dirt floor. At the far end of the room, a garage door had been torn open like the top of a sardine can. Through the gap created by the ruptured tilt-a-door, he could see a white four-wheel drive accelerating away from the house, half hidden by dust as it tore down the dirt track.

He went back into the tunnel and knelt beside Clarrie. 'Sorry one of them got away,' he said, squeezing his hand.

The flames at the end of the tunnel were more intense now. His lungs were being seared by toxic chemical smoke, mixed with the hideous fumes of incinerated flesh that had his stomach on the verge of heaving. His eyes were streaming. And the tears that ran down his cheeks weren't solely the result of eye irritation.

He reached down and, partly as a gesture of farewell and partly to satisfy his curiosity, put his fingertips to the sole of Clarrie's foot. It felt more like rhinoceros horn than skin, not that Chaseling had ever caressed a rhino horn, but this was how he would imagine it. Finally, he squeezed Clarrie's arm and said, 'Goodbye Clarrie.' His voice choked slightly and he found himself fighting off a terrible feeling of loss and grief. It wasn't just the loss of Clarrie. It was as though something in himself had died. The sense of innocence and purity of spirit he had enjoyed as a comparatively innocent medical student, more prone to partying than violence, had vanished.

Rising to his feet, he gagged from the chemical fumes that were much thicker at this height. Crouching down low, he made his way to the end of the tunnel and opened the front door. Bright sunlight flooded in. Staggering slightly, he walked outside and looked down at his upper arm. The knife had sliced deeply into the deltoid muscle just below his shoulder. Blood was splattering onto the dirt. He fished into his pocket for his phone and tapped out the triple zero emergency number.

22 DEATH OF A THOUSAND CUTS

CHASELING SAT PROPPED UP in a bed in Coober Pedy's small hospital. It was a modest facility with 24 beds, but staff displayed a high level of competence as they cleaned, stitched and bandaged his knife wound. They also gave him a blood transfusion, over a litre. And now he had a drip of antibiotics going into his arm as he was interviewed by a khaki-uniformed policeman sitting beside the bed.

The policeman's name was Senior Sergeant Fowler. He had a salt and pepper beard trimmed close to his face. Now he scratched at the beard as he said, 'And you've got no description of this man other than the fact that he was heavy-set?'

'I'm afraid not.'

'Just like the only description you could give of that car was "a white four-wheel drive."'

There was an accusatory, almost hostile tone to the policeman's questions that was starting to grate on Chaseling's nerves. 'There aren't a lot of cars on the Stuart Highway.' He said. 'How do you think he managed to get past your road blocks?'

Senior Sgt Fowler chewed at his lower lip. Chaseling noticed how he had long tufts sprouting from his nostrils that melded into the hairs of his moustache. 'He might have headed across country, down the Oodnadatta Track,' the policeman said.

'Is that a back way out of the desert?'

The Senior Sergeant nodded. Then his mobile phone rang. He had a quick conversation with someone he called "sir." Then he replaced the phone on the bedside table and said, 'The homicide detectives and forensics people have just finished up at St Catherine's. They'll be here within the hour — they're travelling in a light aircraft. The senior officer is Detective Chief Inspector Wolksi, and he'll be coming to see you after he's had a look inside the dugout.' He picked up his phone and got to his feet. 'That will be all for now.'

Giving Chaseling a curt nod, Senior Sergeant Fowler started walking towards the door. Then he paused and turned round. 'The police don't like people taking the law into their own hands,' he said. 'You'll be lucky if you don't go from here to a cell. In fact we've got a room reserved for you down at the station. The previous guest was into finger painting. Created some interesting designs on the wall with his own faeces. We haven't got round to cleaning it up yet.'

'Excellent,' Chaseling said. 'It sounds like an interesting wall mural. I look forward to seeing it.'

The policeman gave a snort of derision and made his exit.

Ali's foot was pressed hard to the accelerator. He glanced down at the speedometer – 170…. 180… The engine was shaking in protest. Behind the car stretched a long plume of red dust. Framed through the windscreen was a straight dirt road stretching to the shimmering horizon. The tiny community he passed through earlier, slowing to a sedate 60km/h, had a sign on its outskirts saying 'YOU ARE NOW IN OODNADATTA, AUSTRALIA'S HOTTEST, DRIEST TOWN.' It was also one of the continent's least populated towns and he hadn't seen a single person, although there were a few cars parked outside a pink-painted roadhouse.

Strapped in the back of the car were two jerry cans of petrol plus a ten litre drum of water. When Ali and Abdul had stayed overnight in Nitarski's dugout a few days earlier, his friend had confided how he was prepared for a sudden departure from Coober Pedy in the event that his past caught up with him. He'd related how there was a network of dirt roads that could take you on a south-easterly route out of the desert. And he'd mentioned the Oodnadatta Track.

As well as Nitarski's provisions, Ali had his brother's day pack containing his $120K mad money. He had a feeling it was going to come in useful. He'd be bringing his departure date for Syria forward and meanwhile he may well have to buy himself out of trouble.

Ali's hands tightened on the steering wheel and his eyes narrowed as he thought of the man who'd brought this misfortune upon him. The man in the tunnel-like hallway of the dugout. The man with blond hair and a darker coloured beard. And glasses – the kind of heavy-framed glasses worn by Austin Powers. Ali was hoping the man with blond hair, beard and glasses had survived the slash of his Jungle Master. Because then he could have the satisfaction of finding him in the very near future and putting him to death very slowly, slice by slice.

Ali was not someone given to historical research, but he once took to Google to study something he'd seen in an obscure Kung Fu movie. In the film, a man had been subjected to a slow execution called The Death of a Thousand Cuts. Ali's scholarly investigations on the web revealed it was common in the old days of imperial China. It took place in public, the unfortunate victim tied to a tree or pole in the village square. It started out with cuts to the limbs and torso which didn't bleed too much. Next, small slices of flesh would be removed. Then larger chunks, moving onto amputation of the ears, nose, hands, feet and genitals. A skilled practitioner could extend the life of a victim for two or even three days. Yes, that's what he'd like to do to the blond man, treat him to The Death of a Thousand Cuts as punishment for Abdul's death.

23 GLEN OF THE OUTBACK

THERE WAS A MAN in the bed next to Chaseling who was starting to drive him crazy. He wouldn't shut up. He'd been admitted to the ward just after the departure of Senior Sergeant Fowler.

The garrulous fellow-patient – the *only* other patient in the little ward – was a man in his mid-fifties with long brown-grey hair tied in a ponytail, a small red snub nose and doll-like porcelain blue eyes with a vacant look that reminded Chaseling of the TV cartoon character Sponge Bob. He had a bandaged ear and his left arm was in a splint.

Speaking in a nasal, broadly Aussie-accented voice, the man said, 'Glen's my name! Glen of the Outback, they call me. So where are you from, mate? Sydney? Oh yeah, I think I might have passed through there once, what's the pub there called?' He broke into a wheezy laugh.

'How did you get injured, Glen?' Chaseling enquired.

'I went the thump with the bouncer at the pub here in Coober Pedy when he tried to kick me out. He got in a lucky punch.'

Glen of the Outback proceeded to regale Chaseling with a series of anecdotes about other pub fights where he'd been the victor, downing Goliath-like opponents with his devastating pugilistic moves, assisted occasionally by the use of ready weapons like bar stools, pool cues and schooner glasses.

Chaseling switched off, nodding politely but not listening to the man's stream of consciousness ramble – until Glen of the Outback claimed that during a stint as a sheep shearer, he'd encountered music legend David Bowie. 'I'm havin' a game of snooker in a little town way out west in New South Wales called Carinda. One pub town, same as this. The bloke I'm playin' is a shearer called Wally, big cunt wearin' a blue singlet and stubbies. Now, I'm about to take a shot, when suddenly this big hairy hand reaches down and grabs hold of my cue and I hear Wally tellin' me, "It's not your shot."

'Now, maybe he was right – maybe it wasn't my turn, maybe he was wrong. But that wasn't the point. I looks at him and I says, "No cunt touches my pool cue! *Outside!*"

'We're about to head out the door when who should walk into the pub – but *David bloody Bowie!* Yeah, the Thin White Duke, in the flesh. Not that there was a lot of flesh – he was a skinny bugger. Next thing there's a film crew setting up, then it's lights, camera, action – and they're filmin' the clip for *Let's Dance*, or a lot of it anyway. Take a look at that video and you'll see that one of the drinkers in the pub is a bloke in an orange T-shirt.' He pointed his index finger at his chest. 'Glen of the Outback.'

Chaseling reached down to his bedside table and picked up his iPhone and clicked onto Google. 'Let's check out your three minutes of fame, Glen.'

The swing doors of the ward flew open. Into the room walked a nuggetty man wearing camel brown trousers and a short sleeved white shirt which had turned grey with perspiration in several places. He was aged around fifty, with a sun-browned face that looked as if it was made of wrinkly, sun-cured leather. His forehead was lined with horizontal furrows which bisected two long vertical creases extending upwards from between his eyes. He looked at Glen of the Outback, then Chaseling.

'Dr Chaseling, I presume,' the man said, approaching his bed. He held out his hand. 'Detective Chief Inspector Peter Wolski, South Australian Police Major Crime Investigation Branch.'

The detective sat down next to Chaseling's bed and told him he had been to the scenes of the two murders in St Catherine's a couple of hours earlier and had just visited the dugout where further blood had been shed. 'I've seen the notes Senior Sergeant Fowler typed up after his interview with you,' said Wolksi, 'so that gives a broad picture of what happened. Now, I'm interested in what the older man...' – he paused as he looked down at a sheet of paper – 'Noelie Jakamara, I'm interested in what Noelie Jakamara said about the man he tracked from the house.'

Chaseling gazed upwards for a couple of seconds as he tried to recall Noelie's exact words. 'He said he was a big, heavy man,' he said. 'Maybe fat, but strong. Wearing sneakers. He thought they might be Adidas.'

The cop ran a hand through his thinning head of light brown hair. 'I've seen some sickening sights in my time. You've probably heard of the Snowtown Murders. People also call them The Bodies in the Barrel Murders. Well, back in the nineties I was assigned to that case and I had a look inside one of the drums the bodies were kept in.'

'*Come to Snowtown, you'll have a barrel of laughs.* Used to have a coffee mug saying that.' It was Glen of the Outback.

The detective ignored the interruption. 'But you know,' he continued, 'the sight of that girl Ruby today was probably the most disturbing thing I've ever seen.'

Glen of the Outback started singing: '*Roo-oo-beee, don't take your love to town...*'

'Glen,' snapped Chaseling, 'why don't you shut the fu – ' He fell silent as Wolski leapt to his feet and, moving quickly, started pulling Glen of the Outback's bed away from the wall. 'I was just singin' a song!' Glen protested. 'One of my favourites, by Kenny Rogers!'

Now the detective was pushing the wheeled bed towards the double swing doors. 'There's no law against singin'!' Glen of the Outback shouted. The end of the bed crashed into the doors, which obediently opened. Now they were out in the corridor and Chaseling heard the squeak of the bed's wheels receding, along with Glen of the Outback's protests.

Like a gunslinger entering the saloon in Dodge City, Wolksi pushed his way back in through the swing doors. As his eyes met Chaseling's, they both burst out laughing. Sitting back down beside the bed, Wolski said, 'Lucky he didn't get a smack in the mouth.'

A nurse burst through the doors, a solidly-built woman with red hair and a matching temper. Advancing on Wolski, she demanded, 'Why did you remove my patient from the ward?'

'He was disrupting a police investigation,' the detective replied. 'So will you be if you don't let me interview this man.' There was a muffled shout from Glen of the Outback out in the corridor. The nurse backed down. 'I'll put him in another ward, but it's one reserved for geriatric patients, so he's coming back here as soon as you're finished.' She did an about turn and made her exit, angrily attacking the swing doors with the heels of her hands.

'OK,' said Wolski, 'now we've got some peace and quiet, I need you to go over everything that happened from the time you left the house where Ruby was killed. I know you've already given your written statement to Senior Sergeant Fowler, but I want to hear it from your own lips.'

Recounting the details of the pursuit through the desert and bloody confrontation in the dugout took well over an hour. Then the detective told him about what they'd found in the dugout – three male body's, Clarrie's plus those of two unidentified males, although one of them was believed to be the dugout's owner Vasko Nitarski. 'His body was burnt to a crisp,' he said.

By the time the detective was finished with him, Chaseling was feeling exhausted. It was a day and a half since he'd had any sleep.

The detective stood up. 'It's not the kind of thing we like to encourage, but you showed a lot of guts, to join in the pursuit of two violent offenders. You're free to leave here whenever you like, assuming you're well enough.'

'Senior Sergeant Fowler was outlining a different scenario, something about admiring the artwork in the cells of Coober Pedy cop shop.'

'Don't worry, that won't be happening. But I'd like you to keep me informed about your whereabouts. When are you heading up to Alice Springs?'

'Tomorrow, I suppose.'

'Leave early. It's a long drive, a thousand Ks. If you drive in the dark, or even as it's getting dark, keep your speed down to seventy or less or you might well hit another kangaroo. You're obviously going to hire a car?'

Chaseling nodded.

'There aren't just kangaroos on the highway. You get emus, and they're on the move during the day. Plus cattle – a lot of the stations around here are unfenced. You don't want to go colliding with a one tonne Angus bull. So my advice is, rent a four-wheel drive. More likely to get you to Alice in one piece.'

'Sounds like a plan.'

They shook hands and the detective made his exit. A few minutes later, Glen of the Outback was wheeled back in by the red-headed nurse. But fortunately he was sulking and remained mute, casting reproachful glances across at Chaseling every now and then like a spurned suitor. Which suited Chaseling just fine. He got his phone and shortly he was talking to the local office of Thrifty Car Rental and booking a Holden Captiva, which looked like a bulky enough vehicle to take on an Angus bull. He said he'd be driving it one way to Alice Springs and they said that was no problem, just drop it at the Thrifty office in Alice.

Then he put in his headphone buds and, keeping his phone angled away from his fellow patient, viewed David Bowie's *Let's Dance* clip. There was indeed a man in an orange T-shirt featured in a number of shots inside an outback pub, but he looked nothing like Glen of the Outback, or how he might have looked a few decades earlier.

Next he phoned his future boss, Dr Hillary Pike, head of the orthopaedic department at Alice Springs Hospital, and as he waited for Pike to answer thought how Hillary was an unfortunate name for a male. A slightly querulous-sounding voice came on the line: 'Yes, hello?'

'Dr Pike, it's Jonathan Chaseling, just getting in touch before starting work on Monday.'

'Ah yes, young Jonathan,' said Pike, his tone warmer, but doing nothing to enamour himself with Chaseling, who hated being called 'Young Jonathan.' Throughout his teens and adulthood till now, he'd always looked younger than his years, which was why he'd grown the beard. But the facial hair only went part way to throwing off his boyish appearance, and he was still asked to show ID at a lot of pubs and clubs.

He told Pike he was planning to arrive in town at seven or eight o'clock the following night. He thought it best not to mention anything about the violence he'd been caught up in.

'You're welcome to join us for dinner,' Pike said. 'It's just my wife Kath and me,'

'I'd love to, thanks.'

'We've also got a spare bed – you can stay with us for a night or two if you like.'

'That's very kind of you.' Chaseling wrote down the address and directions for getting there.

'So how's the trip been so far?' Dr Pike asked.

'Interesting,' Chaseling replied. 'Very interesting indeed.'

After sleeping for a few hours, during which time Glen of the Outback thankfully continued to sulk and remain mute, Chaseling decided to go out and collect his hire car. Which presented a challenge, because he was only wearing underpants and a light blue hospital smock. His shoes and socks were beside the bed but there was no sign of his other clothes. He pulled open the door of his bedside table. On a shelf were his cargo shorts, wallet and phone. No sign of the T-shirt he'd borrowed from the Colonel Sanders lookalike, which had become soaked in blood from his knife wound. *Probably ended up in the surgical waste basket*, he thought.

He looked over at Glen of the Outback. 'Glen, I wonder if you might have a shirt I could borrow or buy off you?'

'Just my AC-DC T-shirt, and it's one of my most treasured possessions.' Glen said. Then the lids of the Sponge Bob eyes lowered in a calculating look. 'I'll sell it to you for a hundred bucks.'

Ten minutes later, Chaseling left the ward wearing Glen's T-shirt, having beaten the price down to fifty dollars. The shirt had once been black but now it was charcoal grey, with the

AC-DC logo across the front in faded red lettering. Out in the corridor, the redheaded nurse loomed in front of him. 'And where are you going?' she demanded.

'Out,' he said.

'Did Dr Prasad say you could leave?'

'I'm coming back,' Chaseling said. 'Just got to organise something down the road.'

The nurse reluctantly moved aside. Then she smiled. And there was something cruel in the smile, matched by a sadistic glitter in her pale eyes. 'Perhaps you'd better give your hair a comb before you go outside,' she said.

'Thanks, I'll be fine.' He made his way to the reception area and headed through a set of sliding glass doors into bright sunlight.

'Dr Chaseling!'

Blinking his eyes as he adjusted to the sunshine, Chaseling saw a woman and man walking towards him. The man had a large, professional-looking video camera on his shoulder and the woman, who wore a navy blue power suit and a helmet-shaped arrangement of black hair, was holding a long, fluffy microphone.

'Leanne Merrick, ABC News.'

There was the click of a camera shutter and Chaseling saw that there was a third person standing further back, a man with a long-lensed stills camera. The man waved and said '*Adelaide Advertiser.*'

'Adelaide?' Chaseling said dully. 'You're a long way from home, aren't you?'

'We took a charter plane up here,' the newspaperman said.

'This is big news, Dr Chaseling,' said Leanne Merrick. She'd stepped closer to him, as had the cameraman attached to her umbilical fashion by the microphone cord. Chaseling noticed that the red light above the video camera lens was lit up. The reporter pointed the fluffy microphone at him and said, 'How did you get involved in this tragic chain of circumstances?'

Chaseling took a deep breath and said, 'I had a car accident – hit a kangaroo – and was given a lift to St Catherine's,' he replied haltingly.

'And what exactly took place at St Catherine's?'

Chaseling swallowed nervously, his eyes flicking towards the *Adelaide Advertiser* photographer, who appeared to double as reporter because he'd also moved forwards and was pointing a palm-sized recorder at him. 'It's probably best that you get those details from the police,' Chaseling said.

Leanne Merrick pointed the fluffy microphone at him like a gun. 'According to the police,' she said, 'you got involved in payback after two people on the community were murdered.'

A sudden gust of wind failed to ruffle a single hair on the TV reporter's lacquered head. Her eyes, hard as her hair, bore into Chaseling accusingly. He tried to control his rising anger. The reporters must have been talking to Senior Sergeant Fowler. Speaking carefully, he said, 'Two innocent people lost their lives in St Catherine's under very violent circumstances. The men responsible fled to Coober Pedy. We followed them. And, there was a bit of a clash inside a dugout.'

'A bit of a clash?' the reporter raised an expertly-plucked eyebrow.

'Well, three people died. I'm sorry, but that's all I can say for now.' He started walking away.

Leanne Merrick and her cameraman broke into a run. And now they were in front of him, the cameraman walking backwards while the reporter had her hand on his shoulder, guiding him. For a seeming eternity, although it was actually less than a minute, they filmed Chaseling walking. The *Adelaide Advertiser* photo-journalist appeared behind the pair and snapped off a couple of shots.

Finally the mini media pack let him go. 'Good luck in Alice Springs, Dr Chaseling,' Leanne Merrick said.

Great, he thought to himself as he walked away from the trio. The cops had told them about the job he was starting the morning after next. He cringed inwardly as he thought about the prospect of his impending appearance on TV and in the next day's newspaper.

He found his way to Coober Pedy town centre. There was a shop with a sign out the front saying 'OPAL DEALER.' He went inside. Under glass on the counter was a glittering display of opals radiating every colour of the spectrum. Some were the size of marbles, others were much larger.

Standing behind the counter was a middle-aged man with a luxuriant growth of grey beard sprouting from his face, the moustache section hanging down low in front of his mouth so that all that could be seen of his features was a red, sun-ravaged nose and a pair of beady eyes which focussed speculatively on Chaseling. An opening appeared in the beard as he parted his lips to speak. 'G'day,' he said.

Chaseling reached into his pocket and produced the opalised fossil shell. 'How much do you estimate this is worth?'

The man took the stone and weighed it in his hand. 'Where did you get this?'

'Oh, just somewhere out in the desert,' Chaseling said.

The opal dealer picked a jeweller's loupe from the counter top and studied the stone. 'It's a black opal, a very nice piece. Look, I have a buyer who might be interested – I can give you $300 for it.'

Chaseling held out his hand to take it back. 'Thanks, I just wanted to get an idea of its value.'

The man reluctantly relinquished the stone. 'OK, make it $600.'

'The price jumped up very quickly,' Chaseling said with a smile as he pocketed the rock.

Just before he reached the door, the man's voice called out. 'A thousand.'

Chaseling turned around. The man had lifted up a hinged section of counter and stepped onto the shop floor, displaying bowed, brown legs beneath a pair of football shorts. 'Fifteen hundred,' he said.

'I might get back to you,' Chaseling said, exiting the shop. Just before the door shut behind him he heard the man yell out *'Two thousand!'*

The car office was just a short distance from the opal dealer. Chaseling handed over his credit card and drivers licence and the man behind the counter tapped away at a computer. Then the man slid the laminated licence across the counter, along with a set of keys. 'It's parked in the yard out back, got a full tank of petrol,' he said.

The Captiva was a solid-looking vehicle which still had a new car smell. He started the engine, then looked in vain for the handbrake. There wasn't one. Then he saw a button below the gear shift with a 'P' on it. Ah! He pressed the button, put the car into gear and it rolled forward.

He decided not to go back to the hospital. There might be more media people lurking outside. And the prospect of spending the night in the same room as Glen of the Outback was not a pleasant one. He drove through the small centre of town looking for accommodation. There was a motel with a sign offering underground rooms. But after his experiences in the dugout, Chaseling felt like staying above the surface for the time being.

On the edge of town he found a place called the Mud Hut Motel, where he paid for a single room. The walls of his above-ground room had an ochre stucco rendering that gave an earthy effect and sunlight spilled in from a window looking out into a leafy back courtyard. He phoned Coober Pedy Hospital and told Dr Prasad he wasn't coming back. Suddenly he was overwhelmed by tiredness and, without bothering to take off his clothes or even his shoes, flopped onto the double bed and fell almost instantly asleep.

When he awoke the room was in darkness, with the dim grey light of dusk filtering in the window. He looked at the red digital display on the bedside clock. It was just after 8pm. He picked up the remote control of the plasma screen TV opposite the bed. Taking off his shoes this time, he propped himself up against the pillows and tuned in to ABC News 24. He didn't have long to wait.

'*Police are investigating five violent deaths in the Simpson Desert,*' a male news anchor said, his face creased in a practiced look of concern. '*Leanne Merrick reports.*'

Chaseling recognised the voice immediately. '*This is the normally quiet Aboriginal community of St Catherine's, in mourning today after two shocking murders last night.*' There was aerial footage of the desert community showing police cars and ambulances parked alongside some ramshackle houses. '*It's understood a 16-year-old girl was stabbed to death and a 61-year-old man was shot.*'

Now the vision on screen switched to the outside of the dugout which had been the scene of further carnage. '*Hours later, three men lost their lives in this underground home in Coober Pedy.*' There was a shot of a forensics officer in a white paper body suit and blue slippers emerging from the front door of the dugout carrying a rifle wrapped in plastic. '*While police have yet to reveal the causes of these deaths, they admit several shots were fired. And they say all five deaths are connected.*'

Now Senior Sergeant Fowler came on screen. '*From what we can piece together at this stage,*' he said, '*there was a pursuit — a car chase from St Catherine's to Coober Pedy. And in Coober Pedy the occupants of the two vehicles had a violent confrontation which resulted in three men becoming deceased.*'

Then came the moment that Chaseling had been dreading – his own appearance on screen. He winced as he saw himself looking into the camera lens with a surprised expression on his face. Then Glen of the Outback's AC-DC T-shirt was displayed in all its faded glory as he was shown walking down the footpath looking extremely embarrassed. Meanwhile Leanne Merrick's voiceover returned: '*This is Dr Jonathan Chaseling, who was involved in the pursuit from the Aboriginal community to the opal mining town.*'

Next there was a head and shoulders shot of him, with the fluffy microphone edging into the bottom of the frame like the woolly head of some grey-furred animal. '*Two innocent people lost their lives in St Catherine's under very violent circumstances, and then I helped track down the men responsible,'* his on-screen likeness said.

Finally Leanne Merrick appeared standing in front of the hospital. *'Dr Chaseling was treated for a knife wound here in Coober Pedy Hospital,'* she said. *'And it's understood he'll soon be spending a lot of time in Alice Springs Hospital, not as a patient but as a newly-appointed staff doctor. Meanwhile police continue to investigate the events that led to five people losing their lives here in the Simpson Desert. From Coober Pedy, this is Leanne Merrick reporting.'*

The male anchor came back on and started to introduce a story about Breast Cancer Awareness Week. Feeling stunned, Chaseling hit the power button on the remote control and the screen went black.

🦘 🦘 🦘 🦘

Ali sat on a fallen log at the edge of a dry creek bed. He had a fire going. He bit into the haunch of a rabbit he'd shot with Nitarski's revolver just before sundown. His hair and beard were tangled and wild and he looked like some kind of demi-beast as he devoured the undercooked rabbit, tearing at the carcase with his canine teeth and wolfing down large chunks of meat.

He'd made it across the South Australian border, back into New South Wales. This meant he was out of the direct reach of the SA police who'd no doubt descended on Coober Pedy. Now he just needed to make it to Sydney, which shouldn't be too much of a challenge, unless the NSW cops were on the lookout for him. In which case, they wouldn't take him alive. He'd go down shooting, or slashing away with the Jungle Master.

24 MONEY TALKS

IT HAD BEEN three days now since Hafsa Fazir had heard from her husband. Before that he'd been phoning every day, spending most of the call talking to their daughter Shahana, the apple of Abdul's eye, although his mistress came a close second. The mistress was a blonde bitch. Hafsa had seen pictures on his phone.

Infidelity aside, Abdul had been a good husband. Unless of course you counted the recent drive-by shooting brought about by his life of crime and his infallible ability to make enemies. Standing in the lounge room of their home in the Sydney suburb of Bexley, Hafsa gazed across at the two bullet holes in the wall. Abdul had been saying he'd fix the damage for two months now, ever since their peace was shattered by a volley of gunshots late one night. Two bullets ripped through the front window and embedded themselves in the wall opposite, just missing a gilt-framed, A4-sized photo of a shirtless, oiled-bodied Abdul flexing his pecs, a ham-like forearm casually obscuring part of what looked like a very impressive six pack.

Fortunately no-one was in the front of the house at the time of the shooting, the family having retired to their bedrooms at the back of the property. Abdul had got the window pane replaced but hadn't got round to fixing the two holes in the wall. And now the indentations of the bullets were a fixture in Hafsa's life.

After the drive-by Hafsa had suggested to Abdul, in the respectful tones of a good Muslim wife, that he leave the family business and get some other job. A normal, legal one. This hadn't gone down well with Abdul, who'd given her a cold stare before driving off into the night to see the blonde bitch. Of course she wasn't a real blonde. One of the pictures on Abdul's phone had clearly shown the black roots to the yellow mane that hung past her shoulders. Plus she had silicon boobs, judging by another photo. *Her tits are even bigger than Abdul's*, Hafsa thought with a smile as she gazed at the picture of her muscle-flexing partner on the wall, while at the same time admonishing herself, asking Allah to forgive her for thinking such a disrespectful thing about her husband.

Hafsa turned to the right and looked at her reflection in an oval wall mirror in an ornate metal frame. She took a few steps closer, till her head and shoulders filled the frame. She took off her *hijab* and shook out her hair so it hung nicely over her shoulders. Her face was still pretty: large, almond shaped eyes, their beauty enhanced by heavy black liner. Her lips were full; an impartial observer might see them as ludicrously full. Encouraged by Abdul after a friend's wife had the procedure carried out, Hafsa had got her lips pumped up. Perhaps she should have asked the girl who did it in a suburban shop to go a bit easier on the filler. Rather than transforming her into a sex kitten, the swollen lips on the woman in the mirror, she thought to herself bitterly, had an almost clown-like appearance.

Her attention moved to her hair, which Hafsa considered her best point, despite keeping it covered most of the time. It was lustrous and dark, with reddish highlights from the Yemeni henna rinse she used once a week. But then her gaze switched to her body, which was running to fat. These days she was struggling to get into a size 14 dress. Unlike the skinny blonde bitch, who looked a size 10 at the most, assuming the zip of the dress wasn't defeated by the bulge of her silicon tits.

Hasfa's body tensed up as she heard the knock on the front door. While not overly forceful, the three beats had a coda of authority, the kind of authority that comes dressed in a blue uniform. She hurriedly put her head scarf back on and was still securing it under her chin as she peered through the peephole in the front door. She saw the distorted wide angle images of two police officers, both women, one young, the other older. Hafsa opened the door, and steadied herself against the edge of the frame. She knew what was coming – she could see it in their faces.

The older cop wore sergeant stripes on the shoulders of her light blue uniform shirt. She had short dark hair and a round face with a jutting, bulldog-like jaw. 'Mrs Hafsa Fazir?' the sergeant enquired.

'Yes,' she said.

Speaking in a deadpan, expressionless voice, the sergeant said, 'It's about your husband Abdul. We regret to inform you that he has been reported dead in South Australia.'

Hafsa flinched, as if hit by a physical blow. 'Abdul – dead?' she said in a shaking voice.

'There will need to be a formal identification process,' the cop said, 'but South Australian police have informed us they believe he is the deceased person.' Her voice took on a hint of compassion as she added, 'I'm very sorry.'

'Very sorry,' echoed the other cop, a tall, long-faced girl.

Hafsa just stood there staring into space for a few seconds. Then she found herself doing something which, as the wife of a career criminal, she'd never have considered in the past – she invited the police inside.

Their official demeanour thawing slightly, the cops followed her into the house. Hafsa said, 'My daughter has just gone to sleep,' she whispered as she led them down the hallway.

Hafsa sat the cops down at the kitchen table while she put coffee, water and a bit of sugar into a little copper pot and heated it on the stove. The bulldog-faced sergeant cast a suspicious glance at Abdul's hookah on a shelf in the corner.

There was an awkward silence as the coffee came to the boil. Then Hafsa set a small cup and saucer in front of each officer and poured the steaming coffee. Hafsa sat down opposite the pair and, looking at the tough-faced sergeant, said, 'What did Abdul die from?'

'We don't have any information on that,' the officer said.

A teardrop rolled down Hafsa's cheek, creating a black streak. She dabbed at it with the edge of her head scarf. The sergeant took pity on her. 'Actually, we *do* have some information about cause of death, but we're awaiting official confirmation by the coroner. But what the hell. It appears Abdul was shot dead, Mrs Fazir.'

Now the young constable spoke up. 'It happened in a place called Coober Pedy in central Australia,' she said. 'The South Australian coroner will release the body within a few days.'

The older cop handed Hafsa a card for a government counselling service. On the reverse side the sergeant's own name and phone number had been written by hand. Hafsa thanked her and placed it on the tabletop. Then she stood up and said 'If you don't mind, I'd like to be alone.'

After they left, she collapsed onto the bed and wept. But Abdul's death hadn't come as a complete shock. She'd always known there was a strong possibility of the policeman's knock, the bland voice announcing Abdul's untimely demise. She'd previewed it in her mind countless times. Apart from the drive-by shooting, Abdul had survived three attempts on his life that she knew of, and there were probably others that he hadn't shared with her. He'd also faced police charges, most seriously for murder, on a number of occasions. But just as he displayed a talent for staying alive, Abdul had showed a remarkable ability to get charges dropped, or else beat them in court. The murder prosecution had been thrown out after the chief witness received a visit from Abdul's psycho brother Ali, who'd threatened to maim the man's family. Various other lesser but nonetheless serious criminal charges, ranging from drug possession to demanding money with menace, had been dropped when serious money changed hands. *Money talks*, that was one of Abdul's favourite expressions.

As she lay on the bed where she would now be sleeping alone, Hafsa thought how Abdul had been the love of her life. True, things hadn't been going well lately, but she still loved him. Her grief-reddened eyes looked up at the ceiling. There was $250,000 cash hidden up in the roof cavity in some boxes of old clothes. The money was going to come in handy. Her income from a partnership in a less than flourishing suburban clothing boutique wasn't going to cover the bills. Yes, she thought, *money talks*. Then she burst into another bout of sobbing. Some time later, once her shoulders had stopped heaving and the tears had almost stopped, she reached for her phone. She had to tell Abdul's relatives.

25 THE PIKES

THE DRIVE to Alice Springs had taken longer than Chaseling had expected. It was after eight and night had fallen when the highway took him through a V-shaped, rifle sight-like gap in a range of bare rock hills and into the small desert town which was to be his home for at least a year – he'd signed a 12-month contract with Alice Springs Hospital. Following the directions given to him by his boss-to-be, Chaseling found his way to a quiet street where there were no fences between the houses. On one side of the street, the homes backed on to an expanse of moonlit desert, the sands dappled with sparse, low-lying scrub. He'd been told to look out for a tall palm tree and there it was, its fronds dead-looking and drooping, in the centre of the otherwise-desolate front yard of a house with a broad veranda running around it. He parked behind a scrappy-looking, ten-year-old Commodore and an equally time-worn Accord, then got out of the 4WD, carrying the bottle of red wine he'd bought at a roadhouse on the Stuart Highway. The main door stood open. Behind the closed flyscreen, he saw the silhouette, of a man, presumably Dr Hillary Pike. The man pulled open the wire door. 'Hello there,' he said. 'Come in.' Chaseling stepped into the house.

Pike was aged around 60 with a raw, pink face speckled with age spots. Sparse reddish brown hair was combed across his scalp. The eyes gazing coldly at Chaseling were small and bird-like behind gold-rimmed glasses of the type favoured by middle-aged Japanese businessmen. He was apparently not inclined towards dressing for dinner, as he wore a rumpled polo shirt, shorts and a scruffy-looking pair of sandals. Nor was he inclined towards washing down his evening meal with a bottle of red, or even his guests doing so. He gazed down disapprovingly at the wine bottle Chaseling held in his hand. 'We don't allow alcohol in the house,' Pike said.

Chaseling went back outside and made as though to stand the bottle on the concrete floor of the veranda. 'Might be better,' said Pike, 'if you put it in the car.'

Chaseling carried the offending bottle of wine back to the Captiva, then went back inside the house, finding himself in a room with a sofa and two armchairs upholstered in a brown and beige pattern that was popular in the late 1970s and early 1980s – his grandparents had a similar lounge suite. A scrawny middle-aged woman with no chin and grey hair cut in a short, mannish style made her appearance. Her face wore a forced-looking smile, revealing long, horse-like teeth. She displayed a higher degree of social skills than her husband as she held out a hand. 'Kath,' she said.

They shook hands, then Kath turned to her husband, who still looked a bit put out, possibly about the bottle of wine, his mouth downturned like that of a sulky child. She said, 'Hill, Jonathan might like a cup of tea before we eat.'

'No, I'm fine thank you,' Chaseling said. Kath retreated back into the kitchen. Chaseling looked around and said, 'OK to sit anywhere?'

Pike nodded, his face still looking far from welcoming. Chaseling sat down on the couch. On the wall opposite was a framed colour photo that showed a younger Hillary and Kath Pike alongside a girl in academic gown and mortarboard hat. The girl's hair was blonde and her skin lightly suntanned in contrast to the lobster-like complexion sported by her father. And unlike her mother, nature had given her a chin. 'So,' Chaseling said, looking across at Pike, who'd sat down in a rigid pose in one of the decades-old armchairs, 'do you have just the one child?'

'Yes,' Pike said. 'She's a school teacher. Same as Kath.' And the silence started ticking away again. Chaseling gazed at a framed certificate beside the graduation photo. It was a community service award from the Rotary Club of Alice Springs. Dr Hillary Pike obviously regarded himself as a model citizen. On a coffee table next to his chair a well-thumbed book lay face-down. Its title, *Building a Multi-Million Dollar Property Portfolio,* gave a strong hint as to where the money skimped on cars and furniture might be going.

Kath emerged from the kitchen holding plates of food which she carried over to a dining nook. 'Come and get it!' she trilled.

Chaseling was feeling hungry; the toasted cheese sandwich he'd had at the roadhouse was a distant memory. He felt disappointed as he took his seat at the table and examined the offerings on his plate: a scrawny leg of roast chicken, supplemented by a small slice of breast meat; anaemic-looking broccoli; a scoop of watery mashed potato; and diced carrots. It seemed that the Pike household wasn't exactly the land of milk and honey. Glancing at the servings on his host's plates, he deduced that they were sharing a runt of the litter-sized half chicken between the three of them. Pike, sitting at the head of the table, had got most of the breast portion and Kath, seated opposite Chaseling, had a wing.

'I'll say grace,' said Pike after they took their seats. Clasping his hands together and with eyes tightly shut, he said, 'Oh Holy Father, we give you thanks for the food we are about to receive. Through Christ our Lord. Amen.'

'Amen' echoed Kath.

Chaseling remained silent, contemplating the food in his plate, and meditating on the fact that there was so much more bare plate than there was food. Kath gave him a disapproving look because he hadn't come out with his own 'Amen.' She picked up her knife and fork and attacked the desiccated-looking chicken wing she'd apportioned herself.

They tucked into the sparse meal wordlessly. Cutlery clattered against porcelain and an old chrome-cased Sunbeam clock on the wall behind Kath marked the passage of the seconds, then minutes, its ticking seeming to get slower, the fabric of time stretching as the Pikes maintained a tense silence.

Chaseling found himself covertly observing Dr Pike, who had a strange and disconcerting eating habit. Whenever he opened his mouth to insert a forkful of food, he stuck out his tongue. It wasn't a full tongue extension like Gene Simmons from Kiss, or a Maori performing a haka; the tongue only came out about halfway, more like a Catholic about to receive the communion wafer. Once the food was in his mouth the tongue would retreat and his lips close as he masticated the food. Above their heads, a fly buzzed; it landed on the wall next to the clock. Chaseling imagined Pike's tongue suddenly extending two metres to attach itself to the fly, before snapping back into his mouth again. The mirth was bubbling away in Chaseling's chest, getting ready to erupt, the corners of his mouth beginning to twitch as he fought to keep a straight face. He gave a snort which he turned into a coughing fit, covering his mouth. Then he took a deep breath and said, 'What's the weather been like lately here in Alice Springs?'

'Hot,' said Pike.

'Definitely on the hot side,' agreed Kath.

'So the Todd hasn't flooded lately?' Chaseling was referring to the river bed running through the town. He'd heard that for all except a few days of the year it was usually just dry sand.

'No,' said Pike.

'Dry as a bone,' said Kath.

Chaseling nodded politely, the tedium of the conversation banishing the laughter he'd been fighting back. 'Alice Springs must really be bearing the brunt of global warming,' he persevered, trying to get some sort of conversation started. 'I was reading how you're getting temperatures of almost 50 degrees here in the desert.'

'Global warming,' stated Pike with an angry timbre to his voice, 'is a myth. I'm surprised that a man of science like yourself would believe in it.' He used his fork to spear a scrap of chicken, which was the last thing left on his otherwise immaculately-cleaned plate. His tongue put in a final appearance, like an actor emerging through the curtains at the end of a play, as he placed the morsel in his mouth. Then the tongue retreated and he masticated the food for a few seconds before swallowing it, Adam's apple bobbing up and down in his skinny, wrinkled neck. 'But then, perhaps it's not so surprising that you subscribe to the fiction of global warming. Because you are a very surprising character, Jonathan.'

Kath reached down to the seat of an empty dining chair beside her and placed a newspaper on the table. Exhibit A. It was a publication called *The Centralian Advocate*. On the front page was a big picture of Chaseling outside the hospital in Coober Pedy. There was an even larger headline saying *'DOCTOR SURVIVES PAYBACK BLOODBATH.'*

'The *Advocate* is part of the Murdoch group,' Kath said, 'so you're also on websites like news.com.au.'

Chaseling's mind flashed back to his encounter with the media in Coober Pedy. The *Adelaide Advertiser* must be part of the Murdoch group too.

Pike leaned forward. A vein had started pulsing in his forehead and his face was brick red. 'Countless people have now heard about the culturally-inappropriate exploits of Dr Jonathan Chaseling, due to be starting a position at Alice Springs Hospital.' The muscles in his jaw tightened. 'Half the injuries we treat here at the hospital are the result of payback in the Aboriginal community. It beggars belief how you could have got involved in a vendetta by one group against another.'

'Hold on for a second,' Chaseling said. 'This wasn't some civil war in the Aboriginal community. We're talking about two violent outsiders wreaking bloody havoc in St Catherine's. '

'You're a great one to talk about violent outsiders,' said Pike with such vehemence that he spat a droplet of saliva onto Chaseling's plate on the final 's' of 'outsiders.' Chaseling still had a bit of food left, but decided he'd now finished and placed his knife and fork in the middle of his plate.

'You,' Pike continued 'are someone who came from down south knowing nothing about what is culturally appropriate and what isn't here in the Territory. What you did went beyond culturally inappropriate. This morning I had a very interesting phone conversation with the general manager at St Catherine's, a Mr Fitzpatrick. He told me how you and your accomplice took his car at gunpoint.'

'Now just hold on!' Chaseling exclaimed. 'What's all this leading to?'

Pike's junior counsel reached down and produced some A4 pages. 'Your employment contract.' Kath's pale grey eyes gleamed spitefully as she regarded Chaseling from across the table. Chaseling gazed down at the loose sheaf of papers she'd deposited on the table in front of him. He picked up the pages and flicked through them. 'What am I looking for?' he asked.

'Page six, clause 39,' she said, looking down at the duplicate in her hand. 'Where it talks about engaging in conduct which brings Alice Springs Hospital into disrepute...'

'... and how employees who do so can be terminated,' her husband finished for her. 'Well, I hope this doesn't spoil this lovely meal for you, but you are terminated. I am summarily dismissing you from the position you were due to start tomorrow morning. Sorry if that puts a sour taste on the lovely meal Kath prepared.'

There were a few seconds of silence, except for the wall clock remorselessly ticking away, as the Pikes looked at him with expressions of acute loathing on their faces.

'Ah well, there goes my career in orthopaedic surgery,' said Chaseling. He leaned back in his chair and fixed Pike with a withering look. 'Firstly, Hillary, or possibly your friends call you Hill, but as the friendship thing doesn't seem to be working out between us, let's stick to Hillary; first off, Hillary, there was nothing even remotely lovely about the meal Kath dished up. It was low down on the scale in quantity, and as for quality, it was the closest thing I've ever tasted to hospital food.'

Kath glared at him with a murderous look not unlike that of the taipan Clarrie had captured. Pike's eyes had widened in a look of outrage. Then he shot to his feet, causing his chair to crash noisily against the wall behind him. The vein in his forehead looked ready to burst as he pointed a finger at Chaseling. 'I know what you *are*, Jonathan!' he said in a kind of half-whisper.

'And what's that?" Chaseling asked.

'*You're a ne'er do well!*' Pike shouted the words. He lowered his voice again and now he sounded as though he was struggling for breath, like someone who has run a race. 'We get a lot of your type here in the Territory. Drunks. Druggies. Men running from their families, from the law. Men running from themselves.'

'Sit down and chill, Hill,' Chaseling said. 'You know, I think I will call you Hill after all, just in case I decide to write a song or poem about what a doofus you are. There aren't many things that rhyme with Hillary; offhand the only words I can think of are "celery" or "salary." Speaking of which, you were talking about my employment contract.'

Pike slowly sank back down into his chair. 'You'll get three months pay, we're paying out the contract.'

'I thought the contract was for twelve months,' Chaseling said.

'With a provisional term of three months.' Pike said.

Kath produced another document and slid it across while her husband said, 'We've prepared a deed of agreement for you to sign.' Now a pen had materialised in Kath's hand, a yellow Bic biro, the soft plastic plug at the end of which had been badly gnawed.

Chaseling took the ballpoint and said, 'So I get three months pay, in a lump sum?'

Pike nodded and said, 'Just initial every page and put your full signature and date on the final sheet.'

'What about my airfare back to Sydney? And there's a removal truck on its way here with all my stuff in it.'

Kath spoke up. 'If you turn to the second last page of the document, you'll see how those costs are included in your package.'

Chaseling looked down and saw that an economy airfare and removal costs back to Sydney had indeed been added to his salary. According to the document, he'd be getting almost $25,000 after tax. Feeling like someone about to make a pact with the evil one, he put his signature and initials to the deed of agreement and passed it to Kath, who then slid across a duplicate.

'Why did you let me get all the way to Alice Springs before telling me this?' Chaseling asked Pike.

'The decision was only made late this afternoon,' Pike said. 'There was an emergency meeting of the hospital board and they agreed with my recommendation that you be dismissed.' Now he stood up again, his chair making a nasty scraping noise against the floorboards. 'There are a number of good motels in town. You might like to try the Desert Rose.'

Chaseling scooped up the papers and got to his feet. At the screen door, he paused, looking across the room at the couple. Pike was still standing, arms crossed, while Kath sat chewing on the end of the yellow biro. Pulling the door open, Chaseling flashed a dazzling smile at his ungracious hosts and said, 'Thanks for an interesting night. Hill, I'm very, very happy that you are no longer my future boss – I suspect your skills as an orthopaedic surgeon are at the same low level as your social skills. And as for you Kath, next time you have guests over for dinner, maybe lash out on a whole chicken.'

'*Get out!*' Pike screamed.

Chaseling made his exit and seconds later his car was roaring out of the driveway, his tyres spraying the Pikes' two crappy old cars with small stones.

26 THE FAMILY BUSINESS

MEHMET FAZIR sat in his windowless office above the Sex Machine strip club in Sydney's seedy night hub of Kings Cross. Aged in his early forties, Mehmet had short dark hair going silver at the sides, where it was shaven to a stubble. The back of his head was flat, a feature he'd shared with his late brother Abdul. There was the vibration of bass-heavy music from the strip club one floor below, where a girl was desultorily performing a naked pole dance. Only a dozen punters were watching the show, but the books would say there'd been fifty, and that they'd bought up big at the bar. However, Mehmet knew he wouldn't be able to get away with laundering the drug money like this for much longer. Strict new 'lockout' laws had almost killed off Kings Cross as a night spot. People were no longer allowed into pubs and clubs after 1:30am and last orders were called at 3am.

But it wasn't the lockout laws, or the challenges they posed in the laundering of criminal proceeds, that were occupying Mehmet's attention at this moment. His eyebrows were lowered in a ferocious scowl as he studied a copy of the *Daily Telegraph* spread out on the desk in front of him. One of the newspapers in Rupert Murdoch's News Ltd stable, it carried the same picture of Chaseling as the *Centralian Advocate* and the story was much the same, although the headline had been tweaked for local readership: *SYDNEY MAN SURVIVES OUTBACK BLOODBATH.*

The previous night Mehmet had received a phone call from Abdul's wife Hafsa telling him Abdul was dead. Stunned, he had phoned directory assistance and got onto the police station in Coober Pedy, where a Senior Sergeant Fowler told him Abdul's body had been taken to Adelaide for an autopsy. It would probably be released within three or four days.

Autopsies are abhorrent to Muslims because they are seen as a desecration of the body. And the body should be buried as soon as possible after death. Mehmet had tried to point these things out to Fowler, but the policeman had been less than sympathetic. In fact he'd been downright hostile.

The cop had not made any mention of Ali. And Mehmet had resisted the urge to ask about him. But now, as Mehmet read the newspaper story, he learned how a hunt was under way for a man who'd fled Coober Pedy in a white four-wheel drive. He wondered what had become of the ute he'd lent Abdul and Ali. The ute registered in *his*, Mehmet's, name. Mehmet picked up his phone and tried calling Ali again. But as it had previously, it went to voicemail.

Mehmet chewed his fingernails for a while, a habit he'd had since childhood. Then he put his emotions aside as the cold, calculating side of his brain took over. He'd have to bring in his cousin Mahmoud to take over Abdul's crucial role in the family business. That would work out OK, Mahmoud had been acting as Abdul's offsider in the purchase of ice from the bikie gangs. He was still young, having only celebrated his 21st birthday last year, but he was smart and ruthless.

Meanwhile, a successor to Ali had already been appointed after his youngest brother's departure for the Middle East became a necessity. The new collector of debts and protector of the drug distribution turf in south western Sydney was Kaho Manakofua. Not a relative, nor, obviously, of Arabic descent. He hailed from Tonga. But standing two metres tall, with a healthy appetite for violence, Kaho had risen from bouncer at the strip club to a trusted lieutenant in the meth business. Whether or not Kaho would be ruthless enough to solve the problem now facing the lucrative enterprise remained to be seen.

The Chinese were moving in, a Triad gang called Big Circle. They were selling imported ice at heavily discounted prices. Low prices weren't the only inducement for dealers to start purchasing their meth from Big Circle. Three days earlier, word had reached Mehmet that a Big Circle leader by the name of Jiang Feng was responsible for a machete attack which had left an ice dealer clinging to life in hospital. The victim was a lynchpin in the distribution network carved out by

Mehmet and his brothers over the past ten years. He'd been hacked across the throat with the machete after refusing to switch over to Big Circle, according to Mehmet's source, who had also told him that other dealers were now very nervous. A mass defection to the Chinese loomed.

Mehmet gnawed at his left thumbnail, then gripped the edge between his teeth and tore away a crescent of nail, exposing the soft, salmon pink flesh beneath. He spat the piece of nail into a waste bin beside his desk.

One brother dead and the other missing; his income under threat. He was feeling very anxious. Mehmet normally didn't drink but he was about to buzz the bar downstairs and get them to send up a bottle of Johnny Walker Black Label when the opportunity arose to relieve his tension in a different way.

There was a knock on the door. 'Come in!' he said.

It was one of the strippers, Nhung, a Thai girl. She'd started work at the club a week earlier. Dressed in jeans and T-shirt, she'd finished her shift and had come to collect her pay.

'Lock the door,' Mehmet told her. He spoke with a strong accent; he'd been in his early teens when the family left Lebanon.

'Why?'

'I'm feeling horny.'

'Not my problem,' she said, remaining in the open doorway.

'I'll give you an extra fifty dollars on top of your pay,' Mehmet said.

The girl shook her head and remained where she was.

'You know,' Mehmet said, 'the Immigration Department has a new freecall service. People can just phone up and tell them about people living here illegally.'

Lower lip trembling, Nhung slowly closed the door, then locked it.

27 ARE YOU IN THE LAND OF THE LIVING?

ALI STOOD beneath the shower in his motel room washing off the outback grime. He was in Broken Hill, the frontier town in the south-west corner of New South Wales. It was here where mining colossus BHP Billiton had started out as Broken Hill Proprietary Limited – beneath the sun-baked surface is a massive deposit of silver, lead and zinc, shaped like a boomerang, with two monstrous arms of rich ore extending deep into the ground. It was in Broken Hill, and the surrounding area, where the movie classic *The Adventures of Priscilla, Queen of the Desert* was shot. A decade before that, the town was taken over by the crew filming *Mad Max 2: The Road Warrior*. The area is beloved to filmmakers because it's in Broken Hill where the vast red desert country begins – or ends, if you are heading east like Ali was. Sydney was now just a day's drive away. But before setting off he'd get some sleep, then steal a set of numberplates. The registration details of the LandCruiser must have gone out to NSW police.

The LandCruiser now stood coated with rust-coloured dust in the moonlit motel carpark, where a group of men – Ali was pretty sure they were miners – were sitting in aluminium-framed camping chairs near their own 4WDs and utes drinking beer. They'd been there for hours, the sound of their voices getting progressively louder, their laughter more raucous, the clunk of the empties being hurled into a bin more violent. Every now and then a bottle would shatter as one of the lads applied a bit too much overarm spin.

In the early hours, when they were sleeping it off, Ali would sneak out there with a screwdriver and remove a pair of numberplates from one of their cars. Then he'd adjourn to his own vehicle and quietly depart the Silver City Motor Inn. Later, when it was light, he'd pull into some secluded location off the road and change the plates.

Walking out of the bathroom with a towel round his waist, Ali heard his iPhone ringing. He picked up the device from the bedside table and looked at the screen. It was his brother Mehmet, who'd phoned several times over the past 24 hours, the first time leaving an anguished voice message saying police had told Abdul's wife Hafsa that he was dead. *'Are you still in the land of the living, brother?'* Mehmet had asked. *'Phone me.'*

There had also been a number of messages and missed calls from his mother Zenah. She'd sounded hysterical, beside herself with grief over the death of Abdul – her golden boy. Abdul had always been her favourite; and he'd reciprocated her love. Unlike her other two sons, Abdul had been a pillar of support since the death of their father Youssif in a car crash three years earlier. Meanwhile Zenah had become cold and distant towards Ali because the head-on crash had been an insurance scam gone horribly wrong. Ali had been the architect of the scheme.

His plan was simple and seemed low-risk. His father and a friend of Ali's, Salim, would drive in opposite directions down a quiet stretch of road, each keeping his speed to around 30km/h or less. Salim would veer over to the wrong side of the road and collide with Youssif's car. The airbags would deploy and the drivers would step from their vehicles unscathed – except for the terrible pain in Youssif's back, which would earn him a hefty insurance payout and disability pension. Salim would claim he'd fallen asleep at the wheel. He'd cop a conviction for dangerous driving, maybe lose his licence for a few months and receive a share of the insurance money. But it hadn't worked out that way.

Salim drove too fast. The force of the collision slammed Youssif's smaller car into a tree. He died at the scene. And instead of getting a slice of an insurance windfall Salim had got three months jail and a two year licence suspension after being found guilty of culpable driving.

Ali put his phone back down on the side table and sat down on the bed. He wasn't going to phone Mehmet or his mother. There might be someone listening in, he reasoned. In fact, his movements could also be tracked through his phone's GPS. He'd turn it off after his sleep. Meanwhile, he needed to use the phone's alarm clock. His fingers tapped in the time of 4am.

He picked up a remote control and switched on the TV. He flicked through the channels until he found something worth watching – a 1980s slasher movie called *Hell Night*. Ali had seen it before; in fact he had the DVD at home. His favourite scene was where a girl was decapitated with a shovel.

28 RENATA, PETRA AND RUDI

ON PRINCIPLE, Chaseling booked into a different motel to the one Pike had recommended. In his room, he opened the wine which hadn't been allowed under the Pikes' roof, or even their veranda. It was a good one, a Taylors Shiraz. He turned on the TV and watched a channel called Imparja. There was a reality show where celebrities were eating deep-fried grasshoppers. He flicked to SBS and watched some world news. More misery in the Middle East. Restless, he got up and had a shower, after which he recapped the half full wine bottle, dressed and went out.

He went to a pub called The Bushranger that he'd checked out on his iPhone. Behind the bar was a young man whose earlobes had been stretched to accommodate a pair of green discs the size of beer bottle tops. A look of recognition swept over the barman's face as Chaseling approached. 'I saw you in the paper!' he exclaimed. 'The massacre survivor!' Chaseling forced a smile and ordered a Cooper's pale ale.

'You're a doctor, aren't you?' the bartender asked, giving him his change.

Chaseling nodded, not looking at the barman but at a girl sitting at a table with a female companion. She had long blonde hair and longer legs growing out of a pair of very brief white shorts. Currently the legs were crossed, but as Chaseling looked, they uncrossed in a piece of body language that recalled Sharon Stone's famous scene in *Basic Instinct*, where for just one or two frames she leaves you in no doubt about the fact that she'd neglected to put on her underpants that morning. This girl didn't reveal as much as the Hollywood star as she re-crossed her legs but Chaseling did get a tantalising glimpse of the border between thigh and outer labia. The girl's startlingly Nordic blue eyes glowed like lapis lazuli as she gazed across at Chaseling while repositioning her legs. Then she was turning to her friend and saying something. The friend – an elfin Audrey Hepburn type with short, dark brown hair – laughed, then looked across at Chaseling. One of her eyes closed in a wink. *Maybe I'll get lucky tonight,* he thought, little knowing just how lucky he was going to get.

'I've got this problem with my, er, *plumbing.*' It was the stretched earlobed man. He was leaning across the bar towards Chaseling.

Chaseling tore his eyes away from the girls and looked at him. 'Really?'

'Yeah. You see, the past few days, when I go for a piss, I get this burnin' feelin'.'

Chaseling was about to tell him to see his GP when a brilliant thought occurred to him. 'Dr Hillary Pike, he's your man,' he said.

'Isn't Hillary a girl's name?'

'Yes, it is indeed, because Dr Pike was born a woman, but he has undergone surgery, which, along with years of hormone therapy, has transformed him into a very convincing man.'

'He's here in Alice?'

'At the hospital. Best urologist in the Territory. As you can imagine, he learned quite a lot about male plumbing before he got it all lopped off, in fact rumour has it that he still has his own male genitalia preserved in a glass jar in his office cabinet. But I digress. The fact is he's a very busy man, huge waiting list. Might be one or two months before you get an appointment.' The barman looked crestfallen. 'However,' Chaseling continued, 'there's a way of jumping the queue.'

'And what's that?' The barman leaned closer. His breath reeked of stale tobacco.

'Dr Pike likes a drink. So all you need to do it take a bottle of gin, preferably Gordon's, to the front desk of the hospital. Say it's for Dr Pike and that you need an early appointment for a penis screening.'

'Penis screening?'

'That's what it's called. You've heard of breast screening for women?' The barman nodded. 'Well, this is the same kind of thing.'

'Thanks!' said the barman. He got a pen and paper. 'Dr Hillary Pike, is that right?'

'He's your man. Say Dr Chaseling sent you.'

'Thanks Doc!'

'No worries.'

Chaseling carried his beer over to the two girls and asked if he could join them. They smiled up at him and the blonde waved him to an empty chair next to hers. 'Where are you from?' he asked.

'Germany,' she said, pronouncing it 'Chermany.'

The blonde, her name was Renata and her friend was Petra, told him how they'd just returned from Uluru. 'Very spiritual place,' Renata said. 'You feel joined to the earth somehow when you look at the Rock.'

I wouldn't mind becoming joined to you Renata, Chaseling thought to himself, edging his chair a bit closer and getting a whiff of coconut tanning oil mixed with a musky womanly odour.

Up on a very small stage, a singer-guitarist, an emo type with a pale face and dyed black hair hanging down over one eye, had just started a rendition of *American Pie*. Raising his voice above the amplified singing and strumming, Chaseling gazed into Renata's eyes and said, 'You look like someone who's very connected with nature.'

'Yes, I am a bit of an earth spirit,' she said. 'And I love the water.'

'So do I!' chipped in Petra from over her friend's shoulder. She picked up her phone from the table and clicked on the photos icon. 'Before Uluru we were in northern Queensland, Airlie Beach,' she said as she scrolled through the images. Then she held up the phone screen outwards, resting her hand on Renata's shoulder as she did so.

On the screen he saw a topless Renata and Petra sitting on the white sands of a tropical beach. Shoulders arched back, Renata was proudly displaying large, sun-bronzed breasts, while beside her, Petra showed off her own more compact mammary endowments, equally attractive to Chaseling in their own pert way.

'Great suntans,' Chaseling, nodding appreciatively. Petra, being further away than Renata, appeared not to understand him, cupping her hand around her ear. Her difficulty in hearing him may have had something to do with the fact that the vocal strains of *American Pie* had now taken on an urgent, angry tone, the singer-guitarist leaning right up against the microphone, the words delivered in a voice that was starting to sound more Robert Plant or Axl Rose than Don McLean. 'Great suntans!' Chaseling repeated, leaning closer to make himself heard, his hand brushing against Renata's thigh. And then the music died.

The performer, who'd been sitting on a stool, leapt to his feet while wrenching the jack plug from his guitar to a buzz of protest from the PA system. He jumped down from the small stage with his guitar strung around his neck and took two or three steps towards Chaseling and the girls, his face a mask of anger. Coming to a halt in the middle of the floor, he screamed, *'How about shutting the fuck up!'*

For a few heartbeats, there was complete silence throughout the room. Then the musician ranted, 'How do you expect me to perform a song like *American Pie* when everybody in the bar is *fucking talking?!'* The last two words were delivered in a hoarse, squeaky shout, like a parade ground sergeant major. The emo's eyes were watery, on the verge of tears. The barman with the expanded earlobes materialised alongside the tortured artist and began speaking urgently to him in a quiet but persuasive-sounding voice. Chaseling saw money changing hands. The erstwhile performer unhooked his guitar and placed it in a case which he then snapped shut with the finality of someone nailing a coffin closed. Then he strode towards the swing doors leading out to the street. Before making his exit, he stopped and did an about-face. 'It was *American fucking Pie,* for Christ's sake! The greatest lyrical song in the history of pop music!' He stormed out. The two German girls clapped their hands. Everyone laughed, even the bartender, who went to the audio desk and put on a recorded track. It was the Village People singing *You Can't Stop the Music.* More laughter.

Chaseling bought a round of drinks – the girls were drinking Castlemaine, Queensland's favourite beer, while Chaseling favoured Carlton Draught, brewed in Melbourne. When he got back from the bar with the drinks the pair told him about their bus journey to Alice Springs from Darwin. 'When it started to get dark, the driver spoke into the microphone and told us we'd be hearing some bumps from the front of the bus,' Renata said.

'He said it would be the sound of the bus hitting kangaroos,' chipped in Petra.

'Sure enough,' said Petra, taking up the story again, 'there were all these bumps in the night.' She gave a little shudder. 'I think we must have left a trail of dead kangaroos along the road.'

Chaseling thought back to his own close encounter of the furred kind, and how the road kill had been turned into bush tucker. 'Have you tried eating kangaroo?'

Renata gave a shudder of revulsion. But Petra announced decisively, 'I want to eat kangaroo.' She picked up a menu from the table and studied it. 'Ah, so! Kangaroo Pot Roast.'

They adjourned to The Bushranger's restaurant for dinner, and Petra did indeed order Kangaroo Pot Roast. Not to be outdone, Chaseling ordered Water Buffalo Fillet (his stomach feeling empty after the Pikes' mean fare).

Renata ordered a vegetarian pizza. 'I grew up in a part of Lower Saxony that people call *die Schweinegürtel*,' she explained. 'It means "the pig belt." There were all these pig farms everywhere and almost every meal at home was pork. It has put me off meat.'

But when the meals arrived, she changed her tune. As Renata picked at her vegetarian pizza, it seemed to Chaseling that she was regretting her choice. She kept casting envious glances at Chaseling and Petra as they tucked into their generous helpings of slaughtered outback wildlife. So he skewered a nice juicy medallion of the gamey-tasting water buffalo with his fork and held it out in front of Renata's mouth. Looking at Chaseling the same way she had when she'd uncrossed her legs, she caressed the piece of meat with the tip of her tongue, then her lips closed around it and her teeth pulled it off the prongs of the fork. She chewed the meat with gusto before swallowing it down. Now Petra was holding out a prime piece of kangaroo meat at the end of her own fork. Renata accepted the offering, eyes narrowing sensually as she chewed. Now another piece of buffalo was being proffered by Chaseling, who had now dispensed with the formality of cutlery and was holding out the meat in his bare fingers. Renata took hold of his wrist and pulled the fingers and meat into her mouth. She then then slid his fingers, now minus the piece of water buffalo, back out from between her lips while keeping his wrist secured in her suntanned hand. After wolfing down the meat, she lifted his hand to her lips again and took the tip of his index finger into her mouth. Looking into his eyes, she caressed the finger with her tongue and then took all of it into her mouth, right up to his knuckle. She slowly removed the glistening finger from her mouth, eyes never leaving his. 'Perhaps I'm not ready to be a complete vegetarian,' she said.

Chaseling was feeling exquisitely aroused. 'Let's go to my hotel,' he whispered in her ear. 'After you've finished eating, of course.'

Renata turned to her friend and said something to her in German. Petra smiled and spoke a brief reply in the same language, the guttural-sounding words a complete mystery to Chaseling, who like most Australians could only speak English. 'What did she say?' he asked.

'She asked if she could join us.'

Chaseling smiled. 'Of course,' he said. He extended his arm around the back of Renata's warm body to stroke Petra's hair while his other hand surreptitiously wiped off Renata's saliva on a serviette.

Petra narrowed her eyes with pleasure and pressed the back of her head into his hand, relishing the touch as though she was a cat. 'Wouldn't want you to feel left out,' Chaseling told the elfin girl.

Petra said she wanted to get something at the backpackers' inn she and Renata were staying at. As they walked there, the girls conversed in German. Chaseling heard the name 'Rudi' mentioned a number of times. And each time the word was uttered, the girls broke into titters of laughter.

When they reached the hostel, Petra disappeared inside, leaving Chaseling and Renata outside for a few minutes, during which time their bodies fused together and their tongues explored each other's mouths.

Petra saw the pair canoodling in the shadows as she emerged from the backpackers' with a day pack slung over her shoulder. She laughed, then, in commanding tones, said *'Raus!'*

Renata and Chaseling detached themselves and the trio walked to Chaseling's motel. He wondered what Petra had in the pack.

Once they got to his room, they were naked within a minute, writhing together on the bed and the girls conclusively confirming Chaseling's suspicion that they played for both teams – in the wildest ways that Chaseling could have dreamed possible. The three of them pleasured each other in a novel variety of positions that ensured no-one was left out. It was a wonder that Chaseling lasted as long as he did, but after half an hour he reached an explosive climax. He rolled off a panting Renata onto his stomach while he regrouped. At this point Petra got off the bed and walked over to the bureau on the opposite wall. There was the sound of a zip as she opened her day pack. She returned to the bed carrying a strap-on dildo. 'Meet Rudi,' she said.

The latex dildo was large and a pinky flesh colour, attached to a red lace corset-like harness and two loops. Petra put her legs in the loops and pulled up the corset, which her friend then laced up tightly from the back. And then the girls were ready for action. Petra climbed atop Renata. Next thing Renata was squealing and moaning as Rudi was put to work and she was given a thorough rogering.

Chaseling was slightly put out by the fact that the dildo was substantially larger than his own flesh and blood member. And the moans coming from Renata sounded more passionate than the vocalizations she'd made when he'd been servicing her. More than offsetting this was his extreme arousal at the sight and sounds of the girls' lesbian ardours.

As Petra thrust away on top of Renata, she turned to Chaseling and, without missing a beat, said, 'Why don't you get on top of her and I'll get on top of you? You can be the meat in the sandwich!'

'Maybe later,' Chaseling said. 'I've got another idea.' He rolled onto his side. Petra ran the tip of her tongue over her lips as she saw that the glory of the Fatherland had been fully restored. Chaseling got onto his knees and positioned himself behind her. '*You* can be the meat in the sandwich,' he said. Petra tensed against him, then let loose a hiss of air as he penetrated her, while below them, Renata was going into fresh paroxysms of passion as she moved at an ever-quickening rhythm against Rudi.

And thus the night, and then early morning, progressed. Renata took a couple of turns at playing Daddy, slipping on the strap-on and rogering Petra. Chaseling valiantly resisted the girls' entreaties to play Mummy. Every time it seemed that he thought he was a spent force, and would have to retire from the wrestling ring for a good spell, if not the night, the feverish antics of the two girls with the strap-on would get him rising to the occasion again and rejoining the sweaty, frenzied bout. Things only came to a close after dawn broke, throwing its opalescent light into the room. Renata gave a gasp of shock. A lot of what they'd thought was perspiration was blood; each of their bodies was streaked with it, their exertions having somehow broken some of the stitches in Chaseling's shoulder. Renata ran to the bathroom. As the shower started running, Petra said, 'I don't mind a bit of blood.' As if to prove the point, she licked at his wet shoulder. He could see her tongue moving inside her mouth as she tasted the coppery blood, then her throat moving as she swallowed it. She patted her hand on the latex-skinned phallus jutting from her groin. 'Like to feel this inside you now?'

'No thanks,' Chaseling said, 'I'm saving myself. Why not take that thing off for a while – you don't want to wear it out.'

A cleansed and unbloodied Renata returned from the bathroom to find her friend and Chaseling enjoying a sexual bout while Rudi lay abandoned on the night stand. As the two had simultaneous climaxes, Renata, lying alongside them with her foot hooked around Chaseling's ankle, closed her eyes and said '*Gute Nacht,*' almost immediately falling asleep. Moments later, Chaseling and Petra were also sinking into a sated slumber, the discarded Rudi lying within Petra's easy reach.

29 AUF WIEDERSEN

RENATA AND PETRA made their departure at 8am. They had a ten o'clock flight to Perth, the final leg of their Australian trip. The three talked about getting together again, in Europe maybe, and exchanged phone numbers and email addresses. Chaseling held each girl tightly as he kissed them goodbye, getting a look of envy from a man across the street walking a small white dog on an extendable leash. Then it was *auf wiedersen*. Chaseling doubted that they'd ever see them again, but Renata, Petra – and Rudi – would forever shine bright in his memory.

He went to the chemist and bought a roll of surgical thread, antiseptic tea tree oil, a pack of needles, Elastoplast and a cotton bandage. Then, after the shop assistant said she'd seen him on the TV news, he also purchased scissors and a razor. She gave him directions to an optometrist where he bought a pair of dark-shaded clip-ons for his glasses. Next he visited a souvenir shop and bought a baseball-type peaked cap.

Back in his room, he cleaned the wound, then sterilised a needle in boiling water before sewing together the lips of the knife slash. Working one-handed, his stitching wasn't textbook standard. It was also extremely painful – he gave a little yelp each time he punctured the flesh. But the thought of presenting himself at the hospital he was due to have started work at today, and possibly running into Dr Hillary Pike, was so repugnant that it overshadowed the pain, along with any concerns about ending up with an uneven, puckered scar across the uppermost part of his left arm.

After re-bandaging the wound, he used his phone to book a flight to Sydney in four days. May as well have a look around the Centre while he was here. But he didn't want people recognising him the way the barman or shop assistant had. So he went back to the bathroom and started snipping at his beard with the scissors. Once he'd cropped it down to a ragged-looking stubble, he soaped up his face and set to work with the razor.

The person who emerged from Chaseling's motel had little resemblance to the man who'd been transformed into a local celebrity by the TV and newspaper reports. The girl at reception certainly didn't recognise the beardless man with a cap pulled down low above dark sunglasses who presented himself at the desk. It was only when he put his room key on the counter and asked to settle his bill that the penny dropped. And then she told him, with a sour, disapproving look on her face, that his room was costing extra because he'd paid for a single whereas he'd had – and here she spat out the word – *'guests.'*

A few minutes later, Chaseling was behind the wheel of the Captiva headed for Uluru. His *'guests'* had done a good job selling its attractions, especially the sense of peace emanating from the giant rock. The sexual healing had only gone so far. His mind remained in turmoil after the violence he'd been caught up in.

Ali had made it back to Sydney. He was in his flat in the Sydney suburb of Bankstown, where people of Lebanese ancestry now outnumber any other ethnic group. The vast majority are law-abiding citizens who have added richly to the cultural fabric of their new country. In Bankstown and its neighbouring suburbs, you'll find some of the world's finest Lebanese restaurants. If you are there on a Friday or Saturday night, you might be lucky enough to see a belly dancer perform as you dip your flat bread into beautifully fresh, home-made *humous* and *tabouli*. The dancer will move to exotic rhythms and melodies that haven't changed much since the days of the Arabian Nights. Meanwhile, members of the Lebanese community have made valuable contributions in a host of other areas, one of the most shining examples being Dame Marie Bashir, Governor of NSW from 2001 to 2014 and an esteemed medical professor, former Mother of the Year and officially-declared National Treasure.

But a minority of the Middle Eastern arrivals have brought mayhem and violence to their new nation. So much so that in 2006, NSW Police set up a permanent Middle Eastern Organised Crime Squad (MEOCS).

The gang members targeted by MEOCS hail from over a dozen different Middle Eastern countries. Among the most violent and troublesome were the Assyrian Kings, whose members came from Syria and Iraq. Equally notorious was another Assyrian gang called Dlasthr, which means 'Last Hour.' Then there were The Afghani Boys, who specialised in extortion, and gang of meth-importing Iranians who called themselves the Sultans.

But, perhaps because they had a much greater representation in the community, it was people of Lebanese descent who tended to dominate the workload of MEOCS, along with the Homicide Squad. There were dozens of organized Lebanese gangs operating in Sydney. Some were clannish groups organised on family lines. Others were run like outlaw motorcycle clubs. A group calling itself Notorious had its own colours – a skull wearing a turban – while displaying a level of chic known as 'Nike bikie,' its designer stubbled-members favouring Armani T-shirts and Nike air max trainers as opposed to the traditional ensemble of beard, dirty jacket and leather boots. Despite the clean-cut look, Notorious allegiants fought dirty when it came to protecting their drug turf in south western Sydney, shooting their rivals in brazen attacks. Even more infamous was Brothers 4 Life, Ali's old fraternity.

Perhaps for sentimental reasons, Ali had a poster of the Brothers 4 Life emblem, featuring a pair of AK-47s, on the wall of his one-bedroom apartment, where he'd just sat down at a table atop which a closed laptop nestled amid a litter of ice smoking paraphernalia, empty coffee cups and other detritus – including two unopened appointment reminders from the psychiatrist Ali's family had insisted he start seeing. He'd been diagnosed as paranoid and delusional and his shrink was pretty sure he was also schizophrenic. *More bullshit! These people knew nothing.* Ali lifted the lid of the computer and pressed the power button. A couple of minutes later he was looking at options for flights from Sydney to Istanbul. He knew he had little time before the heat generated by the disastrous hunting sortie to central Australia would engulf him. There would have been a mass of fingerprint and DNA evidence in the car he and Abdul had hijacked. Plus Ali had left a DNA trail in the house where he'd raped and murdered 'the black bitch,' as he referenced his victim.

What a dump that place had been, the Aboriginal community. How could people live like that? Pondering the question, Ali got up from his chair and navigated his way round the obstacle course of bric-a-brac on the soiled carpet. He went into the bathroom and urinated into a filthy toilet bowl.

After booking his flight to Istanbul in three days' time, Ali picked up the cheap phone he'd bought at his local shopping mall and called a friend, Mustafa Al-Talebi, who specialised in car rebirthings. As luck would have it, Mustafa also ran a side business in illegal weapons. He agreed to collect the LandCruiser, with the Colt .45 in its trunk, from where Ali had parked it in a residential street in the neighbouring suburb of Lakemba. Ali gave Mustafa the street name and told him that the keys were in a scrunched up-piece of paper wedged beneath the left front wheel.

Ali considered calling Mehmet next. But there was that very real danger of a police tap on his brother's phone. No, better to front Mehmet in person. It would not be a happy meeting.

He put his laptop in sleep mode and got out of his seat, stretching his body before walking into the bedroom, which had the feral smell of a carrion-eating animal. As elsewhere in Ali's flat, chaos reigned, the floor half-covered with discarded clothes. But on the top of a gold-painted dresser was a thing of beauty – a pearl-inlayed cigarette box, which Ali now opened, taking out a key with which he unlocked the two drawers at the top of the dresser. He pulled open the left hand drawer and looked down at his collection of switchblades. There were half a dozen of them, nestled in a bed of blue satin and arranged in order of size.

Switchblades fall into two broad categories. There's the traditional flick knife – the leverlock variety where the blade flips out from the side; and there are the so-called 'out the front' knives where the blade springs forth from the end of the hilt. Ali selected a recently-acquired knife of the latter type. This one made a bit of a fashion statement because the hilt had a zebra stripe pattern. Halfway up was a little black release button. Ali took half a step back away from the bureau and slid the button upwards. There was a powerful metallic click and suddenly the hilt had grown an eight-inch long stiletto blade, made of black titanium with the letters AKC stamped into the metal.

AKC stood for the Automatic Knife Company, which operated out of a place called Montiago in Italy. Ali hoped to visit the factory one day. He pulled down on the button of the zebra-hilted knife and the blade did a disappearing act. He carefully put the weapon back in its designated position in its bed of satin. Now he picked out a smaller knife with a hilt made of dark animal horn. This was a leverlock model, a beautifully crafted piece made in Toledo, Spain. Ali pushed up the release button. Suddenly there was a flash of silver and a six-inch blade made of razor-sharp surgical steel flipped out from the side, locking into place with a decisive click. He held the blade in front of his face, admiring the way the steel caught the light. Then he frowned as he noticed a small area of discoloration along the cutting edge. *Must have been the Iranian*, he thought to himself.

The victim had been an ice dealer who'd reneged on a credit arrangement. Ali wondered if he'd seen a plastic surgeon yet – the single slash had cut deeply into the man's face, from the top of the cheekbone to the edge of the mouth.

Ali pulled open the right-hand top drawer of the bureau. Here he stored his knife maintenance equipment, the most crucial pieces of which were the Japanese whetstones which kept the blades so sharp they could slice through a human hair. Another important part of knife maintenance was cleaning. Ali took out a transparent plastic bottle containing a liquid which looked like weak tea. Its label said 'Goo Gone.' He'd ordered it from the United States after seeing it demonstrated on a knife enthusiast's YouTube clip. He poured a small amount of the solvent onto a cloth and rubbed the blade. After checking that the cutting edge was now pristine clean, he gave the blade a squirt of WD40 and a final wipe with the cloth, which was smooth so it wouldn't put any scratches in the metal. He replaced the cleaning equipment and pulled the knife's release button down so it unlocked the blade, which he now pushed back into the hilt, feeling the increasing tension of the powerful spring which had launched the blade in its lightning fast 180 degree flick. The blade clicked into place and he put the weapon in his jeans pocket.

It was a pity he'd have to leave his knives behind when he went to Syria, he thought as he re-locked the drawers. But they should be easy enough to replace when he got there. There would have to be a good selection of blades in the country which now had the distinction of being the beheading capital of the world.

30 THERE'S A MAN CALLED JIANG FENG …

'INTA MANYAK!' (You fucker!)'

'Ma twekhisne! ('I'm sorry.)'

His eyes bright with crocodile tears, Ali was standing in Mehmet's office. His brother stood behind his desk, fists clenched, his face angrier than Ali had ever seen. Reverting to English, Mehmet said, 'You got our brother killed!' He reached down to his desk and picked up a newspaper, furiously turning the pages until he found the story and picture he was looking for. He thrust the newspaper at Ali, who took it from him and looked at the picture with dawning recognition. Reverting to English, Mehmet said, 'This is who defeated you. Looks like a hipster or computer geek, for fuck's sake!'

Ali's ice-dilated pupils narrowed with hatred. It was the man he'd attacked in the dugout. Underneath the picture was a caption saying 'Dr Jonathan Chaseling.'

Mehmet walked round from behind his desk and stood facing Ali, who was slightly taller and substantially greater in girth. His hand lashed out and delivered an open-handed slap to Ali's left cheek. Ali did nothing, just stood looking at his brother with what he hoped was a look of penitence, a slight quiver in his lower lip adding a touch of pathos. Mehmet shook his head as though to dismiss the notion of trying to understand what went on in Ali's sick mind. He went back behind his desk and there was a creaking sound as he sat down in his big black leather executive chair. He picked up his phone and tapped the calendar. 'When did you say you were flying to Istanbul?'

'Next Wednesday.'

'Before you go, I have a job for you. It won't make up for what you've done. Nothing will. But do this for me and maybe, just *maybe*, some time in the future I'll call you my brother again.' He touched his phone's photos icon. Then he extended his arm to show Ali the cruel face which filled the screen. 'There's a man called Jiang Feng who's been causing us some big problems … '

When Ali left his brother's office and descended the stairs of the Sex Machine, he held a rolled-up newspaper – the one with the photo of the blonde man who had been in the tunnel in Cooper Pedy. While his brother had been briefing him on the Triad threatening the family business, Ali's sick mind conjured up a scenario where he castrated the blond man with a switchblade before beheading him with the Jungle Master. He was still visualizing this scene as he emerged onto Darlinghurst Road.

Standing outside the club, beneath a flashing purple neon light saying SEX MACHINE, was a spruiker. Ali knew the man. He was a solidly-built 50-year-old called Ismail who'd been manning the door of the club and exhorting passersby to enter since Ali was a teenager. Ismail smiled when he saw Ali, but his expression changed to one of concern as he saw the mean look in Ali's eyes.

'*Marhaban*, brother,' Ismail said. 'How is life treating you?'

Ali tore his mind away from his fantasy of maiming and killing the blond man. 'Life's pretty sweet at the moment,' he told Ismail. 'About to go away on holiday.'

Ismail nodded, but didn't believe him. Ali did not look even remotely happy; he looked dangerous, ready to do someone serious injury. Then Ismail's attention was diverted by the approach of potential customers – four young men, one of them walking unsteadily. 'Good luck,' he said to Ali, before turning to engage the punters: 'Show starts in five minutes, boys, hottest girls in the Cross, striptease and naked pole dancing, private viewings also available.'

The spruiker's voice faded as Ali walked down Darlinghurst Road, past a bar called the VIP Lounge, where none of the patrons looked like Very Important People, just a bunch of alcoholics and poker machine addicts. It would be good to leave this western decadence behind him for a while, maybe forever, he thought to himself.

But first he had some killing to do. Not just the Chinaman. The newspaper headline had said the blond-haired man was from Sydney. He would have relatives here.

31 COLD CALLING

NOT USUALLY AN EARLY RISER, Ali got up at 6am and sparked up his laptop. He went to White Pages Online and printing out a list of Chaselings living in New South Wales. There were 54 of them, but their addresses were spread all over the state. Some were in country towns he was familiar with. They were crossed off the list. Other locations had to be checked on Google Maps. At the end of an hour he had culled down the list by more than half by crossing out all those living outside Sydney. He picked up the phone and tapped out the first number on the list. The call was answered by an elderly-sounding lady. Ali asked to speak to Jonathan Chaseling and was told he didn't live there, nor did she have any relatives of that name. Unless, of course, Jonathan was a grandson of her second cousin…

Ali had once worked in telesales. It had been a brief career, like most of his work endeavours outside the field of crime, culminating in Ali threatening to kill his manager over an unpaid commission. But during his three weeks of sitting in a cubicle and trying to exhort people to attend a one hour seminar on timeshare accommodation in return for a free night at a Mercure hotel, and getting up and ringing a bell the rare times he managed to secure a client, he had developed a good telephone manner.

He was engaging and friendly as he went through the list of Chaselings. After an hour he hit gold. 'Jonathan hasn't lived here for a number of years,' a pleasant, middle-aged sounding female voice told him. 'In fact he's just moved to Alice Springs. I'm Jonathan's mother. Who's speaking?'

Trying to conceal his excitement, Ali said, 'It's the Apple Store, we've got the new iPad Pro that your son ordered. Now, just confirming, he's *Dr* Jonathan Chaseling?'

'That's correct. Well, perhaps I should give you Jonathan's mobile number.'

Ali had noted down the number and thanked the woman, then after hanging up he circled the address on the White Pages list. Around the circle, he drew a tombstone.

Early the following morning, he drove out to the silvertail suburb of Vaucluse, a part of Sydney Ali had never been to before despite living in the city most of his life. But with the help of his NavMan he found himself driving along New South Head Road. Off to his left, where the land sloped down to the shimmering, sapphire blue harbour, were multi-million dollar homes owned by the rich and privileged. To the right was a cliff line known as The Gap, a popular suicide spot.

The Navman's Australian-accented male voice (there was no way Ali was going to have a woman giving him instructions) told him to turn left into Cambridge Avenue, which was set on a steep hill. The Chaseling family home was located about halfway down the slope. He sat in his car parked diagonally across from it watching from behind heavily tinted windows. At 7.50am the garage door rolled up and a white Lexis ES with a middle aged man behind the wheel drove out, the door slowly descending again as the hybrid car purred quietly away. Then just after 8.30, the roller door ascended again and a grey-haired woman behind the wheel of a silver Hyundai Elantra made her exit. He gave it another half an hour, but no-one else came out of the house and as he drove off, Ali was satisfied the couple lived there alone.

In a bit less than 24 hours time, he would pay them a little visit. With the Jungle Master.

32 THE GODS NEED A SACRIFICE

THE GARGANTUAN ROCK was more than two kilometres long and exuded a powerful sentience, like some ancient, sleeping giant reclining in the desert sands. The Rock took on a spectrum of different shades throughout the day. Right now it was a deep orange colour, fissured with darker, downwards-running grooves, like wrinkles in old skin.

Heading up the side of the monolith in single file was a line of about 20 people, following a narrow track. Leading the way were two teenage girls who had finally put away the phones which were the centre of their universes. Forming the vanguard were an overweight, fortyish man and woman from America's Midwest – they were called Bob, pronounced 'Barb,' and Carol, pronounced 'Keerul.' Bob seemed to be finding the climb most challenging, falling ever-further behind as he slowly dragged himself up the slope with the help of a knee-high chain set on metal posts along the track.

Chaseling stood in the scant shade provided by the parked bus which had brought them here. He thought about the story their guide had told. How the Rock was formed during the Dreamtime by two boys playing in mud after a heavy fall of rain. They'd piled up layers of mud until they built up a massive formation. Then they climbed to the top and slid down on their bellies, raking their fingers in the mud on the way, creating the great grooves running down the side of Uluru.

He heard the door of the bus opening. Tour guide and driver Delilah Tjikatu stepped down onto the dirt beside him. She was a large woman aged around 40 wearing a pair of voluminous khaki shorts and matching short-sleeved shirt with a Parks and Wildlife emblem on each shoulder. While she was beefy, she wasn't fat like the two Americans, more like someone who might have a second job as a wrestler. As she stepped down into the dirt, she shook her head to dislodge a fly that had settled on the tip of her nose the moment she left the vehicle. Chaseling noticed how it was only tourists who swatted flies. The locals employed hands-free techniques like shaking their heads or twitching their eyes and mouths. 'Sure you don't want to climb with the others?' asked the guide.

Chaseling opened his mouth to reply and one of the small, sticky bush flies circling his head seized the moment. It flew into his mouth and landed at the back of his throat. Suddenly Chaseling was bent over double as he hawked and gagged, trying to expel the insect. After finally spitting it out onto the red dirt, he slowly straightened up, red-faced and bloodshot-eyed, wiping his mouth with the back of his hand.

'Congratulations, you've crossed the line,' Delilah said with a twinkle in her eyes.

'What do you mean?' Chaseling's voice was hoarse. He uncapped his water bottle and swigged at it.

'It's like when you're on a cruise ship and you cross the equator for the first time. One of the crew dresses as King Neptune and he covers you in shaving foam. Then you get dunked in the pool.'

'And what,' Chaseling enquired, 'has that got to do with swallowing flies?'

'Just that you've now crossed an invisible line. You've been baptised, Central Australian-style.' She let loose a throaty bellow of laughter.

'Believe me, I've already been well baptised,' Chaseling said, thinking of the bloodbath he'd lived through. He extended his lower lip and let loose a blast of upwards-flowing air to dislodge a fly perched on the tip of his nose. 'Anyway, in answer to the question you asked before that fly came calling, I heard that climbing the Rock was disrespectful, that the traditional owners don't like it.'

'That's right, we don't, because the spirits who live here don't like it,' Delilah said. 'This place is full of spirits. Our ancestors' spirits. But if tourists couldn't climb, we wouldn't get nearly so many visitors. So we put up with it. But some people say it's bad luck for people to climb.'

'What do you mean?'

'Well, since tourists started coming here we've had about 50 people die from heart attacks on their way up the Rock.'

'But surely that would just be the result of extreme heat and poor health,' Chaseling said.

'Maybe.' The guide gazed up at the line of climbers. The two Americans were lagging further and further behind the others. 'I'll tell you one thing – it's definitely bad luck to take away any bits of the Rock.'

'You mean like a stone?' Chaseling found himself reaching down to his jeans pocket and pressing his hand against the opal sea shell that Clarrie and Noelie had said was a bad luck stone.

'Yes, stones, even sand. Take away even the tiniest piece of the Rock and our ancestors can get very upset.'

'What happens?'

The guide raised her wrist and consulted a watch, its silver face glittering in the sunlight and contrasting with the darkness of her skin. 'Tell you what,' she said, 'it's going to be quite a while before that lot reach the top and come down again. I'll drive you back to the resort and you can hang out there for a while and I'll pick you up at say, two o'clock.'

'Sure.'

'And you might like to see something interesting in our offices. They're just next to the resort.'

They got in the bus. As they drove towards the low-slung buildings 15 kilometres away, a stone's throw in outback distance, Delilah said, 'You see, what people don't understand is that to the Australian Aborigine, the land is sacred. We are the land and the land is us.'

Looking back over his shoulder at the crouching colossus framed in the back window of the bus, Chaseling said, 'I can easily understand that.' The opal ammonite seemed to be pressed uncomfortably against his upper thigh. He reached into his jeans pocket and adjusted its position.

The bus pulled up beside an administration block. Delilah led Chaseling into an open-plan office. Against one wall was a large plastic storage box full of brown-red rocks ranging from pebble-sized stones to chunks the size of half bricks. 'Every few days we get a package in the post from someone who took a piece of rock away from here and then had bad luck,' Delilah said. 'A lot of the time it's *really* bad luck. So they send the bad luck back here. Or that's what they hope, anyway.' She pointed to a corkboard on the wall. 'There are some of the letters they've sent with their packages. One woman was diagnosed with cancer a few weeks after getting back to the UK. And there's a letter from a man in Canada whose wife died in a car crash.'

She pointed to a half metre long slab of rust-coloured rock propped up against the wall beside the box. 'That weighs thirty-two kilos, same as a medium to large dog,' she said. 'A family from Adelaide took it home with them in their campervan and put it out in their front yard with a plaster Aborigine on top.' She paused dramatically.

'And?' Chaseling prompted.

'A massive bushfire swept through their suburb and their place burned down. This was one of the few things that survived the fire.'

'How about the plaster Aborigine – I take it we're talking about something like a garden gnome here?'

'Yes we are, a little painted cement black fella wearing a loin cloth and holding a boomerang. They sent us a picture and he survived too, just paint damage.' A smile creased her face. 'Our mob, we're good at surviving the heat, we've been doing it for more than 50 thousand years.'

'So what do you do with these rocks when people send them back?'

'Every few months the elders hold a smoking ceremony, kind of like an exorcism, and they ask our ancestors to forgive the people who've taken the stones. Then we put each stone back where it feels right.'

'And does it work?'

'Seems to.'

As they got back on the bus, the guide's mobile phone trilled. She lifted the phone to her ear and answered the call. It was bad news. *'Oh my God!'* she exclaimed. 'OK, I'll see you there.' She ended the call, started the engine and the bus lurched out of the parking bay. 'It's one of the Yanks. Bob. Suspected heart attack, but hopefully just heat exhaustion.'

The diesel engine roared as she steered the bus onto the bitumen road leading to the Rock. And there was another sound, quickly getting louder – an insistent, machine gun-like clatter. The belly of a helicopter came into view through the windscreen. The chopper, which was painted bright yellow, rapidly got smaller as it made a beeline for the top of the Rock. The sun was lower now and the monolith glowed crimson, as though the gods atop this Mount Olympus of the desert were angry.

Chaseling's hand reached down and pressed against the giant opal in his pocket again. It might be a good idea, he thought, to head down the Stuart Highway and find his way back to the place where he'd found it. Maybe have a little smoking ceremony of his own. But then the rational left hemisphere of his brain, the part that didn't believe in such things as spirits or bad luck, raised its voice, saying, *Listen dude, there's no way a small piece of rock could have conjured up a kangaroo to wreck your car, let alone a pair of murderous psychos to turn your life upside down.*

However, that inner voice of reason somehow lacked a note of conviction. Out here in the strange vastness of the interior, it seemed that the laws of science and logic didn't always apply. It was as though he'd been cast into some other time or spatial dimension. One presided over by an angry god with a thirst for vengeance, like the god of the Old Testament. The helicopter slowly descended and landed not far from where the chain of the walkers' track ended. Two people got out of the chopper and ran through the cloud of dust being thrown up by blades. Then they disappeared from view as the bus got closer to the monolith. Delilah was on the phone. 'His face turned blue, you say? You know, it might be time to start putting climbers through a medical check.'

The bus came to a halt near the base of the Rock and the door slid open. Chaseling got out and walked to where the track up its side began. The two teenage girls were making the final leg of their descent. When they reached the bottom they started running towards him. One of them was sobbing. 'He died right in front of us!' she said.

Running past him, the girls came to a halt in front of Delilah, who had just stepped out of the bus. Chaseling saw Delilah threw out her arms and next thing she was hugging and comforting the pair.

The helicopter took off from the top of the Rock. As it passed over them, Chaseling looked up and said, 'Bob, I strongly suspect you were too far gone for a defibrillator to bring you back. If that's the case, rest in peace.' He watched the helicopter rapidly getting smaller, the sound of its engine and rotors dying as it flew off into the red vastness.

Chaseling approached Delilah and the two girls. 'Are they headed for Alice Springs?' he asked the guide.

'That's right, our local hospital, 450 kilometres away,' Delilah said.

A fly settled at the edge of Chaseling's right eye and refused to go away when he blinked, so he shooed it off with his hand. 'So do you think these two have crossed that line you were talking about earlier?' he asked Delilah, indicating the teenagers clinging to her like a pair of limpets.

Delilah nodded, but didn't say anything. More climbers, including the two girls' parents, were reaching the ground. The girls detached themselves from Delilah and ran to their parents.

'Do you think your Dreamtime ancestors caused Bob's heart attack?'

Delilah gazed up at the massive desert landmark towering above them. 'Our ancestors do occasionally get into bad moods; they have bad days, just like human beings.'

'So you really think that's a more likely explanation than the fact that Bob was verging on being grossly obese? A prime candidate for cardiac infarction?'

'Sometimes the gods need a sacrifice,' Delilah said.

33 KISS GOODBYE

IT WAS 11PM and most of the restaurants lining the Dixon Street pedestrian plaza in the heart of Sydney's Chinatown were shutting down for the night, staff carrying outdoor dining tables and chairs in from the street. But the Happy Friends Karaoke Lounge was still very much open for business, its name flashing in blue neon letters. Guarding the entrance were two green granite lions, plus more pragmatically, an enormous Maori in a black suit which was too small for him, but which emphasized the muscles bulging from his chest and arms. The doorman, face lit up blue every two seconds, gazed impassively at Ali as he approached.

Ali was dressed like a workman. He wore a bright orange fluorescent vest and a leather tool belt and carried a battered-looking metal box. Hanging from his neck was a fake photo ID saying he was employed by Energy Australia. He'd left his ostentatious gold neck chains at home and the tattoos on his arms were covered by a long-sleeved shirt, twin swallows on either side of his neck obscured by a scarf, so the only visible skin inkings were the 'BROS' on his fingers and the teardrop below his eye.

'They're expecting me upstairs,' he told the doorman. 'Problem with the wiring'

The Maori ran a metal detector over Ali's body and got him to open the tool box, his huge brown hands rifling through it for a weapon. 'OK,' he said, 'just go up to the first floor and talk to the girl at reception.'

Ali ascended the stairs, the walls and ceiling of which were covered with mirror panels where he could see multiple reflections of himself. Reaching the top, he walked into a kaleidoscope of more mirrored walls and multi-hued lights. Neon tubing snaked around the matt black ceiling, glowing every colour of the spectrum.

Ali nodded to the receptionist, a stunning Chinese girl with her long hair dyed platinum blonde. Looking as though he knew where he was going, he walked down a brightly-lit corridor, at the end of which he could see and hear a man singing a Chinese song very badly on a small stage. Halfway down the hallway, he passed another, narrower passage to his right, a corridor of numbered black doors which, he presumed, led to private karaoke rooms. Then he was walking into the public karaoke area.

It was a small room by club standards, but the mirrors on the walls made it look roomier. A dozen people sat in red vinyl seats observing the singer perform on a semi-circular stage. The back wall of the stage was a giant video screen, three metres long and two metres high, showing scenes of an attractive young Chinese couple acting out various romantic scenes – walking along hand in hand, looking soulfully into each other's eyes and dancing cheek-to-cheek. At the base of the screen were the words of the song in both Chinese characters and 'Pinyin,' where Chinese words are phonetically rendered in the Latin alphabet.

The man on the stage of the Happy Friends was performing a song which – aptly, as it would soon turn out – was called *Kiss Goodbye*. In the mid-1990s it had been a big hit for Hong Kong singing star Jacky Cheung. Female fans loved the sentimental lyrics and would often cry when Cheung performed the song live.

But the live rendition of *Kiss Goodbye* currently under way was both off-key and out of time. Yet the karaoke performer's audience appeared to be rapt. A girl wearing purple hotpants, showing off dainty legs the delicate off-white shade of a cut potato, swayed her waist length, shining black hair from side to side, her heavily made up eyes never leaving the man on stage. Beside her, a short-haired girl in an anime T-shirt and white jeans tapped the toes of her high-heeled shoes on the floor and silently mouthed the words of the song. One table away from the girls sat three gangster types, young men with heavy gold neck chains and bracelets, baggy trousers, designer sports tops and Nike sneakers. One of them wore a pair of black-lensed Ray Bans. The trio were slapping their hands down on the tabletop in time to the music, or at least as in time as they could get, given the singer's off-putting diversions from the beat.

The man singing into the microphone had an angular face with high cheekbones, cruel-looking dark eyes and thin lips. He wore a tight white tank top and he had muscular arms covered with oriental tattoos. His head was shaven, but as the man turned sideways to present a heroic profile to the audience, Ali saw how the scalp was by no means completely hairless. Growing from the back was a long black pigtail hanging well past his shoulders. Yes, this was him – Jiang Feng. It would be a challenge to kill him while he was on stage. But Ali relished challenges that involved inflicting mortal injury and creating chaos.

He paused at the edge of a small wooden dance floor. Putting his toolbox down at the base of a mirrored pillar, he looked across at the man singing into the microphone. And Ali commenced the Dance of the Buffoon.

Swaying his fluoro-vested torso in time to the music, Ali moved onto the dance floor, where he began waving his arms like a hula dancer. On his face Ali wore a vacant grin and his eyes had a look of moronic rapture as they gazed up at the man on stage.

Feng's lips formed a shape that was half bemused, half contemptuous. He locked eyes with Ali and sang, '*Jiu zai yi zhuan yan/ Fa xian ni de lian/ Yi jing guo shi bu hui zai xiang cong qian* (In the twinkling of an eye/ I see how your face/ has already become unfamiliar, it'll never again be like before.)'

Ali pirouetted on one foot and performed a 360 degree spin, at the end of which he appeared to lose his balance and staggered, taking him closer to the stage. There was a high-pitched titter from the girl in the anime T-shirt. But Ali didn't mind being laughed at. That was all part of the plan. Now he was wiggling his fat hips while his feet performed a comical jig. All the moves were well-intentioned but clumsy. And all the time, he was getting closer and closer to the stage. In fact, Ali was quite a good dancer. But anyone who saw him now wouldn't consider that possible. Nor would they think that the fluoro-vested clown constituted any kind of a threat. He was just some dumb workman.

Ali had now reached the edge of the stage, where he turned to face the audience and did a Michael Jackson crotch-grab. More laughter, both male and female. Now he was facing the stage again, skipping from side to side while gazing enraptured up at the man giving the tortured vocal performance.

Accepting the fact that the fluoro-vested man had now become the centre of attention, Feng hammed it up. Placing a hand over his heart and pouting his lips theatrically, he serenaded Ali, leaning down towards him from the lip of the stage.

'*Wo di shi jie kai shi xia xue/ Leng de rang wo wu fa duo ai yi tian* (It has begun to snow in my world/ So cold that I can't love one day longer).'

Ali performed a heavy-footed moonwalk which took him to the base of the two wooden steps leading up to the stage. '*Leng de yan ying cang de yi han dou na mo di ming xian* (So cold that even my hidden sorrows are all so apparent).'

Ali slowly ascended the first step, pausing to wiggle his bottom at the audience. Then he was mounting the next two steps and stepping onto the stage, where he whirled and gyrated while moving ever closer to Feng.

The pigtailed man gazed into Ali's face as he reached the climax of the song: '*Wo he ni wen bie/ Zai wu ren de jai/ Rang feng chi xiao/ Wo bu neng ju jue* (You and I kiss goodbye/ On an empty street/ Let the wind laugh idiotically/ I can't refuse it).'

Now Ali was right beside Feng, rocking his shoulders from side to side and clapping his hands. The backing track had reached an instrumental break featuring Chinese violins. Feng nodded his head towards Ali and spoke into the microphone in Mandarin. '*Rang wo men gei zhe ge pang gui lao yi dian zhang sheng!* (Let me hear your appreciation for the fat *gwaillo*!)' He put a hand on Ali's shoulder. There was a round of applause. One of the gold-necklaced, Nike-wearing gangsters put his fingers to his lips and whistled.

It was then that Ali suddenly grabbed the hand resting on his shoulder. With his other hand, moving incredibly quickly, he reached down to his tool belt and drew out a yellow-handled screwdriver with a sharpened end. Then he jabbed it backwards as hard as he could into Feng's right eye.

Feng gave a screech of agony as his microphone dropped to the floor with a loud thump. A woman screamed. The final lines of the song started appearing on the giant screen. And this time Feng's vocal performance was truly tortured as he frantically tried to pull out the screwdriver, which was proving difficult to budge because it had torn through the bone at the back of his eye socket and deep into the frontal lobe. Feng collapsed to the edge of the stage, then rolled down onto the dance floor. As he landed face down on the wooden floorboards, the impact propelled the point of the screwdriver even deeper into his brain. His body went into convulsions, his feet drumming on the floor. The song was coming to a close, the giant video screen showing the man and woman tearfully parting at an airport gate, the oriental Ingrid Bergman then boarding a plane.

Meanwhile, Ali had leapt off the stage and pelted across the dance floor. As he ran between the tables, one of the gangsters jumped from his seat and tried to intercept him, but Ali swatted the much smaller man aside and dashed towards the exit. Meanwhile, the music came to a stop – and Ali paused as well. He turned around and yelled 'Stay out of south western Sydney! Bankstown, Punchbowl, Lakemba, they're Lebo-land!'

He took the stairs two at a time. Nearing the base of the stairwell, he saw the dark-suited Maori doorman looking up at him from the entrance. Ali pulled a hammer from his tool belt and as he jumped down the final two steps, threw it at the man's face, scoring a lucky hit as the claw edge slammed into his victim's mouth. The doorman collapsed to the ground, his mouth a bloody pit of broken teeth and torn lips, and Ali leapt over him. Then he was running down an alleyway towards his motorbike, an illegally parked black Honda CB750. He leapt onto the bike and turned the ignition key. He could hear enraged voices, rapidly getting closer. As he kicked the bike into life he glanced over his shoulder and saw a group of Chinese men sprinting down the alleyway towards him, their angry faces lit up starkly in the metal halide street lights. One of them – the man wearing sunglasses – was reaching into the breast pocket of his jacket.

Ali roared away from the curb. He felt the air beside his head being displaced and a jagged hole appeared in the back window of an Audi parked further down the alley. The engine screaming at high revs, he hurtled the wrong way down a short one-way street, then screeched into traffic moving past Sydney Entertainment Centre, about to stage its final round of concerts before being demolished.

Slowing to a legal speed, he steered with one hand as he unclipped his black helmet from the handlebars and put it over his head. *Don't want to go breaking any laws,* he thought with a smile. As he rode home he felt a sense of accomplishment. The Chinese wouldn't be such a threat to the family business now. But he knew that he had sealed his fate and that CCTV images of the karaoke club murder would soon make him an even more wanted man than he already was. So it was a good thing that, in just over 12 hours, he would be boarding a plane for the Middle East and putting Australia behind him as he embarked on the next chapter of his life, fighting in the Syrian war zone and beheading people.

There was just one final matter to deal with before he left. And it was something that set his heart pounding and curled his lips into a sadistic grimace as he rode across the Gladesville Bridge. Because it would involve getting in some beheading practice – on the blond-haired man's parents.

34 ROAD RAGE

THAT NIGHT Ali slept peacefully. He always did after he'd committed an act of extreme violence. No waking up screaming and cursing as he usually did. This morning more blood would be shed. A lot of it.

And so, feeling energised and bursting with his own particular twisted blend of *joie de vivre* after murdering Feng the previous night (his morning smoke of ice also no doubt helped), Ali took another trip out to Vaucluse.

Wearing his fluoro vest again, he drove his car out of the basement car park of his apartment block at 6.15am. The car was a Nissan Skyline R34 painted such a brilliant shade of metallic blue that it was hovering on the edge of purple. And the highly-tuned 1482cc engine had twin turbos which made the car go like a rocket. But as Ali drove down a stretch of freeway, then hooked up with Parramatta Road, the engine was drowned out by the sound of death metal music blasting from 150-watt, three way speakers. It was an album by Australian band Sadistik Exekution. As he turned off Parramatta Road and started skirting round the eastern edge of the city, he began singing along with one of his favourite tracks (although, technically this wasn't singing, because the voice coming out of the speakers, and being emulated by Ali, was a shouted demonic growl): *Kill, kill, kill, violence is saving your soul/ Sweeping you away as dust,/ Sadistik Exekution/ We are death, fuck you all, die, die, die!*

By the time he reached the edge of Bondi Junction, not far from his destination, the final track on the Sadistik Exekution album had just finished. He was stopped at a set of traffic lights ogling the bouncy breasts of a girl crossing the road when his contemplations were interrupted by the roar of a car engine to his left. He tore his eyes away from the girl and gazed sideways. Beside his car was a red Mazda RX-7.

Ali had nursed a vehement hatred for RX-7s and their drivers ever since watching the movie *Fast and Furious: Tokyo*

Drift, which featured a burnout between a Skyline and an RX-7. Much to his distress, the RX-7 had won.

The RX-7 driver challenging Ali was a man in his thirties with a stylishly unruly mop of wavy dark hair. He was looking across at Ali with a half-smile. His foot pressed down on the accelerator again, harder this time, making the RX-7's rotary engine howl. He raised his eyebrows as he stared unblinkingly at Ali.

Ali was pretty sure the man was a Jew. He had that look about him, even though he wasn't quite sure what the look consisted of. But there were a lot of Jews in this part of Sydney. In fact, he'd just passed a synagogue called Temple Emmanuel. Even if the man wasn't a Jew, he needed to be taught a lesson, to be shown who was boss.

As the lights blinked from red to green, Ali plunged down his right foot and his car made a screeching take-off, the turbo chargers screaming as the car shot up through the gears. Within a couple of seconds, Ali's speedo had hit 80km/h and it was still climbing as he glanced into his wing mirror to see the RX-7 driving sedately away from the lights. *Fucking wimp,* he thought to himself. *Didn't have the balls to take on the mighty Ali.*

But then Ali's moment of glory was destroyed by two flashes of light from a grey box mounted high on a metal post he'd just driven past. Then he saw the sign saying it was a 40 km/h school zone. He voiced a stream of obscenities as he slowed down.

For a few seconds, the berserker fury took hold. A hot flush engulfed his neck and started to work its way up his face. He thought how satisfying it would be to engage in some serious road rage with the RX-7 driver. Force him off the road, then beat him to a pulp. But then, in a rare display of self-control, Ali managed to turn back the red tide. The flush slowly started fading from his skin as he took a series of deep breaths. *Stay focused,* he told himself. *You're flying out of the country later today and you won't be coming back, so a speed camera conviction doesn't mean jack shit.*

He stopped for another set of lights. The RX-7 pulled up level with him again. At first Ali resisted to urge to glance sideways at his *bête noire*. But then machismo pride and curiosity made him turn his head. The man was smiling smugly and Ali could see his shoulders shaking. The cunt was laughing at him.

Ali lowered the passenger side window so the man could see him clearly. He raised his hand, forefinger extended in the Islamic State salute, then made a throat-slashing gesture. That wiped the smile off the cunt's face. Now he was no longer gazing smugly across at Ali but looking up at the traffic lights as his fingers drummed nervously on the steering wheel.

Ali made a sound that was half snort, half laugh. After looking around to see that there wasn't a camera at this intersection, he roared away when the lights turned green. In his mirrors, he saw the RX-7 turning down a side street, smoke rising from the back wheels as the driver took the corner at speed. 'Loser!' Ali said. Then he smiled. The duel with the RX-7 driver was a nice little prelude to the morning's main event.

35 DEATH COMES KNOCKING

EVELYN CHASELING was a germophobe. After taking four strips of bacon out of a packet and placing them on a hot pan, where they started sizzling and spitting, she went to the sink and washed her hands in liquid germicidal soap. Then she picked up a small nail brush and gave her fingertips a good scrub, thereby erasing all traces of the contaminants she feared lurked in the uncooked bacon. Next she rinsed her hands under the tap, the water almost painfully hot. Then, holding her wet hands upwards like a surgeon, because there were all sorts of infectious microbes that could be lurking on a towel, she went to the fridge and got out a packet of eggs. After breaking two of them into the pan, she returned to the stainless steel double sink and again washed her hands of any germs that might have been on the surface of the egg shells, or the fridge handle for that matter. The backs of her fingers and hands were ravaged by dermatitis from the repeated washings, the skin inflamed and flaking. Her palms were a study of deep furrows that would probably be fertile ground for a fortune teller.

As you might imagine, meal preparation could take a long time in the Chaseling household. Or at least it did when Evelyn was the chef, which was why her husband Craig prepared their evening meals. Putting together a dinner with multiple ingredients could involve twenty or more scrubs of Evelyn's hands. This not only lengthened the food preparation time, but multiplied the chances of the end product tasting of antibacterial solution.

While she was never going to get a job as a hand model, the rest of Evelyn Chaseling was pleasing to the eye. Aged 56, she had collar-length blonde hair streaked with white. The skin on her face was lightly tanned, with few lines, and even her neck was relatively unwrinkled for someone who had lived over half a century. She wore shorts and a T-shirt, as she didn't need to get ready for work for another half hour. She was a university academic – a lecturer in English literature – and started work at nine.

Craig, a senior partner in a law firm, would be out the door directly after breakfast, at 7:50 on the dot, just as he'd done for 30 years. A tall, distinguished man with wings of white hair at the side of his head and thinning iron grey hair on top, he was already dressed in business shirt and trousers, although his feet were bare. He sat at the kitchen table reading a copy of the *Sydney Morning Herald*. There was no conversation between the couple. They had reached a stage in life where they spent most of their time together in companionable silence.

The doorbell rang.

The Chaseling home was fronted by a two-metre tall brick fence painted mustard yellow, the same shade as the house. There was a sturdy wooden gate which was a glossy Brunswick Green to match the home's window frames, exterior doors and upstairs balcony balustrade. Ali lifted his tattooed finger away from a button set at shoulder height beside the gate. There was the faint sound of a bell ringing. A short time later he heard a door being unlocked, then footsteps on a stone surface. The lens of a peephole set into the centre of the gate darkened.

'Can I help you?' said a woman's voice. It was the woman he'd spoken to on the phone. The blond man's mother.

'Electricity,' Ali said. 'Come to read the meter.' He held his fake Energy Australia ID up to the peephole.

'But we've got one of those new smart meters and it reads itself,' said the voice on the other side of the gate.

'The smart meters aren't as smart as they're made out to be,' Ali said. 'These ones need recalibrating, so until they get fixed it's back to manual readings.'

'I see,' the voice said. 'Another thing – we're with AGL, not Energy Australia.'

'We've just taken over AGL,' Ali lied, hoping the woman wasn't a stockbroker or someone else in the know. 'Got our new ID badges yesterday.'

'Yes, it does look very new,' Evelyn Chaseling observed as she looked at the pristine, unscratched ID card that continued to almost fill the wide angle vista provided by the peephole. Just above the top of the card she could also see the man's eyes. And she didn't like the look of them. They were dark and forbidding, like two holes in the ground. Then she chided herself for being racist. The man looked Middle Eastern and by thinking unkind things about him she was engaging in the same kind of blanket ethnic stereotyping that ran rampant through much of society, thanks to the media.

She unlocked the gate and pulled it open. As she stood there looking at him, the misgivings resurfaced; those eyes definitely looked scary, but then she rebuked herself again for nursing such unkind thoughts (although she'd definitely be giving the outside gate handle a spray of Glen 20). 'Come in and close the gate behind you,' she said. 'The meter's just over there.' She indicated a Brunswick Green-painted metal box at the end of the terrace.

Ali clicked shut the gate. At the same time, he pulled up the edge of his fluoro vest and grabbed the knife from his belt. Then he leapt at Evelyn, launching himself upwards from the base of the two stone steps leading up to the terrace. She gave a little cry of shock and reeled away from him just in time to avoid the blade of the Jungle Master as it sliced through the air. She ran for the doorway. Now she was inside and pushing the door shut. But just before she got it closed the silver blade of the Jungle Master appeared through the gap. With a metallic clunk, the edge of the door slammed into it. Then Ali put his shoulder to the door and pushed hard.

As the door flew open, Evelyn ran down the hallway, the urgent pattering of her bare feet echoing off the walls and white-tiled floor. Close behind, Ali snatched a yellow and black device with a pistol grip from the side pocket of his fluoro jacket, pointed it at the woman and pressed the trigger.

The taser's two barbed prongs flew through the air and bit into Evelyn's back, which arched as she received a 50,000 volt shock. With a shriek of agony, she collapsed face downwards to the floor, her legs twitching.

A moment later Ali was straddling her, sitting on her back as he grabbed her hair and pulled her head upwards. In his other hand he held the Jungle Master, its blade resting against her throat. Evelyn Chaseling's eyes were glistening with tears as he slashed sideways, releasing a cascade of crimson arterial blood. The dying woman let loose a little sigh and he released his grip on her hair.

He heard the sound of footsteps and looked up to see an enraged-looking man running towards him. The man was wearing a business shirt, tie and suit trousers, but no shoes or socks. He was wielding a rolled up umbrella, the large golf variety. Holding the umbrella like a sword, he charged towards Ali, who was still hunched over the body of his victim.

The man was a metre away as Ali leapt to his feet brandishing the bloody-bladed Jungle Master – just in time to knock aside the steel-tip of the brolly so that it brushed past the side of his face. Meanwhile one of the man's bare feet slipped in the pool of blood that had gathered around his wife's head. His arms windmilled as he fought to regain his balance, then his other foot slipped on the skating rink-like surface and he fell heavily onto his back. Ali pounced.

As Craig Chaseling struggled to get up, his hands pushing down at the floor, Ali's knee cannoned into his stomach. Craig made a sound that sounded like *'Oooomph!* as the air was driven from his diaphragm. He was beginning to suck in a breath when the blade of the Jungle Master slashed into the front of his throat, cutting deeply into the windpipe. And the last sound that he ever made was a dreadful bubbling gurgle as the Jungle Master severed his carotid artery.

Ali's face was that of a madman. His eyes bulged from their sockets and flecks of white foam were gathered at the edge of his lips like a dog in the grip of rabies. Taking a handful of the man's hair, he hauled backwards to expose the slashed throat.

Then he proceeded to put to good use the knowledge he'd gained out in the desert.

A very short time later, no more than 15 seconds, the head was all but severed. Ali put the Jungle Master down on the tiles and took the head in both hands. Just as he'd practiced with animals out in the bush, he placed his hands on either side of the head and gave it a violent twist, so forceful that the head ended up doing a Linda Blair and staring backwards at Ali. Then, gripping the sides of the head, Ali pulled upwards. There was a tearing, crunching sound like the stalk of a banana peel being broken, only much louder. And Ali held the head in front of him like the Aubrey Beardsley drawing of Salome clutching the severed, blood-dripping head of John the Baptist. The only thing spoiling the moment for him was the furious expression on the man's face. His upper lip was curled in a snarl and his eyes stared at Ali with hate. 'You should chill out, man,' Ali told the head. But his levity was forced and he couldn't look into his victim's eyes.

He placed the head down sideways on a clean area of floor beside the body. He picked up the Jungle Master and wiped it on the front of his fluoro vest. Time for the next beheading.

Less than a minute later, he was rising to his feet carrying the woman's head by the hair, a cascade of blood falling from the ragged stump of her neck. He took two steps to where the man's head lay and swore as he saw that in the time he'd decapitated the woman, a lake of blood had flowed from the jagged stump of the man's neck and spread across a section of floor tiles to engulf the head. As he picked it up Ali saw that one side of its face was coated with crimson blood, giving a particularly disturbing cast to the angry expression the man's face had set in as he died.

Carrying a head in each hand, Ali turned left at the end of the hallway and found himself in a large, elegantly furnished lounge room. A pair of royal blue couches formed an L-shape. Filling the space in front of the couches was a knee-high glass-topped table with a vase of purple-pink hydrangeas in the middle. Ali's Adidas-clad feet stepped onto a polished wooden floor, then sank into a red and black Bukhara rug as he headed for the fireplace at the end of the room. The hearth had grey marble surrounds and a mantelpiece on which stood an antique clock and half a dozen framed family photos, most of them featuring the smiling face of the blond-haired man who'd been the cause of all his recent woes.

Pausing in front of the mantelpiece to examine the photos, Ali saw how they were arranged in chronological order from left to right. As he studied them, he saw that in an older family photo, the couple he'd just murdered, whose blood-dripping heads dangled by the hair from his hands, were pictured with the hated blond man and an older sister. But in a recent family snap, the parents were with the blond man and another adult male, a short guy with a goatee. Leaning in closer to study the goateed man's features, Ali saw how he and the girl in the earlier picture were one and the same. *These rich cunts, they get up to all kinds of weird shit,* he thought. He placed the woman's head down on the floor to give himself a free hand. Then he reached up and casually swept the framed photos and clock from the mantel.

The room filled with the sound of breaking glass as the objects smashed on the grate and floor. Ali took the man's head in two hands and placed it on the mantelpiece, positioning it to the left so Mum could be on the right, about a foot away. But there was a problem.

The man's head had a bit of vertebra sticking out from the base of it and didn't want to sit up straight, even when leaning against the wall behind. Ali placed the head on its side and bent down to pick up the second display in his nightmare tableau.

He had severed the woman's head cleanly so when he set it down on the mantelpiece it sat stably. Then he lifted up the man's head and positioned it tight up against the woman's so its weight was being partially supported.

Like an interior decorator contemplating his work, Ali gazed critically at the display. The man's head still had a marked lean to the right, but it would have to do.

36 MUM SENDS HER LOVE

IN THE MIDDAY SUNLIGHT the opal looked as though it was alive, a protean creature with crimson fire blazing away in its depths while a multitude of other colours danced on its surface. Chaseling carefully wrapped the stone in a tissue and put it back in his pocket.

He was at a place known as Ellery Big Hole an hour's drive out of Alice Springs. It was a deep billabong with a sandstone rock face on one side and a small beach on the other. After his swim, he would go back to Alice, refuel the car and drive south down the highway. He would stay the night at a roadhouse, then go back to the place where he'd found the opal. And replace it underneath the slab with the remains of its rightful owner.

The search results from Google about souveniring stones from Uluru had not been encouraging. Far from it. Story after story about people being bedevilled by misfortune after taking away pieces of rock. Some of the reports were carried on sites specialising in the paranormal, but a lot of others came from reputable news sources like the UK Daily Telegraph and Australian Broadcasting Corporation. Most likely it was all a self-perpetuating myth. But if the stories about angering Uluru's dreamtime spirits were true, it made sense that it would also be very bad karma to take rocks from other sacred sites, especially a burial ground.

No-one else was at the Big Hole, but after taking off his clothes and shoes he kept his underpants on in case other people arrived. Plus there was also the chance of some biting, nipping creature lurking beneath the still waters of the little lake and attacking the organ which had brought such pleasure to the two German girls.

He walked to the edge of the sandy bank and took a running dive into the water. The cold pounded at his skull like an army of little men wielding sledgehammers. He popped up from beneath the surface like a cork, giving a gasp of discomfort. Standing in shoulder-deep, water, he thought that he might just leave it at this and go back to bask in the warm sunshine.

But then he thought to himself, *You're not chickening out, are you?* And his shivering, goose-bumped inner wimp found some backbone. He plunged back under the water and resurfaced a couple of metres away, where he started ploughing along in a powerful freestyle, striking out for the orange-grey wall of rock rising up on the other side. After reaching the opposite bank, he rested against the rock face for a few seconds, then, no longer bothered by the cold, he started to swim back towards the little beach, thinking about the long journey he was about to undertake back to the burial site.

Walking up the sand bank, he was surrounded by a halo of water droplets as he shook his head to repel a small squadron of flies attempting to land on his face. He picked up the light blue towel he'd borrowed from the motel and started drying himself.

His iPhone rang. He reached into his bag and as he looked at the screen, his face lit up with a smile. It was his mother's mobile.

'Hi Mum!'

'Mum sends you her love, but she can't come to the phone right now.' The man's voice was harsh, and he delivered the words in a rapid burst. He gave a little snigger, a snort of air from the nostrils. 'Dad can't talk to you at the moment either.'

'Who is this?'

'We last met in a tunnel in Coober Pedy. You ought to remember me – *cunt!*'

Fear flashed. 'How did you get hold of my mother's phone?'

'I've just created a nice little display for Mum and Dad's mantelpiece.' There was a longer snigger – several snorts interspersed with high-pitched little whinnies. 'I'll send you the picture now.'

'*What have you done to my parents?*' Chaseling screamed. But the man had already ended the call.

In the Ellery Big Hole carpark, Jason Clarence, a 28-year-old quality control manager from Manchester, stepped out of the battered camper van, which was painted with psychedelic flowers, a peace sign and the words 'REVOLUTION IS IN YOUR HEART – LIBERATE YOURSELF.'

Draped around Jason's sunburned neck was a beach towel and he wore just a pair of board shorts and sandals. 'Can't wait to sink into Ellery Big Hole,' he said in a broad northern accent as he looked at the surface of the water glittering between the white branches and silvery leaves of some ghost gum trees.

'That sounds indecent,' said fellow-Briton Nina Russell from the other side of the van. Nina, a 27-year-old business development manager, spoke in the more rounded tones of someone brought up in the Home Counties. A redhead in denim shorts and a pink bikini top, she was stepping into a lime-green plastic life buoy that had a grinning dinosaur head rising from it. She was pulling the ring up over her slim hips when the scream rang out.

The scream was long and agonized. Jason and Nina stood looking at each other for a few seconds. Then there was a second scream, even more bloodcurdling than the first. Then the sobbing started.

'I don't feel like going for a swim any more,' said Jason, opening the driver's door of the Mitsubishi Budgie camper which had carried them halfway across Australia. 'Not here, anyways.'

'No, I don't either,' said Nina, stepping back out of the pool toy and throwing it through the open side door of the van.

Half a minute later, the Budgie pulled out of the carpark. Nina was looking at her phone and telling Jason how the aquatic centre in Alice Springs had a double loop water slide.

Ali dropped the iPhone to the floor. He went out into the hallway, where he opened the door of a cupboard and looked inside. Hanging there was a man's light cotton coat. He tore off his bloodstained fluoro vest and put on the coat. Next to the cupboard was another door that was part open, revealing a vanity unit, shower and toilet. He went inside and washed his hands. The water ran red as he rinsed off the gore. He hurriedly dried his hands on a pristine white hand towel which quickly turned pink as he wiped off the blood stubbornly clinging to his hands. He threw the towel to the floor and headed back out into the hallway.

Making his way to the front door, he tried to step around the sea of gore surrounding the two headless bodies, but there was so much of it he couldn't avoid one foot slopping into the edge of the puddle. Then he was running towards the open front door. He paused as he reached the doormat just outside and wiped his feet.

After opening the front gate out to the street, he had a quick look-see. No one in sight. Closing the gate behind him, he walked quickly to his car. Seconds later, he was speeding away.

He'd driven less than a kilometre when he realised how fine he'd cut it time-wise. As he passed the towering white obelisk of Macquarie lighthouse perched on the clifftop at the edge of the ocean, he heard a siren and saw flashing blue lights rapidly approaching from the other direction. A police car screamed past.

Ali smiled. He'd got away with it. Beheading people felt good. There'd been the same thrill he had experienced when he plunged the screwdriver into the Chinaman's eye the previous night. But on top of that there'd been a feeling of ecstatic arousal as he sawed into his victim's necks with the wicked steel teeth of his Bush Master. His smile broadened into a grimace as he thought about the orgy of beheading he would revel in once he got to Syria.

Constable Kylie Doyle and Senior Constable Neville Bowman got out of the white Holden Commodore, which had the word POLICE in big letters on each side along with the NSW police insignia, with its motto declaring '*Culpam poena premit comes* (punishment swiftly follows crime).'

The officers walked up to the tall, green-painted wooden gate. Senior Constable Bowman, a 31-year-old ex-rugby player going to seed, his belly thrusting out belligerently from his light blue uniform shirt, raised his hand and pressed a white button set at shoulder height. They heard the faint sound of door chimes from inside the house but couldn't hear anything else. After standing listening for half a minute, the policeman pressed the button again, holding his finger down longer this time. Then he felt his colleague tapping him on the arm.

Constable Doyle, her blue eyes wide under the police cap, was pointing downwards. Senior Constable Bowman looked down and at the base of the gate he saw a pink footprint, so indistinct that they hadn't noticed it at first. But now that it had been pointed out to him, he could see that it had probably been made by a sneaker. And the chances were that the substance adhering to its sole was blood. His eyes tracked along the concrete footpath and he could just make out a second print, more ghostly than the first and only visible now they knew what they were looking for.

'I'll radio the station,' he said, putting his hand to the device near his shirt collar. But Constable Doyle was having none of that. The suntanned, athletic-looking 23-year-old, with long black hair held up by clips plus her police cap, took a step back, then delivered a hefty kick to the gate with the thick rubber heel of her boot. There was the sound of wood snapping, and the gate yielded slightly.

'What the fuck are you doing, Kylie, I said we should wait!' exclaimed Bowman, who operated by the maxim that there's safety in numbers, especially when you positioned yourself at the rear of the pack.

Constable Doyle had worked alongside Bowman enough times to conclude that he was a spineless idiot who froze at crucial moments like this one. So she ignored him, delivering another powerful kick to the gate. The frame splintered in the middle, beside the lock, and the gate flew open. They saw a trail of pink prints on the terracotta tiles, fading as they headed towards where they were standing. The front door of the house hung open, ominously so.

Constable Doyle pulled her Glock from its holster and stepped onto the tiles, being careful to avoid the footprints. Senior Constable Bowman drew his gun too as he followed his junior and much ballsier colleague through the gateway, up the steps and into the white-tiled hallway.

'Oh God!' said Constable Doyle as she saw the two headless bodies.

Gazing over her shoulder at the two corpses, a man and a woman, lying in a large puddle of congealing red-black blood, Senior Constable Bowman pressed the send button on his radio. 'Senior Constable Bowman here reporting a double homicide at the address we were despatched to in Cambridge Avenue, support urgently required….' He started backing away down the hallway, towards the sunlight framed in the front door, while Constable Doyle just stood there transfixed, looking down at the bodies and wondering what had happened to the heads. She flicked off the safety catch of the Glock and, in a loud, forceful voice, called out *'Hello!* Is anyone there?'

'Shut up, Kylie!' Senior Constable Bowman whispered. He was now at the doorway. He turned and hurried out of the house, down the two steps and out the open gateway.

Inside the house, the policewoman called out again: 'Police! Is anybody there?'

The house was silent.

Senior Constable Bowman sunk into the driver's seat of the Commodore and turned on the radio – not the police one, but his favourite station, Nova FM. *Yes, best not to contaminate the scene, wait for the experts to get here,* he told himself as he turned up the volume so he could appreciate the Adele song *Hello*. All he could think of was two headless corpses.

37 THE FRIDGE

WORKING AS A MORTUARY ASSISTANT had its perks, Mal Kite thought to himself. Well, one perk, anyway. You could rob the dead. And he had a feeling that the latest arrival at Glebe Morgue, the largest and busiest mortuary in Australia, might yield ripe pickings.

Kite was a thin-faced man in his early thirties with greasy-looking brown hair hanging in a limp fringe that stopped just short of his deep-set eyes. His mouth was perpetually open, exposing top and bottom incisors which were long and yellow, like a rat's. The once-white lab coat hanging from his bony shoulders had, over the five years Kite had been working at Glebe Morgue, taken on a shade that matched his teeth.

He stood looking down at the body of a 60-year-old man on a steel trolley. The man looked as though he'd been affluent – expensive shirt and shoes, well-trimmed hair and immaculately manicured fingernails. The body also wore another sign of affluence, one that may have figured in his death – white powder inside his nostrils.

Earlier, police at the death scene took custody of the man's wallet, jewellery and other personal items of value. But it was amazing what the cops missed. What raised Kite's hopes about this particular cadaver was the fact the man's death had taken place at Star City Casino. He could be a high roller with a wad of cash stuck down his shoe, or in his underpants.

But before Kite could search for cash and anything else of value (drugs were a common find, so much so that Kite ran a side business as a dealer), he had to be alone with the corpse. And right now, his manager Col Morrissey was in the room with him.

They were in a section of the morgue called the Identification Room, first port of call for cadavers. Morrissey, wearing a pristine white coat, sat behind a computer. Kite stood holding the edge of the gurney where the body of the white-nostrilled man reclined. Now he pushed the gurney forward onto a set of floor scales. 'One hundred and one kilos,' he said.

Morrissey entered the figure in the morgue's MMS (Mortuary Management System), which automatically subtracted the 23kg weight of the steel trolley to record the man's real weight – 78kg. He hit the enter key and stood up from the work bench. 'OK, I'll leave you to tag him and put him in the Fridge,' he said.

Kite smiled, revealing a blackened upper first molar. This was the opportunity he was waiting for. 'No probs,' he said.

'Don't forget to get those two bodies ready for the viewing at eleven o'clock,' added Morrissey.

'Okey-dokey.'

Morrissey's white-coated form disappeared through the swing doors of the Identification Room. Kite stood still for a few seconds, his head cocked to the side like a dog. The corridor outside the Identification Room was quiet. Kite's rubber-gloved hands reached into the front pockets of the body's white moleskin jeans. No joy.

The groin area of the moleskins was stained yellow with urine. 'Didn't your parents ever toilet train you?' Kite whispered as he rolled him onto his side. He slipped his hand into the left back pocket – and struck pay dirt. His fingers emerged with a wad of cash, at least half a dozen dark yellow fifties and a few 'lobsters,' the orange twenties. He transferred them to his wallet, then rolled the body onto its back.

He went round to the other side of the gurney and started undoing the man's belt. Now for the less than pleasant task of looking inside the underpants. *Could be a nice bag of blow in there*, he thought, nostrils twitching. But sadly, this was not to be. All Kite found was a set of genitals. He quickly re-zipped the man and did up his belt, then rolled him onto his back. 'Time to go into the Fridge.' he told the corpse, rearranging an arm hanging inelegantly over the side of the trolley. He walked over to a line of coat hooks and grabbed a padded parka which he put on over his dust coat.

The Fridge, officially called the Refrigeration Room, occupied almost half the floor space in Glebe Morgue. There was room here for 250 bodies, although at the moment there were just 102.

As Kite wheeled the gurney through a set of swing doors, his face shone white in the glare of a rack of fluorescent lights set along the ceiling. Cold air hit him in the face – the temperature here was four degrees Centigrade, about the same as a domestic fridge. On either side of him rose metal racks where bodies were stacked four high.

The dead were enclosed in giant blue bags made of the same kind of woven plastic as a tarpaulin. The corpse Kite had just robbed would remain unbagged because it was awaiting a post mortem. He steered the trolley into a vacant bay alongside two other unbagged corpses. One of them was an old man in striped pyjamas who still had a hospital drip feed going into his nose. The other was a younger man, his body reduced to a scarecrow by disease, drugs or both. His face was a hideous port wine purple colour, while the rest of his body, clad in singlet and underpants, was pale. The purple discolouration, called lividity, occurs when blood collects in the lowest lying parts of the body – for instance a head hanging over the edge of the bed. Kite locked the wheels of the gurney, then walked to the far end of the room where there was a separate set of doors leading out to the Autopsy Room. He had to collect those bodies for the viewing.

The Autopsy Room was the second largest area of the morgue. It had a row of 14 stainless steel tables with channels around their perimeters. On one of the tables lay the eviscerated body of a woman, her torso cut open with a Y-shaped incision from pubic bone to sternum. The top of the woman's skull had been removed and now surgical-gloved hands reached down and lifted out the pink, glistening brain.

The hands belonged to forensic pathologist Dr Sophie Nicolides. As well as gloves she was garbed in a plastic apron, plastic arm protectors, a shower-type cap and surgical mask. Plus she was wearing large, thick-lensed glasses. Earlier she had cut into the woman's scalp and peeled it away forwards and backwards to expose the top of the skull. Then, using a vibrating bone saw that made minimum impact on soft tissue, she cut into the top of the skull at a level just above the ears and eyebrows. The saw made a complete circuit of the head before the pathologist removed the crown of the skull like the top of a boiled egg. Next she'd used a scalpel to carefully cut away the tissue anchoring the brain to the skull. And now Dr Nicolides stood holding the brain in both hands. It was the size of a large coconut, and slowly dripped blood onto the tiled floor as she transferred it to a set of scales alongside the autopsy table and recorded its weight – 1.49 kilos.

She heard the toneless whistle that heralded the appearance of Mal Kite. You never actually heard his footsteps, not until he was right beside you, but his whistling was like a knock at an invisible office door. Looking up from the scales, Dr Nicolides saw the rat-faced assistant standing alongside two bodies that she'd conducted post mortems on earlier in the morning. 'Morning Mal,' she said, her voice slightly muffled through the surgical mask.

'Morning doctor,' he replied. 'These two ready for viewing?'

'Yes. But be careful when you wheel them out because the heads are just held in place with pillows.'

Kite looked down at the man and woman on the gurneys. They'd both been decapitated. In fact when they'd arrived at the morgue, the heads had been in separate bags from the bodies. Half the man's face had been coated in blood on arrival, but during the autopsy Dr Nicolides had cleaned it off. Kite pressed his foot down on a pedal beneath the man's gurney and unlocked the wheels As he pushed the gurney out of the autopsy area, Dr Nicolides was bent over the brain she'd removed, cutting into it with a razor sharp, long-bladed knife. In a procedure she and her colleagues called 'breadloafing,' she would divide the brain into 12 slices, each one centimetre wide, then examine them for abnormalities.

Kite wheeled the gurney out of the Autopsy Room and down a corridor, at the end of which he had to take the trolley round a tight corner. Despite the pathologist's warning to be careful, he took the bend a bit too quickly, the centrifugal force dislodging the head from the pillow it rested on. Craig Chaseling's head fell to the floor and rolled along like some kind of uneven bowling ball before coming to a standstill against a white-tiled wall.

Moving quickly, because it wouldn't be a good look if this little mishap was witnessed by any other staff, Kite retrieved the head and placed it back in position. There were some specks of dirt on the forehead and cheeks of the waxy-looking face, so he brushed them away as best he could with his gloved fingers.

After wheeling the cadaver into the viewing room, Kite got the second body and this time took particular care when he steered the gurney round the corner. 'Don't want you losing your head as well,' he told the dead woman. He did quite a lot of talking to the corpses. In fact, when he thought about it, he probably talked to them more than he talked to his colleagues.

38 WRITING ON THE WALL

CHASELING SAT in a room that was like the waiting area of a second-rate doctors' surgery. The walls were peach-coloured and the carpet, light grey with a pink weave, was badly stained. On the wall hung, slightly crookedly, a framed picture of an Australian pastoral scene – grazing sheep, silver-trunked gum trees.

A door opened and Bonita Spinelli entered the room. She was a social worker employed by the NSW Health Department to ease the trauma of relatives viewing their loved ones at Glebe Morgue. She was short but solid and dressed in a dark grey skirt and well-pressed white shirt. A laminated ID card hung from her neck. Her heavily made up face was set in a look that was meant to convey concern and compassion – red-lipsticked mouth pursed, powdered forehead creased.

Minutes earlier, Spinelli had greeted him in the reception area. After ushering him into the waiting area, she'd gone off to check with morgue staff that the bodies were ready for viewing. Now, speaking in her hushed, even-toned voice, she said, 'We can go into the viewing area.'

Chaseling rose from his seat and followed her to the end of the room, where she opened a door. They entered a mutely lit area with the same pastel décor as the waiting room. The social worker touched his arm. 'I feel your pain,' she said in a half whisper.

'Thank you,' Chaseling said. Then he started to become a bit embarrassed as the social worker retained her hold on his arm, doe-like brown eyes gazing up into his with contrived empathy. He added, 'I'd like to get on with it please.'

Spinelli's expression morphed into a frown for a second before she reset her features into the little half-smile, matched by the concerned look in her eyes. She let go of his arm and walked over to the side of the room, where she pressed a green button on the wall. A pair of doors started to slide open like stage curtains. 'I'll leave you to your grief,' she said.

As the social worker made her exit Chaseling's eyes started to glisten. On the other side of a narrow, waist-high wooden counter reclined his parents. Their gurneys had been arranged lengthways next to the counter. Each body had a green and white hospital blanket pulled up to the base of its chin, hiding the shocking decapitation injuries. The nearside arm of each body had been placed above the blanket.

Chaseling stood over his mother's body. He took her cold hand and gave it a squeeze. 'Goodbye Mum,' he said, his voice choked and reedy-sounding. Then he pulled down the sheet. He had to see what the monster had done to her.

A white towel had been draped over what was left of his mother's neck. He lifted it away, and reeled back in shock as he saw the jagged strips of bloody flesh, rope-like tendons, the white cartilage of the severed windpipe and vertebrae. He fought back the urge to vomit as he replaced the towel.

Next he farewelled his father. Leaning over his body, he saw some specks of dirt on the side of his father's face. He pulled a tissue from a dispenser on the countertop and wet it with water from a bottle he'd brought in with him, then wiped away the dirt. Then he gazed at his father for what would be the last time. It was a shame, he thought, that he wore such an angry expression because in life he had radiated happiness.

And then it was as though a spark of his father's anger flew out of the body and started sizzling in the pit of Chaseling's stomach. A single word was echoing through his mind. In fact, he could almost see it spelled out in the air in front of his father's body, like the letters written by a dismembered hand on the wall at Belshazzar's feast – *'payback.'* The thought of revenge held back the flood of tears that had been building up, so that when Chaseling emerged from the Viewing Room his eyes were red but dry. His mouth was a letterbox slit.

In the waiting room, the social worker had been joined by a bald man in a grey business suit who looked as though he might be a cop. Aged somewhere in his late forties or early fifties, he was tall and slightly stooped. He advanced on

Chaseling. 'Mate,' the man began, 'sorry to trouble you at this time. Nick Beauchamp, Homicide Squad.'

They shook hands. Beauchamp reached into the breast pocket of his jacket and gave him a business card. Before pocketing it, Chaseling noted that Beauchamp was a Detective Superintendent, so he was high up in the food chain.

'While we're handing out cards,' said Bonita Spinelli, 'here's mine.' Chaseling put her card in his pocket without looking at it.

'Any time you want to talk,' Spinelli said, 'day or night, I'm here for you.' She looked at the man-sized watch on her wrist. 'Now if you'll excuse me, I've got another viewing to prepare for.'

As the social worker made her exit, Beauchamp said, 'Perhaps we could get a coffee. There are a few things I'd like to discuss with you.'

The detective barely moved his lips as he talked. And what lip movement did take place was confined to one side of his mouth. Chaseling wondered whether the habit had been brought about by years of clandestine conversations with informants in bars and other public places. 'Good,' he told the cop. 'But how about something stronger than a coffee? I could do with a beer right now.'

Beauchamp gave a slight smile. 'I'm not averse to that,' he said.

Ten minutes later, they were drinking schooners of Young Henrys in a pub called the Forest Lodge Hotel, popular with students from nearby Sydney University. Chaseling drained almost a third of his in one mighty gulp. The detective produced an e-cigarette which he sparked up, blowing a plume of vapour towards the ceiling. A young barmaid with breasts almost bursting from her low-cut shirt suddenly appeared alongside their table. 'No smoking inside and that includes e-cigarettes,' she said in a feisty Irish voice.

Beauchamp took another puff of the e-cigarette and reached into a jacket pocket. He opened a small leather wallet and showed the girl his silver and blue NSW Police badge. She seemed unimpressed. 'No exceptions,' she said, her foot starting to drum impatiently on the wooden floor.

The cop exhaled vapour towards the barmaid. 'Don't worry sweetheart, it's just vanilla essence, perfectly harmless.' He switched off the e-cigarette. 'You can expect a visit from the Licencing Squad,' he muttered.

'Sorry, I didn't quite catch that,' the girl said.

Resorting to sexual harassment, the cop gazed lasciviously at her chest. 'What I said was, "A pair of tits like yours restores my faith in God."'

Her face red with a mixture of anger and embarrassment, the girl returned to the bar.

'You were about to tell me who murdered my parents,' Chaseling said.

'Was I?' the detective said. He took a healthy swig of his Young Henrys. 'OK, I will. Unfortunately he's left the country, so at the moment he's out of our reach. And yours.' He reached into the breast pocket of his jacket and produced a folded A4 page which he smoothed out on the table. Staring up at Chaseling was a black and white image of the killer. He had a mop of dark hair that looked as if it hadn't been combed for days, along with a beard and moustache in equal need of grooming. Dark eyes, accentuated by the almost bruised-looking skin below the eyes that is often possessed by people of Arabic descent, stared up from the page. Chaseling read the text below the picture:

FAZIR, ALI.

D.O.B. 29/04/1988 - 177CM.

Below that it said *BANKSTOWN,* followed by a long string of numbers. 'That was the last time he was charged, by the hard-working officers at Bankstown police station,' Beauchamp said. 'It was for malicious wounding, slashing a man's face open with a knife. Charges ended up being dropped, strong suspicions that the victim and witnesses were threatened. But suffice to say, Ali Fazir is a very sick puppy. Been in trouble with the law since his teens, served time in a juvenile correctional facility for rape and after that he went on to notch up a string of convictions for other serious offences – drug supply, assault, demanding money with menace. Employs good lawyers so apart from his year in juvenile detention, he's only ever done six months' jail time. But we were about to charge him with murder – he shot another gangster. We were just building up our case against him. Oh, and he's almost certainly the killer who plunged a screwdriver into the eye of an ice dealer in Chinatown a few days ago. We'd know for sure if the club where it happened could provide surveillance footage, which they say they can't, that there was some major glitch in the video equipment that night. I don't believe a word of it, of course, but there it stands.'

'You said he's flown the coop,' Chaseling said. 'Where to?'

'He flew to Istanbul two days ago,' the cop said. ''We don't know where he's gone, although we strongly suspect it's southern Turkey.'

'Why's that?'

'Because it turns out that Fazir was an associate of a number of local men suspected of having Islamic State connections. A number of them have gone to fight in Syria – via southern Turkey – because there's still an open border and southern Turkey is very close to the Islamic State strongholds in northern Syria.'

'How the hell could he get out of Australia when we're supposed to be stopping these people leaving the country?'

'Well, that's the thing,' Beauchamp said. 'Turns out that he was on an ASIO watch list, but unfortunately the spooks didn't see him as a big enough threat to notify Border Control – or NSW Police.'

Chaseling contemplated his empty glass. 'I'm having another beer, if the barmaid is still talking to us.' He got to his feet. 'Will you join me?'

Superintendent Beauchamp drained the last few drops of his Young Henrys and, speaking conspiratorially through the side of his mouth, said, 'I think I could force another one down.'

39 CONTROL + ALT + DEL

GILBERT BUCKLEY was 27, just a year older than Chaseling. But he was ageing prematurely due to an unhappy combination of genes and lifestyle. The mousy brown hair on his scalp was thinning, while his body was thickening, his belly straining against a rumpled T-shirt that declared *'TECH SUPPORT: control + alt+ del.'* An old pair of black jeans completed his outfit. Possibly, Chaseling reflected, the jeans were the very same ones Gilbert had been wearing when they met at a Doctor Who Society meeting at the University of Sydney seven years earlier.

Tapping a dirty fingernail against the glass of a wall unit displaying his first-run *Star Wars* figures, Gilbert said, 'You'll note how this Snaggletooth is wearing a blue jump suit, not the conventional red one. Collectors therefore refer to him as the Blue Snaggletooth. Plus of course he's the same height as the other figures in the line. When Lucasfilm saw how their height-challenged Snaggletooth had been depicted, the company got the manufacturer to redesign the figure.'

Chaseling, sitting on the edge of a single bed littered with *Phantom* comics, nodded. His face had the thoughtful expression of a student being imparted a pearl of wisdom by The Master. 'So how much did you pay for the Blue Snaggletooth?'

'Seven hundred and fifty US dollars,' Gilbert said as he turned away from the wall display and started to navigate a narrow gap between an early 1980s arcade table and a one-metre high, gold-coloured Dalek, a sole remnant from his brief flirtation with Doctor Who. 'Someone has already offered a thousand.'

Making the final leg of the journey through his cluttered room, Gilbert's face was cast in a bilious glow from the phosphor screens of two 1980s computers – a Commodore 64 and an IBM 3270. Then he eased himself into the old leather executive chair he'd found in the street. He rolled the seat forward and his stomach pressed against the edge of his work station, which was located next to the bed where Chaseling reclined.

Gilbert touched the space bar on his keyboard and the 27 inch screen on his iMac lit up, displaying a mass of desktop folders every bit as cluttered as his room décor. He hit a key and his email inbox came on screen. He opened the email Chaseling had sent earlier from his laptop, copied the URL for Ali Fazir's Facebook profile and pasted it into the address bar.

A second later the image of Chaseling's nemesis appeared on the top left of the screen. His hair and beard looked combed and clean-looking, in contrast to the police photos Chaseling had been shown. Ali Fazir was wearing a backwards-pointing black baseball cap and a dark grey sweater. His thick neck was adorned with several avoirdupois ounces of glittering gold chain. He was striking a rapper pose, forefingers pointing outwards in a move that was also chillingly reminiscent of the Islamic State salute. The top of the page showed a bright blue car with mag wheels which shone a brilliant silver in the sunlight. Chaseling wasn't big on car makes and models, but thought it might be a Nissan Skyline. The panel of intro information about Ali Fazir simply said *Lives in Sydney, Australia.'*

'Now, the problem that we have is that his privacy settings are tight,' Chaseling said. 'We can't send him a friend request. But there's some revealing stuff in the 'about' section. We can also see his timeline – a lot of stuff about cars, tatts, metal music, girls. And his most recent postings are from his little holiday in central Australia.' Gilbert's cursor lingered over an image of Ali, sunburned and bedraggled-looking, but grinning broadly as he stood with his foot resting on the body a kangaroo lying dead in the red dirt. Clutched to Ali's chest was a rifle with a telescopic sight. Above the pic was text saying *'RIP Skippy the Bush Kangaroo. Never liked that show anyway!'*

Gilbert scrolled down to the previous posting, made two days before the kangaroo was killed. It was a picture of Ali holding up the severed head of a camel by its ears. The caption said *'My new knife works very well.'*

'Jesus Christ!' exclaimed Gilbert. 'And you want to go after this psycho?'

'I want to make friends with him,' Chaseling said.

His idea was to create a Facebook account for an attractive young woman – a woman who Ali would find irresistible. So that when she sent him a friend request, his eager finger would tap on 'Confirm.' His new girlfriend would share the fact that she was just about to leave Australia for the Middle East. Which would hopefully prompt Ali to reveal his location.

'Interesting idea,' Gilbert said. 'But your mate Ali might smell a scam when he sees they have no mutual friends and that none of this bogus woman's postings are more than 24 hours old. No, the simplest solution is just to hack into his account. And all we need to do that is to find out his email address. His fingers danced on the keyboard. 'I think the Nissan Skyline might give us the key here. So let's have a look down his timeline...' He scrolled the cursor down the page. Pictures and text flashed past in a near-blur. Then the screen went still and the cursor arrow quivered above a picture of Ali standing in front of the blue Skyline. '*"My new R34 NISMO edition,"* Gilbert read out. '*"Hard to part with the R32, but this babe has better curves and my mate Walid has done an amazing custom paint job on her."*

Gilbert started scrolling down Ali's timeline again. 'That means he must have sold the R32 and probably posted stuff about it,' he said. The screen fell still again and he looked at a picture Ali had posted. 'Yes, there *is* a Santa Claus,' Gilbert said.

The cursor hovered over a shot of a car's back window. Stuck inside the window was an A3-sized FOR SALE sign. '$30,000 ono,' Gilbert read out. 'There's a phone number, plus his email – *Psychosheikh666@gmail.com.*'

Having discovered Ali's email address, Gilbert then crafted a one sentence message he'd be likely to open. After that he took to Google images, hunting out a suitable picture that Ali would also hopefully feel compelled to click on. 'OK, here we go,' he said, dragging an image onto his desktop. It was a back view of a car, a Skyline R34, same model as Ali's, taken at night from behind, highlighting the car's sleek looks, the fat tyres and the signature tail lights – on each side there were two circles of red, the outer ones larger. The picture also provided a nice view of the Skyline's twin exhausts.

Gilbert then hunted down some pictures of high performance track cars spurting fire from their exhausts. Next he went to his desktop and clicked on the *Ps* icon. And soon, the miracles of Photoshop had created an exciting image where tongues of flame were shooting from the mouths of the two exhausts. 'Ok,' Gilbert said. 'Finally we infect the picture with a nice little virus, a Remote Access Trojan, also known as a "RAT."'

A page of letters and numbers – strings of raw data in stark white text against a black background – filled the screen. He highlighted a line of text and pressed ENTER.

A new screen of text appeared. 'OK, now I'm embedding the RAT – actually, this system refers to it as a "payload" – in the PDF,' Gilbert said. He called up a new screen. 'And now we're just checking that all our settings are correct …' He briefly eye-scanned the screen '… which, they are, so we're ready for blast-off.' He pressed the ENTER key.

Ten minutes later, Gilbert was ready to press the 'send' button of a message from the Hotmail account he'd just opened. The message was headed '*Ur R34 is shit, bro!*' The body of the message simply said, *If you want to see a fully-cocked R34, check out MINE!*' At the bottom of the message was a PDF attachment.

Gilbert's reasoning was that dissing a young Arab guy's car was in the same league of insults as informing him that his Mum was a whore. Ali would get so riled he'd click on the PDF without smelling a RAT. 'And then we'll take over his phone, laptop or any other other device,' Gilbert said, clicking on *Send*.

It was past midnight. Chaseling stretched and closed up the Phantom comic he'd been half reading as Gilbert worked his magic. 'I'll head off, and check with you in the morning,' he said, putting a foot on the floor and swinging around the other leg to stand up. But no sooner had he risen to his feet than a box appeared on Gilbert's screen. 'I can't believe it!' he exclaimed. 'He's taken the bait immediately!'

Chaseling sat back down on the bed and watched as Gilbert, with a flurry of taps, took control of Ali's device and installed a keylogger. 'OK, the Force is with us,' he said after his fingers performed a final tap dance on the keyboard. 'I'll call you in the morning and give you a progress report.'

Chaseling stood up again, stretching his body. 'Thanks Gil,' he said.

Gilbert slid back behind the keyboard and said, 'Now if you'll excuse me, I'll get back to my game of *Civilization IV*, where I am on the verge of achieving world domination, which you may or may not know is defined as having 65 per cent the world's land and a population 25 per cent bigger than anyone else's.'

Chaseling began to make his exit. As he walked past his friend's kitchen, a huge brown cockroach darted across the countertop and disappeared into a litter of unwashed crockery. *Gil might be on the brink of ruling the world,* he thought, *but he needs to tidy his kitchen and get some roach traps.*

At the door, Chaseling said goodbye to Gilbert, who appeared not to hear him, his face lit up by the flickering light of the Mac screen as he razed another city in pursuit of global domination.

Out in the dank corridor, Chaseling summoned the lift. Travelling down to the ground floor, he thought about the upcoming meeting with his sibling. He wasn't looking forward to it. Most dealings with Chris tended to be traumatic.

40 MORTAL KOMBAT

CHASELING WAS SITTING WITH HIS SISTER Christine, who now passed herself off as his brother Christopher, on a park bench.

Late afternoon sunshine danced on the surface of a small lake in the middle of Centennial Park, an oasis of lawns, trees and waterways on the eastern edge of central Sydney. Chaseling had insisted on having the meeting on neutral territory because he knew what Chris's reaction would be.

'*You killed them!* You weren't the one who chopped their heads off, but you killed them!'

Without looking at Chris, Chaseling gazed across at the lake, where a duck had just landed on the water, sending a circle of ripples. 'I was thinking, maybe we could scatter their ashes here.'

'You won't be getting your filthy hands on their ashes. And I don't want you at the funeral – *murderer!*'

Chris's voice, unusually high for a man's, offered the only clue that he'd started life as a female. Chaseling turned to look into his sibling's face. It was red with anger, the flushed skin contrasting with the blonde hair, worn in a close cropped style with a quiff at the front. There was a 'soul patch' of darker hair underneath his bottom lip. Earlier in his trans-gender journey, he cultivated a full goatee, but he'd down-sized now that his overall appearance was incontrovertibly male, right down to a bulge in the crotch of his jeans.

Three years his senior, Chris had looked and acted like a boy since they were children, when she'd played boys' games and favoured boys' toys, usually *his* toys.

In time, as childhood progressed, he came to accept the situation. He reasoned to himself that he was lucky having a sister who he could share boyish pursuits with. Another reason for his passivity was his sibling's flashpoint temper and propensity for physical violence. Whenever Chaseling fought back while trying to repossess his favourite toys, clothes, computer games and other prized possessions, she would punch, kick, bite or scratch (occasionally all four), employing all the physical strength at her disposal in a way that, as the years progressed, left a trail of battle scars on Chaseling's body and a store of traumatic memories in his head. Adding insult to injury had been the fact that his parents almost always sided with Chris when they got into physical fights, saying things like, 'She's a *girl!* What kind of man are you?'

He came to realise that the real reason Chris was allowed to get away with it was that her commandeering of his possessions freed his parents from having to buy their daughter boys' toys of her own. It was a kind of *de facto* way of them giving her such things. And for the time being, they could continue to live the fiction that there weren't any gender issues with their 'tomboy' daughter.

It all reached a nasty climax on Chaseling's sixteenth birthday. His parents' present to him had been the computer game *Mortal Kombat: Deadly Alliance,* the latest manifestation of the popular film and gaming franchise which first appeared in the early 1990s. The fighters looked more realistic and there were exciting new combat styles and storylines.

The day after his birthday, he arrived home from school looking forward to going into battle against the soul-sucking sorcerers Quan Chi and Shang Tsung. Sitting down behind the Xbox unit in his bedroom, he'd opened the case of the *Mortal Kombat: Deadly Alliance* disc. It was empty.

He stormed into his sister's room. There she was, headphones over her short hair, Xbox control in her hand and a look of violent intent on her face as her avatar Blaze slugged it out with Shang Tsung. He strode over to her console and pressed the eject button. He snatched the disc from the tray and turned to face his sister – just in time to see her fist flying towards him in a powerful uppercut that slammed into the tip of his jaw. Chaseling's head snapped backwards and he fell to the floor, which came into violent contact with the back of his skull. He passed out.

Fortunately the floor was carpeted, so the neurological damage was minimal. He returned to fuzzy consciousness lying on his back. As he slowly pushed himself up from the carpet, something round, flat and silvery rolled off his chest. It was the *Mortal Kombat* disc. Into its playing side, his sister had used some sharp implement to scratch a roughly-rendered but recognisable profile of a dragon's head, the *Mortal Kombat* logo.

He'd gone looking for Chris. It was time, he thought, for a fight to the finish – their own all-deciding bout of mortal combat. He was bigger than Chris now. And at this moment he felt just as mean.

She was in the kitchen putting away the fruit knife she'd used to ruin the disc. Seeing the look on his face, she'd slammed the utensil drawer shut and bolted for the door. Chaseling had caught up with her out in the backyard, spear-tackling her to the lawn, where he sat on top of her with one hand round her neck and the other raised in a fist above her face.

'You should know,' he said in low, menacing tones, 'that I'm totally willing to beat you to a pulp if that's what it's going to take!'

'Game on!' Chris sneered, her voice slightly hoarse from a restricted airway as his fingers tightened around her neck. 'You haven't got the balls for it.' She started heaving and wriggling her body, trying to dislodge him.

'I'll also tell Mum and Dad about the hormone injections you're having.' Chaseling looked at his sister's chin, where pale, downy hairs sprouted, the wispy beginnings of the goatee she would later cultivate.

Chris started to look worried; she ceased her struggles and gazed up at him with a calculating look. 'What exactly do you want?' she said.

'I want you to leave my shit alone. And I want you to stop committing acts of physical violence against me.'

Chris thought about this for a good 20 seconds. Ceasing her appropriations of his property didn't present too great a challenge. But she wasn't sure about the stopping the physical violence part of the proposed treaty. All her life she had casually assaulted her younger brother; it was going to be a difficult habit to break. But then again, she thought to herself, there was always *verbal* abuse. She nodded. 'OK.'

Soon afterwards, she left home to share a house with fellow students from the University of Sydney, where she was doing a Bachelor's degree in international studies. The regime of androgens continued and she started wearing a special binding bra which concealed her breasts. Then, just after graduating from university, she underwent an operation known as Top Surgery where the breasts were removed and upper chest recontoured into a more masculine shape.

As a convincing-looking male, Chris managed to score a plum job as an assistant to Australia's delegation at the United Nations in New York. Chaseling was bemused to see his abusive sibling beginning a career in the world of diplomacy, but she had obviously managed to keep her temper in check. She flourished in the UN role, then went one on to snare a senior position with the Australian Trade Commission in London. It was in the UK where Chris had taken the final step in her transformation with a series of operations which removed her uterus and ovaries and constructed a penis out of skin from her stomach. Finally her labia were sewn together to create a scrotal sac containing a pair of prosthetic testicles.

And now Chaseling no longer thought of his sibling as 'she.' The person sitting alongside him on the wooden bench possessed all the male *accoutrements*, except for the voice. Chris tried to offset the high pitch of his voice by speaking in a gravelly tone, but it always sounded contrived; at least it did to Chaseling's ears. 'I'll be hiring security people for the funeral,' Chris said, 'and they'll be under instructions to keep you out.'

Chaseling gazed into Chris's accusing eyes and said, 'I kind of said my goodbyes at the morgue.'

Suddenly a bunched fist came flying towards Chaseling's face. But he was ready for it and caught the fist in his open palm. Then his fingers closed around Chris's knuckles. He squeezed as hard as he could, his grip fuelled by decades of bullying. He could hear his sibling's knuckles cracking, on the point of fracturing.

Chris gave vent to a strangled-sounding moan – and burst into violent sobbing, tears gushing from his eyes, shoulders heaving. Chaseling released his grip. The next thing, he was hugging Chris tightly and crying too. They remained like that for some time, locked together in their grief, drenching the shoulders of each other's shirts, bodies shaking.

After a while, Chris pushed him away. 'Don't think the touching little scene we just acted out changes anything,' he said. His eyes, red from crying, were screwed up in a look of hatred. He reached into a front jeans pocket for a handkerchief and blew his nose. As he lowered the handkerchief, he said, 'Just keep out of my life from now on. I never want to see you again after this.'

Chaseling felt a stinging sensation in his neck. Sunset was approaching and the mosquitoes were emerging from the damp hideaways where they lurked in daylight hours. He brushed away the insect and got to his feet. After stepping clear on the bench in case Chris decided to kick out at him, he said, 'I'm going to track down the animal who did it – his name's Ali Fazir.'

Chris held his gaze for five or six heartbeats. 'Maybe you could behead him,' he said.

'I'll see what I can do.' Chaseling raised a hand in farewell and turned to go.

'It still won't change anything,' Chris said.

Chaseling remained silent but as his feet tramped across the lush grass carpeting the edge of the lake, he thought to himself, *oh but it will, it will avenge five deaths.* There was a flapping of wings. He looked up and saw the black silhouettes of fruit bats fluttering across the darkening sky.

Reaching the top of a grassy rise, he turned and looked back towards the lake. Chris was gone. A pair of ibis fossicked near where he and Chris had been sitting, stabbing their long beaks into the earth in search of worms. His mind replayed some happy scenes from his childhood that had taken place on the lawns of this park. He saw his father standing with Rufus, the family's Golden Retriever, at the Sunday dog training classes which had completely failed to curb the recalcitrant Rufus's disobedient tendencies. He could smell the roast chicken laid out on a picnic table by his mother alongside a bowl of her special mayonnaise and curry sauce. He pictured the boomerang he'd bought on a school excursion to La Perouse sailing through the air and instead of coming back, touching down on an island in the middle of one of the park's lakes. He remembered the thrills he'd experienced one magical day playing hide and seek here with Chris and two friends called Hans and Karl.

Hide and seek. It had been one of his favourite pursuits early in his childhood. He'd always preferred being the seeker, rather than the hider.

His phone rang. It was Gilbert. 'He just logged onto Facebook, so here's his username, which is the same as his email address – *psychosheikh666@gmail.com.*'

Chaseling opened the Notes app of his iPhone and tapped in the address.

'Are you ready for his password?'

'Yeah.'

'*Torture,*' Gilbert said. 'He uses the same password for his email account if you want to get into that. Dude, I'm starting to get a very bad feeling about this.'

41 CALL TO PRAYERS

THE WAILING CALL TO PRAYERS from the mosque jolted the slumbering Ali into consciousness, propelling him from a supine to a sitting position, bloodshot eyes blinking rapidly. His hair was matted and dirty-looking. A nerve twitched below his left eye, so that for half a second the blue teardrop on his upper cheek came to life and rippled.

He stood up and swished open the flimsy white curtain beside the bed of the hotel room. And he saw why the wailing was so loud. Just 50 metres from his window, a sandstone minaret rose above his hotel and the surrounding buildings. The balustrade below the pointed top of the tower was ringed by cone-shaped speakers blasting out the chant, which now appeared to come to an end, the final words echoing off the rocky hills overlooking the city. But no, it hadn't ceased, the *muezzin* had merely paused for breath and now he started to sing another long, meandering phrase.

Ali sat down on the bed and grabbed his phone from the nightstand to check on the time – 3.15pm. His eyebrows lowered in a scowl as he recalled the email message that he'd received just after he checked into the hotel around midday. The text rubbishing the beloved car he'd had to leave behind in Australia. When he'd clicked on the link he'd seen a back view of a silver R34 spitting fire from its exhaust pipes. Big deal, that was easy to do, you just needed to invest in an exhaust flame thrower kit for about $150. Apart from the flames, there was nothing that made the car any hotter than his own beast. Or ex-beast. The car, motorbike, his knife collection – he'd left all his prized possessions behind. Various friends and relatives were 'minding' them, but Ali knew he'd never be getting behind the wheel of his R34 again or breaking the speed limit on his Honda 750.

The *muezzin* hit a series of high notes which Ali found excruciating. 'Shut the fuck *up!*' he yelled.

Ali's nerves were not in a good state. It was two days since he'd had a hit of ice. Going through passport control in

Istanbul, more than 20 hours after leaving Australia, it was obvious he was strung out. His hand trembled as he placed his passport down on the wooden counter. His face twitched and his forehead was shiny with sweat. On the other side of the desk, a man with a black moustache opened the passport and compared Ali's photo with the frazzled-looking individual standing before him before bringing down his rubber stamp with the ferocity of someone killing a blood-sucking insect.

Then when Ali got to the customs barrier and tried to pass through the 'Nothing to Declare' portal, he was stopped and taken to a side room where he was frisked and his luggage searched. Much to their disappointment, the customs officials didn't find anything illicit and finally Ali was allowed to walk out of the international terminal, with just one more plane journey to go, a flight to southern Turkey on a regional airline called Pegasus.

And now Ali was waiting in Antakya, a small city with a population of around 250,000, for a man called Najim to contact him. Najim was a 'fixer' who would get Ali across the Syrian border less than 20 kilometres away. Ali would pass himself off to border guards as an aid worker.

The room where Ali waited was located up three flights of worn marble steps and had what the adventurous traveller might call 'Old World charm.' An interesting installation of pipes ran up one wall of the bedroom – there were seven in all, he counted them – while in the bathroom there were cracks in the wash basin and once-white tiles. The toilet flush was a corroded lever protruding from the wall. And now, making Ali's environment even more unpleasant, was the unwelcome serenade from the mosque.

Eventually, the call to prayers came to an end. There were now just muffled traffic noises filtering in from outside. Perhaps he'd go out and see what Antakya had to offer.

Chaseling was staying in the guest room at his grandparents' house. He sparked up his laptop and logged in to Ali's Facebook account. He clicked on the 'friends' tab. Ali appeared to be a popular guy – he had 296 friends. Chaseling started clicking on the names beside the thumbnail friend images.

Ninety minutes flashed by before his cursor rested on the bearded face of someone called Fady El-Chamy. He clicked on the name, then the 'About' tab of the man's Facebook page – and shouted, *Yes!* The text in the box said 'Aid worker. Lives in Raqqa, Syria.'

Chaseling started flicking through the man's timeline. And it immediately became clear that the endeavours Fady El-Chamy was engaged in were not humanitarian ones. Fady was pictured holding an assault rifle, then out in the desert in the back of an open truck with several other men, their fists raised in victory salutes. Chaseling's heart started pounding with excitement as he studied a posting from two months earlier. It was a picture of El-Chamy outside a hotel.

'This is where the brothers stay before heading south,' the posting stated. *'Not the Hilton, but clean and cheap – the same way I like my women! (SMILEY FACE EMOJI)'*

The sign on the building behind him read 'Hotel Elanur.'

🦘 🦘 🦘 🦘

After leaving his key at the first floor reception desk, Ali headed out into the street. The pedestrian plaza outside the Hotel Elanur was buzzing. He leered at two young women who were walking past. Turkish chicks were *hot*, he thought to himself. Only a minority wore veils and these two were in tight blue jeans and figure-hugging tops. *'Marhaban,'* he said as they passed – the greeting was one of many words that the Arabic and Turkish languages had in common – but the girls studiously ignored him. 'Sluts!' he said, loud enough for the girls to hear and, he hoped, understand.

He turned into an alleyway, walking idly without any particular destination in mind. He passed a barrowman selling fruit and nuts, while on the other side of the alleyway were two middle-aged men in suits sitting outside a café drinking tiny cups of coffee. A scrawny ginger cat ran in front of Ali, who tried to kick it, prompting a look of outrage from an elderly veiled women walking in the other direction with a basket of pastries.

Ali suddenly paused as he saw a sign set high on an ancient stone wall: 'Cindi Hamami. Historical Turkish Bath. Since 1516.'

Maybe, he thought to himself, he could sweat the withdrawal pangs from his system, let the toxins ooze out in the steamy atmosphere of a Turkish bath. He passed beneath an arched stone entranceway and down a tiled passage. Then he walked through a doorway to the right into a huge, church-sized room with a domed ceiling. In the middle of the room, half a dozen men with towels round their waists stood round a table drinking tea and smoking cigarettes. Another two men reclined on the red-cushioned divans lining the wall, puffing away at hookah pipes. Ali could hear the bubbling of the smoke passing through the water. Then he heard a voice to his right. He looked round and saw a swarthy-faced man behind a battered wooden counter. The man was saying something to him in Turkish. Ali shook his head and asked, 'You speak English?'

The man pointed to a sign on the wall that said, 'TURKISH BATH 12 LIRA. MASSAGE 20 LIRA.' At this point another man materialised. He wore a singlet and what looked like striped pyjama bottoms. He was huge, built like a heavyweight wrestler. He flexed a set of long, thick fingers and smiled at Ali. 'I give good massage,' he said.

Ali hurriedly shook his head. 'No thank you.' The kind of massage he liked was one from a naked Thai girl. The massage man retreated.

Glancing around the huge room, Ali didn't see the steam and sweating bodies he was expecting. Then he saw a red and white striped door open outwards. A cloud of steam escaped as a man emerged, his body dripping wet, with a damp towel around his waist. An attendant approached and handed the man a towelling dressing gown, then held up a large towel as a modesty shield and averted his eyes as the man discarded his towel and slipped into the robe. He adjourned to one of several intricately-carved wooden changing cubicles set along one wall.

Ali paid the counter attendant 12 lira. The man locked Ali's valuables in a small wooden box, giving him a key to take into the steam room with him. He was also given a thin towel. The man indicated a line of bright orange, open-toed plastic slippers on the floor. Ali slung the towel over his shoulder and discarded his Adidas sneakers, hoping none of the other customers would take a shine to them, and slid his feet into a pair of slippers. He shuffled across the stained white marble floor towards the changing cubicles.

Before Ali reached the cubicles, one of the men around the central table broke away from the group and approached him. The man, who had a bulbous nose and unshaven face, held up an unopened packet of luxury length cigarettes which shouted the brand '*Alhamraa*' in tall letters. No health warnings, unless they were in the small Arabic text at the bottom of the pack. 'From Syria,' the man told Ali in a heavy accent. 'Good!'

'No thanks,' said Ali, retreating to his cubicle. After removing his clothes and fastening the towel around his waist, Ali headed towards the red and white striped door. He opened it and went inside. A swirling, warm mist was rising to a domed, green-stained ceiling, much smaller and lower than the ceiling in the other room, and peppered with half a dozen holes the width of a man's body to let the steam escape. Through the fog Ali saw 10 sweating men, mostly overweight like himself, sitting on a large raised slab of grey marble. Like him, they all had flimsy towels wrapped around their waists. Ali was grateful, because he'd been half expecting male genitalia to be on ugly display. He sat down in a vacant spot on the stone plinth. Beads of moisture were already forming on his body and it wasn't long before the droplets started to coalesce into little rivulets.

Every now and then one of the other men would rise from the slab and go into an open- fronted room, using a plastic bowl to sluice down his body with water from a marble basin before making his exit through the red and white striped door. Following this example, after about 45 minutes, when he felt he'd done enough sweating, Ali sluiced himself down, then left the steam room.

As he emerged, he felt calmer and cleaner. And it could have been his imagination, but walking to his changing cubicle, he felt lighter.

'Good?' enquired the swarthy-faced man as he collected his valuables from the wooden box.

'Yes, good,' Ali replied.

He returned to his hotel, where the elderly male receptionist told him, 'Someone to see you.'

A man rose from a couch near the desk. Aged in his forties, he had nut brown skin, a wiry body, and a close-cropped black beard and hair salted with white. But his most distinctive physical feature by far was his left eye, which was crossed, appearing to be gazing sideways out the window while his right eye looked straight ahead at Ali.

'I am Najim,' the cross-eyed man said.

42 A CRUEL PLACE

NAJIM LED ALI down a narrow street flanked by shops selling pastries, clothing, hand-made soaps and cheap electrical goods. They conversed in Arabic. Najim told Ali he was from Damascus and had come to Antakya soon after the Syrian civil war broke out in 2011. He ran a carpet shop in the nearby bazaar.

They sat down at a café table near the entrance to the bazaar and Najim ordered *çay* for both of them. The tea quickly arrived in small glasses and it was only just below boiling point. While Ali let his brew cool down, Najim, who appeared to have Teflon lips, tongue and fingers, sipped his *çay* (which was pronounced *chai*, same as the Indian version). He nodded his head towards the line of bare brown hills that were starting to turn pink in the late afternoon sunlight. 'Syria is on the other side,' he said. 'We will take you there in four, five days. Just waiting for three other brothers to arrive from the UK. I will drive you all across together.'

Ali looked at Najim, wondering if the crossed eye could see, whether his brain had to decipher a set of double images. 'When I get there,' he said, 'how soon before I go to the front line?'

'Oh,' Najim said, a gold tooth gleaming at the edge of his mouth, 'in Raqqa you'll be right on the front line from the day you arrive.' He produced a packet of cigarettes and offered one to Ali, who shook his head.

'So,' Najim said, 'what do you think of the *Ulu Cami?*'

Ali gave him a blank stare. 'What's that?'

'The mosque almost next door to your hotel,' Najim said, the good eye gazing at Ali searchingly.

'It's very impressive,' Ali lied glibly. In truth, he hadn't been in a mosque or even said any prayers since fleeing the central Australian desert. After all the dark things he'd done, he didn't see much point on trying to get on Allah's good side, despite the many verses in the *Quar'an* about Allah's propensity for forgiveness.

'There's another mosque, just three hundred metres down this road, that you might like to see,' Najim said. 'The *Habib-i Neccar Camii*. Have you heard of it?'

'No, I don't think so.'

'It's Turkey's oldest mosque. Habib-I Neccar is entombed there. Not his whole body, just his head.'

'Really?' Ali leaned forward in his seat. Anything to do with decapitation always piqued his interest. 'Who was he?'

'He was a holy man who tried to stop the pagans stoning two messengers sent by Prophet Jesus. The pagans cut off his head and rolled it down the hill. At the place where it stopped rolling, the mosque was built.'

'Is the head on display?' Ali asked.

'No brother, it might put people off their prayers to have a two thousand year old head staring at them.'

'Tell me,' Ali said, 'have you beheaded anyone?'

The question was so left of field that, for a few seconds, Najim just sat there with his good eye gazing quizzically at Ali. Then he said, 'As it happens, I have. Two Kurds. It was before I came to live here in Antakya, at the beginning of the war.'

'I've had a bit of beheading practice myself,' boasted Ali. 'I can cut the head off a man – or a woman – in less than twenty seconds.'

Najim took a sip of tea, then said, 'Out on the battlefield, you may find that things are different. You may want to prolong the agony of the person you are beheading. That's what I did with the two Kurds. I deliberately chose a blunt knife to slow things down. It took almost five minutes for each of them to die. They both squealed like pigs!' The inside of his mouth glittered as he gave a hearty chuckle. Ali laughed along with him, thrilled at finding a kindred spirit.

Ali looked up at a woman who suddenly appeared beside their table. She was dressed in a biblical style, ankle-length robe and a threadbare veil. In her arms was a young baby, its face pinched and unhappy. The mother was holding out her hand to Ali. He scowled and shook his head. Najim reached into his pocket and gave her a couple of coins. She thanked him and moved on.

'That woman was a refugee from Syria,' Najim said. 'They have no money. There are many here in Antakya.'

'The world is a cruel place,' Ali said.

Najim's good eye glared at Ali. 'You have a hard heart, my friend. But I suppose that will help with a lot of things when you get over the border.' He drained his tea. 'Come – I have a bit of work for you to do.'

Najim led Ali into the *Uzun Çarsi*, a centuries-old covered bazaar. It was a sprawling, stone-paved maze of narrow, winding alleyways, like something out of an Indiana Jones movie. Muted sunlight filtered down from dusty skylights onto shops and stalls selling all manner of goods, the proprietors standing in their doorways exhorting passersby to step inside.

They passed a glittering display of bangles, rings and necklaces that looked fit for Aladdin's cave and, as the man standing in the entrance to the little shop told Ali, were very reasonably priced. The man's voice faded and there was a chorus of shrill piping sounds as Najim led Ali past a shop where dozens of canaries, parrots and other birds perched and fluttered in small cages. Then Ali found himself looking at the window display of a little clothing boutique. There was a faceless mannequin in the window, her prominent nipples jutting from beneath a tight sweater like cherries on an ice cream sundae. Ali licked his lips. Up ahead of him, Najim paused outside a shop where rolls of carpet were standing up in front of the window. Inside, Ali could see more carpets mounted on the walls and spread out on the floor. Najim motioned to follow him inside.

They were greeted by a young woman wearing a purple veil, black trousers and a long-sleeved, coat-like garment, light blue in colour, which ended just below her knees. Her oval face was pretty and Ali ran hungry eyes over her curves.

'My daughter Asna,' Najim said, giving Ali a warning look. He pulled back a curtain with a pattern of gold quarter moons against a dark blue background. Ali found himself being ushered into a small storeroom. On the floor were two long wooden boxes. Najim got Ali to help him lift one of them onto a two wheeled trolley, positioning it upright. It was very heavy.

Najim secured the long crate with a pair of octopus straps, then they hoisted an identical, equally-heavy box onto another trolley and strapped it in place. They rolled the trolleys out of the shop and, wheels bouncing along the cobblestones, headed for the street.

Najim had a late model Toyota HiAce van. They loaded the boxes and trolleys, then got in and Najim drove out into the afternoon peak-hour traffic. Ali soon saw that peak hour wasn't so chaotic in this modest-sized city. The traffic was heavy, but it moved, and the van made steady progress as they headed out of the city centre, past ranks of five and six-storey apartment blocks, their balconies crammed with satellite dishes and drying clothes.

After 15 minutes, gaps of vacant land began to appear between the apartment blocks. The hills to their left were closer. Najim turned left onto a sealed road which took them past a weed-infested lot where children's play equipment stood in a state of neglect, a ride-on horse lying on its side, the seat of a swing with a broken chain dangling in the dirt. On the other side of the road were half a dozen modest-sized cement block houses. Outside one of them was an overflowing rubbish skip. Perched atop the skip were two cats, one tortoiseshell and the other black and white. They tensed their bodies, ready to flee, as the van drove past.

The bitumen road surface gave way to dirt. They passed a roofless, half built house with weeds growing up through the concrete base slab. Najim turned onto a side road and now they were driving past a small grove of trees where an old man and woman with walnut brown faces were picking olives, placing them on a sheet spread out on the ground.

After passing an ancient stone house where the olive pickers probably lived, they drove past a stretch of wasteland, its only occupant a limping dog scavenging around some bushes. The hills got steadily closer till they rounded a bend into a little valley where the road came to an end alongside a cement block house surrounded by a two metre high cyclone wire fence. Parked out the front was a white Range Rover coated with a film of cinnamon-coloured dust. Najim parked the HiAce behind it and as they got out of the vehicle, Ali could hear the throbbing of a petrol-powered generator from the rear of the property. Najim unlocked a tall, black-painted iron gate. Then he opened the front door of the house and called out to someone. A man appeared in the doorway. He was sturdily built, with a bald head, the top of which was strangely pointed, like an unusually elongated egg. He had bushy black brows above expressionless eyes and a curly, dark brown beard with no moustache.

The man followed Najim to the car and helped them unload the boxes. As well as the two heavy wooden ones, there were several cardboard cartons labelled 'Medical Supplies' in English, French, Turkish and Arabic.

Inside the house, the décor was Spartan in the extreme – a dusty cement floor, some cheap chairs and a formica-topped table littered with numerous tools plus rolls of wire, soldering equipment and various other paraphernalia – Ali's eyes were drawn to an ice cream tub of chunky metal bolts and ball bearings. The wavering strains of Arabic music, thin and compressed as though from a phone or other small device, spilled from a bedroom where Ali could see a mattress and striped prayer rug on the bare floor.

Najim introduced the bearded man as Ibrahim. 'If you want to know how to make a bomb, Ibrahim will teach you. He is a master bombmaker.'

Ibrahim gave a modest smile.

'Soon he will be making a dirty bomb,' Najim said. 'We have sourced some highly radioactive material and when it arrives Ibrahim will turn it into the ultimate weapon of terror.'

Ibrahim said, 'As well as making bombs, I make excellent tea. Would you like some?'

Ali nodded and Ibrahim went into the kitchen.

'What's in the boxes we took from the bazaar?' Ali asked.

Najim went to the table and got a crow bar. 'Why don't you open one and have a look?'

Half a minute later Ali was looking down into the crate he'd prised the lid from. Inside were 10 AK-47s, packed in two layers nose to tail with separate compartments at one end of the box for the bullet magazines and webbing straps. Ali picked up one of the weapons. It felt good. Solid, but not too clunky. The metal had a waxy feel. His nostrils savoured the cloying, almost sweet aroma of gun oil.

He pointed the AK-47 at the front door of the house and pulled the bolt back. '*Die, motherfucker!*' he screamed as he pulled back the trigger. There was a nice, decisive click. Ali imagined a Syrian government soldier collapsing to the desert floor.

Najim laughed again, but it sounded forced this time. 'It's best not to press the trigger. There could be a bullet in the chamber.'

Ahmad loomed in the kitchen doorway. 'Everything OK?' He was looking at Ali with his bushy eyebrows raised and a faint sneer on his lips, an expression that said, *This isn't kindergarten, brother.*

Najim said, 'Ali was just about to put the rifle back in the box.' Watching Ali replace the weapon, Najim said, 'You will soon be very proficient with that gun. Mr Kalashnikov will be your best friend.'

Replacing the weapon, Ali noticed something sharing the same compartment as the shoulder straps. And his eyes lit up with excitement. There were a number of black-hilted combat knives in polyester sheaths. He reached down and grabbed one, pulling it out of its pouch. He held the blade in front of his face and inspected it. The knife wasn't quite as long as the Jungle Master he'd left behind in Australia, but looked more than capable of beheading *kufr*. Stamped into the metal were the letters 'KA-BAR.'

'American,' Najim said, not knowing that Ali was a knife *aficionado* who was already familiar with the brand. But what the Syrian said next was news to him. 'The company has just started selling a new range of knives and swords for killing zombies. I think it's meant to be a joke, although with the Americans it can be difficult to tell. We might include some of them in our next order, they look as though they'll be good for beheading when we want to make it swift.'

Ali slashed the combat knife through the air. The air displacement sounded like a sharp intake of breath. 'Can I take this back to the hotel with me?' he asked eagerly.

'Not a good idea. Wait till you get to Syria before you start carrying these toys around with you. These weapons will go into Syria secretly, not at the official crossing we'll be using. Ibrahim will cut the fence and drive across the desert in the four-by-four.'

As Ali replaced the knife in its sheath and put it back in the crate, Ibrahim emerged from the kitchen carrying three steaming glasses of *çay* on a battered brass tray. Seeing Ali looking down wistfully at the boxful of death, he said, 'Don't worry my friend, soon you'll be using those weapons battling the pig Assad, the filthy Kurds and our other enemies.'

'And beheading them?' Ali asked hopefully.

Ibrahim smiled. 'If you want, you'll be able to play football with their heads'.

43 INSHALLAH

EASTERN SUBURBS Memorial Park has two funeral chapels built around its crematorium, located in the centre of a large, sprawling cemetery on the edge of Botany Bay. Chris Chaseling, dressed in a black suit, was greeting people before they filed into South Chapel. His face was set in a look of contrived-looking grief. 'Where's Jonathan?' asked a 78-year-old family friend he knew as Auntie Joan.

'Oh, he decided he had other things to do,' Chris said. Above them, a passenger jet roared through the sky after taking off from Sydney airport a few kilometres away. Chris wondered if his brother was on the flight. 'Yes,' he said, 'Jonathan can always be relied upon to let you down.' He placed an arm on one of Auntie Joan's bony, hunched shoulders and ushered her towards the chapel entrance. 'The service starts in five minutes,' he said. 'I'll be saying a few words, then Father Keegan will take over.'

'Thanks Christine.'

Chris's body froze, a mortified expression on his face. He slowly looked down at Auntie Joan. She was gazing up at him with a mischievous gleam in her sunken eyes, while her red-lipsticked mouth, slightly smudged after kissing someone's cheek a couple of minutes earlier, was curled upward at the sides into a cruel smile. '*Chris*, I meant to say. Chris, Jonathan loved his parents very much. And he's more of a man than you'll ever be – in more ways than one.' She shook his hand off her shoulder and with an arthritic limp, headed towards the chapel entrance.

🦘 🦘 🦘 🦘

Chaseling had actually flown out of Sydney 17 hours earlier. And now the Emirates Boeing 777 was about to land in Dubai. One of the tall, attractive, overly made-up stewardesses wearing the distinctive pillbox hat with a token veil flowing to the shoulders went down the aisle checking that lap belts were fastened, window shades open and seats upright. There was a middle aged, *hijab*-wearing woman who still had her seat tilted back. Speaking to her loudly and slowly, the flight attendant said in an English-accented voice: 'Please press the button in your arm rest and return your seat to the upright position, madam.' Chaseling could see the girl's foot beating out an impatient rhythm on the cabin floor. It was as though the additional height afforded by the pill box hat had given her a disproportionate amount of attitude, Chaseling thought wryly. Then his thoughts switched to deep vein thrombosis.

Sitting to his right in the middle of a row of three seats was a large man who hogged the armrest for the entire trip. Worse still, his plump bottom overflowed into Chaseling's zone. With the result that Chaseling had spent the night pressed up against the window, recoiling from body contact with the plump man, who reeked of stale talcum powder. Every time he tried shifting position, his own bottom and hip would come into unpleasant contact with the elephantine left buttock of his fellow-traveller. There'd been the nightmare of waking from a brief but deep slumber to find himself pressed up against the fat man like a Siamese Twin.

At the end of his evening of putting his body into all kinds of cramped, uncomfortable positions, his legs felt numb and he wriggled his feet to try and restore circulation as the plane descended from a cloudless sky over an expanse of bare, biscuit-brown desert.

In Dubai he had to spend five hours in transit before boarding another Emirates flight for Istanbul. But as it turned out, the time was passed quite tolerably, reclining on a double bed in a hotel located inside the airport terminal.

The room cost US$300 and the man at reception, who appeared to have gone to the same Attitude School as the cabin attendant, gave him a frosty look when he jokingly asked whether they had a special half-day, Love Hotel rate. But he got a few hours' sleep, showered and changed into fresh clothes.

The Dubai-Istanbul flight was painless – a mere four hours and 52 minutes – and the person in the neighbouring seat was a small, skinny, non-armrest-hogging man. Chaseling whiled away the time watching two inane movies, then managed to get some more shuteye before the plane began to descend towards Istanbul's Ataturk Airport, named after the great military leader who crushed the ANZAC landing at Gallipoli a century earlier. He hoped his own mission wouldn't turn out a dismal failure like the disastrous World War I invasion attempt that had claimed the lives of so many thousands of Australian soldiers. He'd done some more trawling through Ali Fazir's Facebook and email accounts but hadn't come up with any further clues as to his whereabouts. All he could do was follow the trail to Antakya.

At Istanbul, he was due to connect with a 90-minute evening domestic flight to Hatay, the airport gateway to Antakya. But when he presented himself at the Turkish Airlines desk, he found himself joining a queue of people, most of whom appeared pissed off. The man in front of him spoke good English. 'The flight to Hatay has been cancelled and there isn't another until tomorrow morning,' he explained. 'I think they are organising for us to stay at a hotel.' He spread his hands, palms upwards, and smiled. *'Inshallah.* That's a word we say a lot in Turkey.'

'What does it mean?' Chaseling asked.

'God willing.'

44 EYE FOR AN EYE

CHASELING SPENT THE NIGHT in a hotel a few kilometres from Ataturk Airport, with Turkish Airlines footing the bill, and at 9am boarded an Airbus A321 which took him over the perpetually snow-capped mountains of central and southern Turkey to Hatay.

A swarm of taxi drivers converged on him as he emerged from the modest terminal of Hatay airport at 11:20. And soon he was being driven away in a small yellow taxi with a spider web of cracks across its windscreen. Just outside the airport, in a field off to their left, Chaseling saw around 20 veiled women bent over picking knee-high cotton plants.

The taxi driver, a large, fleshy man in his forties, explained, 'Refugees. From Syria. Many, many Syrians in Antakya now, three thousand maybe. Big problem.'

'Why is that?'

'Different culture,' the driver said. He didn't elaborate, other than to lower his window and spit out a gob of grey-yellow phlegm in the direction of the field workers.

🦘 🦘 🦘 🦘

The taxi stopped opposite a narrow, four storey building that announced itself as 'Hotel Elanur.' Just to reinforce the message, below was a marginally smaller sign declaring 'Elanur Hotel.' The outside walls were painted pink and the structure had an air of past grandeur – Chaseling guessed it was well over half a century old. But it looked new compared to the domes and minarets which rose beyond it, while at the foot of the steep hills that closely overlooked this part of the city, he could see clusters of ramshackle, whitewashed stone houses probably dating back to Biblical times. He had read on the Lonely Planet site that Antakya was originally known as Antioch and had been one a vital link in the Silk Road between Europe and the East.

He mounted a set of steps to the first floor reception desk, where an elderly man gave him a room for an incredibly reasonable 50 Lira with breakfast included (one Turkish Lira was worth roughly 40 cents US).

There were no lifts and the room was up a further two flights of stairs. The first thing Chaseling did was wash off the grime of his 24 hours of travel under the lukewarm water which dribbled from the antique showerhead.

Feeling refreshed, Chaseling left his room and headed down the stairs to the street. The pedestrian plaza outside the hotel was a teeming mass of people. Turkish music blared from a shop selling phones and tablets; a cloud of cigarette smoke rose from people sitting at an outdoor café – it seemed as if a hefty percentage of the population here contributed to the profits of tobacco companies.

His nostrils detected the aroma of roasting meat. Behind the front window of a restaurant was a man wearing a white bus boy hat and short-sleeved shirt which revealed an incredibly hairy pair of forearms, with almost no skin visible beneath the pelt of thick black hair. The hairy-armed man was using a machete-sized knife to carve slices from a huge cylinder of red-brown meat revolving on a vertical rotisserie. This was the kind of eatery Chaseling had patronised, usually late at night after consuming several beers, on countless occasions back in Sydney. He went inside.

On the way in, the hairy-armed man looked across at Chaseling and smiled. '*Doner kebab*,' he said, adding in English 'You like?'

'Yes, I like,' said Chaseling.

The meat arrived with a small side plate of fresh basil leaves and whole chillies. Chaseling was hungry and wolfed it all down, except the chillies, which he left alone after an experimental bite set his mouth on fire, necessitating several cooling sips of *Efes* beer.

He went back to the hotel. The old man was at his station behind the desk, alongside which was a leather couch. Chaseling sat down and looked towards the nearby stairwell.

Good. He had a grandstand view of anyone coming up or down the stairs. He turned to the old man and said, 'I'd like to try your Turkish coffee.'

'Our Turkish coffee is very good,' the old man said, pronouncing 'Turkish' '*Teer*kish.' Then he yelled out a two syllable word in Teerkish which sounded like someone's name, projecting his voice towards a kitchen facing a small dining area beside the reception foyer. A tall, attractive girl with short black hair appeared. She wore blue jeans which tightly encased a pair of long legs, above which was a white kitchen smock. They made eye contact.

A short time later, the girl returned with coffee, which was beautifully presented in an intricately-etched little metal pot, atop which was a dome-shaped metal lid covered with swirling Arabic designs. Chaseling lifted the lid and saw that nestling within the pot was a small, round, white porcelain cup of steaming coffee, dark and viscous-looking like treacle.

The girl was standing there looking at him expectantly. He reached down and plucked the cup out of its recess before raising it to his lips and taking a sip. The coffee was scalding hot, but its taste was potent and earthy. He gave the girl the thumbs-up sign. She smiled and adjourned back to the kitchen.

Chaseling turned to the old man and said, 'Are there many other tourists at this hotel?'

'No,' the man said, his face mournful. 'Tourists stay away now because of war in Syria. Right now only you and one other man, you and he are only foreign guests.'

'And what country is this other man from?' Chaseling asked, his heartbeat starting to soar.

'Well, that is interesting thing,' the old man said. 'He is from Australia, same as you.' He raised an eyebrow. 'Is he friend?'

'No,' Chaseling said. 'It's a just co-incidence.' Taking a final, sediment-rich sip of coffee from the little cup, he heard a gurgling from deep in his abdomen. At the same time, his bowels told him it soon might be good to find a toilet.

His body tensed as he heard footsteps coming down the stairs. It was only a female cleaner carrying room service trays left outside guests' doors. The phone at the reception desk trilled and the old man began a conversation. Chaseling thought to himself, for the umpteenth time, *just what am I going to do when I come face to face with Ali Fazir?*

Given that he wouldn't be able to inflict the payback he craved, otherwise he might find himself spending the rest of his life in a nightmare Turkish prison straight out of the 1970s movie *Midnight Express*, what exactly was his game plan?

Revenge, in the dangerous light of a foreign country, was not all that practical. The bottom line was that he'd probably have to settle for attacking with words, which sadly wouldn't give him the same kind of satisfaction as driving a stake through the man's heart or inflicting some other grievous, if not fatal, injury. But at least he would be able to vent some of his anguish.

He heard heavy male footsteps coming down the stairs. The body came into sight before the face, a pair of thick-thighed legs in blue jeans, a belly bulging from a Green Bay Packers jersey. And even before Chaseling saw the unkempt beard and hair, the cruel dark eyes and slash of a mouth, he knew this was his man. He could feel the evil radiating off him.

Ali was holding out his room key and was just a metre away from the desk when he saw Chaseling. His eyes widened. He threw down the key, then did a quick about-face and made for the stairs. As Ali started pelting down the single flight of steps to the street, Chaseling was moving quickly past the reception desk. 'Actually we *do* know each other,' he told the old man as he vaulted down the steps.

When he reached the bottom the swing doors at the hotel entrance were only just coming to rest. Chaseling burst out into the street, where he stopped and looked around – just in time to see Ali, who had his phone to his ear, dodging around a man carrying a huge bronze calabash of tea in a shoulder harness. Now he was heading down a shop-lined alleyway, shouldering aside a teenage boy in a brown leather jacket who hadn't got out of the way quickly enough.

The alley intersected with a narrow but busy two-lane road. Ali ran in front of a car, prompting a squeal of brakes and a blast of a horn. He paused for a second in the middle of the street as a motorcyclist roared past, then dashed to the other side, where he disappeared beneath the domed entrance of a shopping bazaar.

The seconds ticked by as Chaseling stood at the edge of the road waiting for a break in the traffic. He threw caution to the winds and ran out onto the road. The traffic parted like a Biblical sea. Then he was on the other side and running into the bazaar.

The *Uzun Çarsi* was busy and Chaseling had to navigate his way through a gaggle of people. There was no sign of the man he'd come halfway across the globe to confront. He broke into a half-run, almost getting his arm burned by a cigarette-smoking man stepping out of a luggage shop.

Up ahead, he got a glimpse of Ali's head bobbing up and down. He was keeping up a rapid pace, weaving through the stream of shoppers. And he still had the phone to his ear.

Quite a few of the other people in the bazaar were either talking into phones or tapping things into them. And so Chaseling didn't think there was anything unusual about the man standing in the entrance of a carpet shop talking into an iPhone 6s, other than the fact that one of the man's eyes was hopelessly crossed, while the good eye was fixed on Chaseling.

Up ahead, he saw Ali glance over his shoulder before, phone still at his ear, he turned into another, smaller alleyway snaking off to his right.

Chaseling increased his pace from a half-run to a three quarter run, the equivalent of an equine canter, his feet slithering over the smooth, time-worn cobblestones. As he turned into the side passage, he feared he'd lost Ali. Here there were no shops, just a courtyard where people sat drinking coffee and *çay*. Then the passage narrowed, with pitted sandstone walls pressing in from the sides and a stone ceiling which was only just high enough for Chaseling to avoid bumping his head. His footsteps echoed as he hurried down the passage.

Ali came back into sight again. He was pushing aside a waist-high safety barrier painted with diagonal black and yellow stripes. Then he ducked around a corner and was out of view again. Chaseling ran to the safety barrier. It had been left partially open and he slipped through the gap, finding himself in a gloomy area where there were the shells of a number of old shops in the early stages of renovation, the old rock dividing walls being rebuilt using cement bricks. At first there was no sign of Ali, but then he came into sight again as the passage took Chaseling round a winding corner.

The alley had come to a dead end. Ali stood against an ancient stone wall watching Chaseling approach. His face had a smug look, the eyes lit up in a dreadful gloating expression. 'I killed your parents and you're next,' he said, giving a snuffling chuckle.

Trying to keep his voice level, Chaseling said, 'Congratulations, you'll make it into the serial killer league.' Despite his levity he was terrified. But he took a few steps closer to his adversary. They were now just two metres apart. As he gazed at the murderer with a look of what he hoped was cold disdain, he saw the other man's eyes shift slightly. They appeared to be looking at something just over Chaseling's right shoulder. He was starting to turn around as his vision exploded.

🦘 🦘 🦘 🦘

People strolling past the carpet shop saw nothing unusual as Ali emerged wheeling a trolley, strapped to which was a rolled-up *Kilim* rug. The diamond-patterned rug was a large one, the roll standing three metres high, its girth substantial – some men wouldn't be able to encircle it with their arms. 'Be careful!' cautioned Najim as the wheels bumped heavily on the cobblestones and the trolley almost overturned. Ali tensed his arms and kept the trolley on track, forcing a woman in a red veil to step rapidly aside. Najim made an apologetic gesture as they passed the woman, spreading his hands, then tapping the tip of his index finger to the side of his head while nodding towards Ali.

🦘 🦘 🦘 🦘

When Chaseling came to, his body was restricted as though he was in a tight cocoon. The back of his head was pounding and he could feel the sticky wetness of blood on his neck. His face was pressed against some kind of coarse, prickly material, which had been rolled around his body, confining his movements to wriggles of his head, feet and hands. The feeling was horribly claustrophobic. Equally discomforting was the churning feeling in his bowels. He was close to having an attack of diarrhoea.

He was in a moving vehicle. There were the muted sounds of other traffic – the engines and horns of cars and motorbikes, the rumble of buses. He started to open his mouth to call out for help. But his lips wouldn't open. They'd been gaffer-taped shut. So instead of being a cry for help, the sound that he made was a nasal-sounding groan like the bleating of a sheep.

Ali leaned round from the front seat and snapped, 'Shut the fuck up or I swear I'll cut off your dick and shove it down your throat!' Beside him, Najim's face remained impassive as he drove, his face turned slightly to the side to compensate for the lack of vision in his left eye.

Chaseling accepted that none of the sounds he was capable of producing were going to help him and fell silent. Gradually, the surrounding traffic died away. Now the roll of carpet – with his body inside it – was tumbling to the right as the vehicle turned left. The car wheels crunched over the stones of an unsealed road. Perhaps 10 minutes later, the vehicle stopped. Chaseling could hear Ali and Najim talking. The car's engine was switched off and Chaseling heard the men getting out and walking to the back of the van. There was the click of the rear doors being unlatched. The carpet roll was manhandled onto a trolley and secured with straps. Najim unlocked the front gate of the property and led the way as Ali navigated the trolley through the broken bricks, tiles and other rubble in the front yard, then down the side of the house.

In the back yard, Najim pointed to a small stone shack. The shack looked very old, Ali thought as he steered the trolley towards it. The mortar was crumbling in several places, but the stonework was thick and solid. Najim turned the corroded metal knob on an ancient but sturdy timber door and Ali wheeled the carpet inside.

The inside of the shack was illuminated by stripes of light spilling in through the rusty metal bars of a window recess which faced the low afternoon sun. Ali manoeuvred the trolley into a vertical position. Then he unclipped the octopus straps and pushed at the carpet roll, which toppled to the ground, prompting a muffled shout from Chaseling. Ali and Najim shoved the carpet with their feet. The next thing Chaseling knew, he was spinning as the carpet unrolled. His body performed several revolutions before he found himself lying on his back on a dirt floor. Silhouetted against an open doorway were two men – Ali Fazir and the cross-eyed man. The cross-eyed man turned and disappeared out into the sunlit back yard. Ali took a step closer to Chaseling's prone form. 'You just chill out here for a while till I come back.' He gave a little giggle.

Najim reappeared with a battered old iron bucket. He threw it down on the dirt floor beside Chaseling, who was propped up on one elbow and slowly unpeeling the strip of tape from his mouth. Najim reached into a side pocket of his cargo pants and pulled out a half-full bottle of water. He threw it down beside the bucket and then he and Ali grabbed the carpet and dragged it back out through the doorway. Najim came back in and wheeled out the trolley. Then the door was closing and there was the sound of a key turning. A few seconds later Chaseling heard a two-stroke engine starting not far away.

Chaseling shakily got to his feet and walked over to the metal bucket lying on its side on the floor. There was an urgent groan from his large intestine. He stood the bucket right way up and quickly peeled off his jeans, followed by his underpants. Then he squatted over the makeshift lavatory – and his bowels exploded.

His captors hadn't been considerate enough to leave any toilet paper. He reached down to the ground and picked up the water bottle. He uncapped the bottle and cleaned himself up as best he could, using up all the water.

Inside the house, the main room looked emptier than it had the previous day. Ali looked around but there was no sign of the wooden boxes of weapons or cardboard cartons of 'medical supplies.' He glanced into the bedroom Ibrahim had been using and saw the mattress and prayer mat were gone.

Following his gaze, Najim said, 'He went into Syria last night, in the Land Rover. He'll be back tomorrow, *inshallah*.'

'I was hoping to use one of those combat knives to send our prisoner to paradise,' Ali said.

'We should take him into the hills and kill him there,' Najim replied.

'No, better to do it now,' Ali said. 'The guy is a troublemaker, the sooner the better. We can dump his body later.'

Najim went into the kitchen. Ali heard the sound of a drawer being pulled open. Najim came back into the room holding a large, black-handled kitchen knife. 'How about this fine blade?' he said.

'That will do the job very nicely, brother,' said Ali.

Petrol fumes from the generator drifted into the shack, partially masking the smell from the bucket. Chaseling picked up his underpants from the floor and put them on, followed by his jeans. Just as he was just securing the top button of his Levi's, he saw a shadow at the bottom of the door.

He reached down and grabbed the bucket he'd just emptied his bowels into. Then he darted to the side of the doorway. He heard a key turning in the lock.

Ali burst into the room brandishing his knife, blinking as his eyes adjusted to the reduced light. As he pushed the door all the way open, his peripheral vision took in the form of Chaseling standing to his right. Ali turned and lunged at him. At the same time, Chaseling let loose with the bucket.

Liquid shit flew through the air. Ali started to raise his hands to deflect it, but not in time to prevent the noxious substance drenching his head and shoulders, some of it going into his mouth.

The effect was dramatic, stopping Ali in his tracks as his upper body bent over and retched. The hand holding the knife hung down loosely at his side while a stream of green bile shot from Ali's mouth. As he heaved, Chaseling kicked at his knife hand. The weapon clattered to the ground but Ali seemed oblivious, giving vent to further gags and hawks.

Chaseling reached down and his fingers closed around the wooden handle of the knife. Ali finally seemed to become aware of the peril he was in. He was trying to wipe shit from his face as he turned around to face Chaseling – who employed the wall of sound technique favoured by Clarrie when he ran at taipans, giving a bloodcurdling and extremely loud yell that was amplified tenfold in the small stone room: *'Yaaaaaaaaagh!'* At the same time, he slashed the knife towards Ali in a deadly arc. Ali remained frozen to the spot, a light of dawning realisation in his eyes just before, with a sound like wet paper being ripped, his belly was cut open.

Ali backed into the stone wall, then slowly sank to a sitting position. His shit-splattered face had an open-mouthed, wide-eyed expression of terror. He held his hands over his stomach as blood gushed between his fingers.

Chaseling was panting and the white-knuckled hand which held the knife was trembling. He started backing out of the room until one of his feet bumped into the base of the door frame. He paused there for a moment looking at Ali, who said something, but the words were obscured by the sound of the generator spilling in from outside.

'Didn't catch that,' Chaseling said in a shaky voice. He took a step closer to Ali, who remained slumped against the wall, his hands held over the terrible horizontal belly slash.

'Help me.' Ali's voice was a grating, agonised rasp. 'You're a doctor,' he said. 'You've got to help me.'

'You know,' Chaseling said, raising his voice above the sound of the generator, 'since my early teens I've been an atheist. Used to read a lot of books by people like Christopher Hitchens and Richard Dawkins, neither of whom you would have heard of, so let's move on. The point I'm leading up to is that I'm now hoping there is a god. Or at least, I'm hoping there's a *hell* – a fiery pit where you will be prodded by devils with red-hot pitchforks and who will tell you over and over again that your car is shit. Bro.'

A furious red flush broke out on Ali's neck and spread up his face, till his eyes were red and bulging. 'They're booking you in at reception right now,' Chaseling taunted. 'Be sure to say "hi" to your brother for me.'

Up till now, Ali's hands had been clamped over the knife slash. But with the mention of Abdul, he clenched his fists, which wasn't a good idea because a loop of bloody intestine popped out of his belly and he had to hurriedly push it back in.

Chaseling walked out of the shack, closing the door behind him and turning the key which had been considerately left in the outside lock. He heard a hoarse, angry shout from inside. He pocketed the key and walked away, knife in hand, the sound of the dying Ali's protests drowned by the chugging of the generator.

Reaching the back door of the house, Chaseling paused and listened. Just audible, almost drowned out by the generator, was a TV. It sounded like a sports broadcast. He opened the door and slipped inside.

He was in a concrete-floored hallway. Ahead loomed the open doorway to a brightly lit room. The sports commentary got louder. Holding the knife at waist level, Chaseling stepped into the room. The cross-eyed man was sitting in a chair watching a football match. Seeing him, the man jerked up in his seat.

'Turn it off!' Chaseling said, waving the knife towards the TV set.

The cross-eyed man reached for a remote control and pressed the red on/off button. The room became silent, apart from the insistent throb of the generator outside. One of the man's eyes was fixed on the knife in Chaseling's hand while the crossed one appeared to be examining the kitchen off to the left.

Chaseling advanced on the cross-eyed man. His vague plan was to threaten him with the knife, then somehow tie him up. But Najim had other ideas. He leapt to his feet and reached round to the back pocket of his jeans. His hand reappeared holding a bone-handled flick knife.

Click! A blade snapped out of the hilt and locked in place. Najim laughed, and slashed the stiletto through the air. He took a step closer to Chaseling, his eye unblinking, fixed on him like a cobra's.

'That's not a knife!' Chaseling said, echoing the immortal line from the *Crocodile Dundee* movie as he brandished his much larger weapon. Despite his levity, he had no idea about the tactics he'd deploy in the impending knife fight. Somehow though he felt calm, fatalistic. *Que sera sera.*

'Seven,' Najim said in heavily accented English. 'I am seven when I stab my first person, in Damascus. An older boy try to steal the cakes I buy at bakery. But I say "no." He knock me to ground. He kick my face so bad I get blind in this eye.' He pointed up to his crossed left eye. 'But still I keep hold of bag with cakes inside. Then I take knife from my pocket.' He tossed the knife through the air again and his right hand caught it, while keeping his eye fixed on Chaseling.

'Don't keep me in suspense, I'm dying to find out what happened,' Chaseling said, tossing his own knife from hand to hand and catching it far less adeptly.

'I stab him in stomach. Then in eye. Left eye, same as this one.'

'Eye for an eye,' Chaseling said, his mind blanking in and out with fear. He suddenly remembered his first close encounter with knives in his early teens, when he and his sister/brother-to-be had managed to spend some quality time together during a weekend away on their grandparents' hobby farm. They had spent countless hours throwing a kitchen knife at a paperbark tree. By the end of the two days they were both excellent knife-throwers, although it hadn't done their gran's carving knife much good.

As he stood waiting for the cross-eyed man to make his move, Chaseling began to picture how he and Chris held the knife, how far they stood from the tree. Najim saw the faraway look and seized his opportunity. With a feral snarl, he launched himself at Chaseling. But instead of lunging at him with the blade, he aimed a vicious kick at Chaseling's groin. *Get your adversary down on the ground.* That was one of the first lessons Najim had learned in the alleyways of Damascus, paying for the tuition with the sight of his left eye.

Chaseling sidestepped and slashed at Najim's leg, but the cross-eyed man had already pulled his foot away. And now he came in for the kill, launching himself at Chaseling with the knife held low, his arm pivoting back for a belly stab. Chaseling threw himself sideways again but the wicked blade of the stiletto sliced along the edge of his ribs. He gave a yelp of pain and jumped backwards. Gold glinted in the cross-eyed man's mouth as he let loose a throaty chuckle.

Chaseling's mind flashed back again to the day he and his then-sister had done permanent damage to the tip of his grandparents' carving knife a decade and a half earlier, recalling the simple but effective techniques they employed to hurl it into the soft bark of the tree. Then an image of his beheaded father appeared before his eyes. He saw the look of rage on his father's face. And his own fury erupted.

Moving with a skill he did not know he possessed, Chaseling changed his grip on the knife so he held it with the back of the handle pressing into his palm. At the same time, he took a long step backwards. He lifted the knife behind his head. As he had done that weekend on the farm all those years ago, he moved his hand like someone chopping wood. At the end of the arc, when his arm was straight, he released his weapon, giving a primal cry of rage as the knife left his fingers.

Everything happened in slow motion. Najim was lunging forward, his good eye gleaming as he held the stiletto at stomach-level. The kitchen knife flew from Chaseling's hand in a blur of flashing metal and shot through the air for just over two metres before embedding itself in Najim's neck next to his trachea. Najim's stiletto fell from his fingers and clattered to the floor as his hands flew up to the knife protruding from his throat. He pulled at its black handle and the blade slowly came out, making a sucking sound as it came loose, at which point a one metre long jet of bright red blood shot from his neck. Najim held a hand to his throat, the pressure of his fingers only serving to give the pulses of arterial blood greater trajectory, so the next crimson spurt shot a full three metres across the room and splattered onto the whitewashed wall. Now the Syrian had both hands at his throat. His breath was a bubbling, gurgling rasp.

Chaseling rushed to the work bench on one side of the room and grabbed a crow bar. He ran at the cross-eyed man, who held up a hand to protect himself while keeping the other hand at his throat in a vain attempt to quell the blood shooting out at one second intervals. Using all his strength, Chaseling brought the crowbar down. There was a snap as it broke the cross-eyed man's arm. The Syrian gave a screech of pain. Chaseling lifted the crowbar again and brought it down on the top of the man's skull. Najim fell to his knees. Chaseling hit him a third time, slamming the bar into the man's forehead just above the eyes. Najim collapsed backward onto the cement floor. He let loose a long, rattling breath, a cluster of red bubbles forming around his ruined throat, then fell still.

Chaseling let the crowbar drop from his trembling fingers and took vague note of the fact that Najim's wonky eye had somehow straightened up during the fatal beating. Both eyes were now staring out of the ruined head in the same direction. But they were quite lifeless. Chaseling staggered to the bathroom.

He emerged ten minutes later, just wearing his jeans, his head, hands and chest dripping water. He hadn't been able to bring himself to use the filthy towel hanging from the shower rail. Holding his shirt to the knife slash across his ribs – the wound was six inches long, but, thankfully, shallow – he walked across to the work bench. He found some electrical tape and patched up the slash. Then he gazed into the open doorway beside the bathroom where there was a pile of scrunched up clothes on the floor beside a bedroll.

Another minute later, after rifling through the clothing, he emerged from the room wearing a crumpled long-sleeved T-shirt with Arabic writing across the front, hoping the words didn't say 'Death to the infidel' or anything else inflammatory. He walked over to a small table next to the seat where the cross-eyed man had been sitting. He found his own phone alongside the dead man's. There was also a bunch of keys, among which was a vehicle ignition key and the little black box of a car door opener. He pocketed them, then walked down the back hallway.

Out in the back yard the generator was still roaring away in its little wooden shelter alongside the shack. Chaseling flicked the power switch and killed the engine. Then he looked in the barred window of the shack.

Ali was every bit as dead as the cross-eyed man. His eyes were already glazing over and the dirt floor around him was dark with blood. Having said his goodbyes earlier, Chaseling didn't linger. He walked round the side of the property into the front yard. The front gate was locked but it opened with one of the keys he'd taken.

A minute later he was driving away in the HiAce. He started going into a state of shock. His body shook and his head was a jumble of images and fragmented sound bytes – the sound of the knife slicing open Ali's belly; the sickening thud of the crow bar as he'd slammed it into the cross-eyed man's skull. He took deep breaths and tried to keep his mind focused on the dirt road in front of him. It was getting dark; better turn on the headlights. After rounding a bend, he saw the lights of a main road. He thought back to when he had been transported in the carpet. He remembered rolling to the right when the van left the main road, meaning it had taken a left turn. And so at the main road he turned right.

Keeping to a sedate 50 kilometres an hour, he drove into Antakya. Box-like apartment blocks on either side of the road gradually gave way to grander, older buildings. Now he could see the dark waters of a river to the left, running parallel with the road. He thought he was probably close to his hotel, which was near the river. He steered the van down a side street and found a parking space. He left the key in the ignition, thinking it likely some eligible candidate, a Syrian refugee perhaps, might take custody of the vehicle. Then he walked along a footway beside a waist-high stone wall bordering the river, heading for a bridge that he was pretty sure was just a stone's throw from the hotel.

In the distance, a siren howled. *Get out of Turkey ASAP,* he thought. He walked along a pavement running above the steep, concreted bank of the river. Out on the water, a fish jumped, a splash of silver above the inky surface. On the bank below him, Chaseling saw a man holding a long fishing rod which was bent over as he reeled in the line. The fish broke from the water again, closer this time, then disappeared beneath the surface as the fisherman kept turning the reel. Now the man had a long-handled net and was dipping it into the water. He pulled it out again with a large, ghost-white fish flapping away inside the mesh.

At the hotel reception desk, the old man looked shocked when he saw the state Chaseling was in. 'Are you sick, sir?'

'Yes, I am. A bad *doner kebab*. I'll be leaving in the morning.' He collected his key and turned to go up the stairs.

'Did you see the other Australian?' he heard the man's voice calling after him.

Chaseling stopped and turned around to face him again. 'I did,' he said. 'He's staying at a friend's house tonight.' He continued up the stairs.

In his room, he stripped off his clothes and went into the bathroom to shower. He paused and gazed at himself in the mirror. Staring back at him was a very different person from the geekish Doctor Who enthusiast who'd begun this journey. There were twin furrows in his cheeks that hadn't been there before and a different look in his eyes. He had crossed a threshold. He was a killer.

45 DEJA VU

CHASELING ROLLED his new, ocean-blue RAV4 to a standstill and looked down at his phone to check the GPS coordinates. He was here.

The moment he opened the door, the heat hit him, a searing dry blanket of air that sucked away at the moisture in his body. A fly settled on his mouth and he let loose a hiss of air to blow it away.

He walked off the stony verge of the red dirt road onto the edge of the parched plain, which was flat and featureless apart from a low-slung mesa on the near horizon. As before, he headed for the mesa, using it as a bearing.

After about five minutes a small stand of mulga loomed in front of him. And there it was – the sandstone slab. In his hand was the opalised ammonite. He bent down and placed it on the ground. Then he grabbed the end of the slab with both hands and hauled upwards. As he tilted it up on its edge, he gave a gasp of surprise as he saw what had taken up residence beneath the rock since his last visit – a colony of bull ants.

The ants were two centimetres long, heads and thoraxes an angry red-orange, abdomens jet-black. They had built a labyrinth of tunnels in the dirt. A mass of them swarmed around a cache of white eggs, grabbing them in their mandibles and moving them to safety into deeper recesses of the tunnels, while others spilled out of the nest. One of them was on his hand and Chaseling gazed down in horror as the insect lowered the tip of its abdomen to the base of his index finger, just above the knuckle.

A bull ant's sting barb is hollow, like a hypodermic needle. And the formic acid it injects is so potent it throws some people into anaphylactic shock. As the ant sunk its barb into his skin, it felt as though a red hot needle had been plunged into his finger. The pain almost made him let go of the upended rock slab and send it crashing down onto the swarming mass of ants and eggs below. Somehow he managed to support the rock with one hand as he shook the insect off his finger just as it was lowering its wicked abdomen for a second assault. He looked down at the opal fossil on the ground near his right foot. He hooked his foot around the opal and kicked it into the nest.

Chaseling lowered the slab back into position and beat a hasty retreat, performing what looked like some kind of primal dance as he hopped from foot to foot and stomped down onto the earth in an effort to dislodge the dozen or so furious bull ants which had settled on his boots. But one of the ants, a particularly large one, transferred itself from the top of his boot onto his sock. And then Chaseling felt insect feet on his lower leg as the ant moved from his sock to a new landscape of skin where it anchored itself on his leg hairs as Chaseling stamped his feet. Then it lowered its jet black rear, plunging the venom barb half a centimetre into Chaseling's skin.

'Aaaaaaaaagh!' The pain this time was even more intense, centred on a fiery point four or five centimetres above the ankle. And now the Dance of the Ant went into its final movement as Chaseling balanced on his right leg while raising his left leg and frantically slapping at it, trying to kill his attacker.

But the bull ant was made of tougher stuff, maintaining its uncompromising grip on his leg hairs. And through the protective layer of denim, its armour-plated body was able to resist the impact of Chaseling's slaps – enough, at least, to give him a little goodbye present. It lowered its rear end to Chaseling's leg again. He let loose another howl of pain.

The bull ant finally decided it was time to bail out and landed feet first in the red dirt. Then it reared its body upwards like a spider poised to strike, its pincers opening and closing. Chaseling raised his foot to squash the insect. But then something made him keep the foot in mid-air. It was the feeling that, despite all the suffering the ant had inflicted on him, there could be some kind of karma at work here, a penance he must serve for violating the ancient bushman's grave.

He slowly lowered his booted foot to the ground and took a step backwards. The ant, completely fearless, remained on its haunches for another few seconds before getting back on all sixes. Then it marched away across the red dirt back towards the rock slab.

Chaseling looked down at his index finger – just below the knuckle was a raised, fiery red bump with an angry white centre pulsating with white-hot pain. His lower leg was suffering similar agonies. He put the pain aside for the moment. It was time for the smoking ceremony.

He found a clear area of dirt where there would be no danger of bushes catching fire. Then he reached into the back pocket of his jeans and pulled out a crumpled and dog-eared piece of paper. It was a folded-up newspaper page. He unfurled the tabloid-sized sheet. It was a page from the Daily Telegraph with his picture and story headed *SYDNEY MAN SURVIVES OUTBACK BLOODBATH*. He'd found it in his parents' house. Now he scrunched up the sheet into a rough ball, not too tight otherwise the flames mightn't take hold, and placed it down in the earth. Next he collected some dried tufts of spinifex grass and placed these around the paper ball. He picked up some mulga twigs which he placed in a teepee shape around the pyre, then got a plastic lighter from his pocket and sat down cross-legged in the dirt.

He clicked the lighter and the newspaper caught alight, a tongue of flame expanding into a fiery red ball as the page burned. Flames started dancing in the grass tussocks and within seconds they were ablaze too. And now the bone-dry mulga twigs were starting to smoke and with a whooshing sound like a gas cooker being lit, they were engulfed in fire. Chaseling got back on his feet and quickly collected some larger pieces of wood from the ground around him, adding those to the pyre. He sat down in the dirt in front of the crackling fire and gazed into the flames. Then he addressed the spirit of the long-dead bushman.

'I am so sorry,' he said. 'You were a man of few possessions and you took just two of them to the grave with you – your rock knife and your opal. When I took the opal, I knew I was doing the wrong thing, but I did it anyway.'

The fire quickly burned down to red embers, then ashes. Chaseling remembered how the old man in St Catherine's had mixed the alkaline fire ashes with his *pituri* leaves. Perhaps the ashes would act as an antidote to the ant stings. He took his Swiss Army knife out of his jeans pocket and snapped open the main blade, which he dipped into the remains of the fire, lifting out some powdery white ash which he deposited in the palm of his hand. He got a second scoop of ash, then reached into the breast pocket of his shirt and pulled out a little tube of sunscreen. He took off the cap and squeezed some of the creamy lotion onto his palm, where he mixed it in with the ash, creating a gritty grey paste. He rolled up the leg of his jeans, exposing an angry bite above his ankle and a second further up his inside calf muscle. He coated each bite with the paste, which he then rubbed into the inflamed flesh so the ash would penetrate. Next he daubed his index finger, which was starting to swell up like a sausage. Then he waited to see if his bush medicine would work.

It *did* work. Within minutes the pain and swelling started to ease as the powerful alkaline compounds in the ash neutralised the acid injected by the ants. And as he sat there, Chaseling's troubled mind eased too.

The guilt he felt about taking the opal from the ancient bushman's grave lifted. So did the bitter remorse he felt over the deaths of his parents. He started to feel grounded, connected to the earth he was sitting on. Time to head for St Catherine's and pick up his dot paintings from Lester. He stood up and kicked some loose earth over the embers. With one trouser leg still rolled up to his knee, he walked back to the car.

He felt that he was ready to pick up his life again after the chain of tumultuous, life-changing events which had begun out here in the desert. Perhaps, he thought, in a distinct sign of recovery, there might be some female backpackers with deeply tanned legs at the roadhouse.

Three hours later the wheels of the RAV were crunching across an expanse of dirt outside a place called Spud's Roadhouse and he pulled up alongside one of the petrol bowsers out the front. He filled the gas tank and went inside to pay. On the door was a sign saying 'NO SHIRT, NO SHOES, NO SERVICE.'

A roadhouse is a combination petrol station and outback pub. As Chaseling's eyes adjusted to the artificial light, he found himself walking towards a bar decorated with hundreds of car numberplates from all over the world. Perched on a stool with his back to Chaseling, a customer was tilting back his head as he took a swig from a bottle of beer. There was something worryingly familiar about the man's ratty-looking pony tail, brown at the end but the rest of it multiple shades of grey.

As Chaseling stepped up to the bar, the man swivelled round and he found himself looking into a familiar pair of doll-like eyes.

'G'day mate, Glen's the name, Glen of the Outback. You might recognise me from that David Bowie clip that they filmed in an outback pub.'

Glen of the Outback lifted a stubby of VB to his lips and took a deep swig. He didn't appear to recognise Chaseling.

Chaseling massaged Glen's ego. 'I think I *do* remember you! Weren't you the bloke in the orange T-shirt?'

Glen preened, running a hand through the thinning hair at the top of his head. 'Correct! Join me for a stubbie of amber fluid and I'll tell you about some of the other amazing outback adventures of Glen.'

'I'd love to, but I'm headed up north,' Chaseling said. He had been planning to stay at the roadhouse – there were two barrack-like rows of cabins at the side of the main building. But facing the prospect of becoming a captive audience to Glen of the Outback again, he made a snap decision to drive to the Aboriginal community.

A solidly-built middle-aged man, possibly Spud himself, appeared on the other side of the bar counter. Chaseling paid for his petrol, then waved goodbye to Glen of the Outback and headed for the exit. Glen's voice trailed him: 'I was also in that Mad Max film they shot near Broken Hill, *Thunderdome* – did some kung fu moves in one scene, because Glen of the Outback is a double black belt, and *mate*,' he placed an angry emphasis on the word, 'Glen doesn't like people turnin' their backs on him and *WALKIN' AWAY WHEN HE'S FUCKIN' TALKIN'!* The last words were shouted.

Chaseling left Spud's Roadhouse and walked to the car, half expecting Glen of the Outback to burst out of the building and launch himself into the air towards him while giving vent to a high-pitched, Bruce Lee-like cry. But Glen remained inside, regaling Spud with another exciting chapter of his life.

Seconds later Chaseling was driving away through the desert.

The sun had disappeared below the horizon. He looked down at the instrument panel to check his speed – just under 75km/h – then his eyes scanned the scrub growing on the sides of the road. A bright yellow and black kangaroo warning sign loomed ahead of him. *This was where he'd had the crash!* The sign had already been replaced. Someone had fired a bullet through the metal, leaving a jagged hole in the kangaroo's head. On the ground, near the base of the pole, he could see some bits of his old car – pieces of shattered radiator, some twisted air con piping – lying forlornly in the dirt.

When his eyes moved back to the road in front of him he saw a kangaroo. It was launching itself from the verge onto the blacktop. He jammed his foot down on the brake pedal. But he was too late.

The tyres screeched, then *THUMP!* The nose of the RAV4 slammed into the unfortunate animal…

THE VOICE OF THE MAN on the phone screen was casual and conversational, like someone telling a story in a pub or other relaxed social situation. But his appearance was far from mundane. He wore a lime green wig and his face was painted chalk white, contrasting starkly with huge crimson lips and the pair of black crosses over the unblinking eyes.

'I was eight years old when I first started dressing up as a clown. Not just dressing up (my mother made me a special outfit), but wearing makeup like I am now.

'It took me a while to understand why so many of the other kids at the fancy dress party avoided me that day. But when I got a bit older, I learned that a lot of people are very scared of clowns.

'From this first dalliance, I moved on to pranks in my early to mid-teens where I'd leap out in front of unsuspecting people in full clown regalia. They say my gran – I used to call her GM – they say GM already had a bad heart, that it was only a matter of time, but I felt very guilty about that particular mishap. Well, I did for about a minute, but look, you can't go through life racked by remorse. And just between you and me, Leanne, GM's death gave me a thrill.'

'OK, we'll use the first few sentences of that in at 5pm and some longer grabs in the main news.' Bob Hordern, known to all and sundry in the Channel Eight newsroom as 'Mad Bob' because of his hypomanic nature, delivered the words in a rapid-fire burst to the raven-haired, 30-something female reporter holding the iPhone. Mad Bob's eyes seemed to be bulging a bit more than usual as he asked, 'So why do you think you're the lucky recipient of this message?'

Leanne Merrick raised a black, fashionably thick eyebrow. 'His three victims – well, the three victims after his grannie – were all women in the public eye. One of them was a TV presenter.'

'And they were all strangled?'

The eyebrow arched higher. At the same time, she raised a hand to her throat. 'That's correct. I'm surprised you're not familiar with the case, Bob.'

'That was when I was head of news at Fiji TV and deliberately cutting myself off from the horrible things happening elsewhere in the world.' He gazed nostalgically into space. 'Ah, the kava, the dusky-skinned girls –'

'We were talking about the killer clown who escaped from the loony bin at Long Bay,' Leanne interrupted. 'The one that you want me to put together a package about in half an hour.'

Bob tilted his wrist and consulted a battered old diver's watch on a hairy wrist. 'Make that 25 minutes,' he said. 'And you'd better call it the Forensic Hospital, not the loonie bin.'

'Do you want me to call him the Killer Clown?'

'Ooh yeah!' There was a gleam in the exophalmic eyes as Mad Bob foresaw a sure ratings win over archrivals the Seven and Nine networks.

Leanne played the rest of the killer clown's message. 'Yes, I get a big thrill from snuffing the life out of fellow human beings. And I don't know why, but my favourite victims are women with dark hair. Women like you Leanne – I've often admired your lovely mane while viewing the news.

'Anyway, just thought I'd say hi. Maybe we can catch up some time.'

The final couple of seconds showed the clown reaching forward to switch off the device, his pale eyes briefly filling the screen before the clip went to black.